The

Glass Swallow

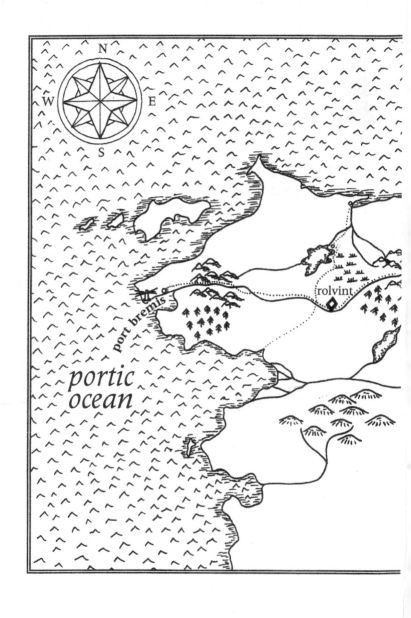

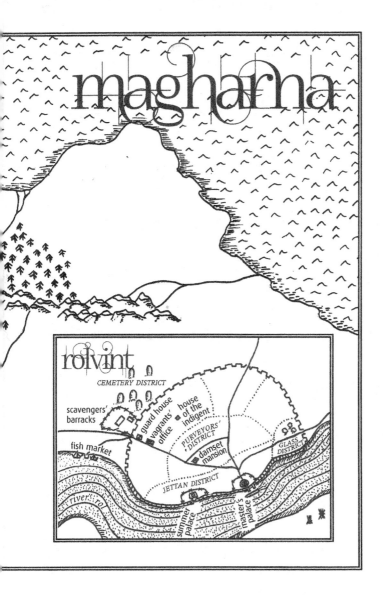

Also by Julia Golding

In the 'Companions Quartet':

Secret of the Sirens
The Gorgon's Gaze
Mines of the Minotaur
The Chimera's Curse

The Ship Between the Worlds

Dragonfly

Wolf Cry
Young Knights of the Round Table
Young Knights: Pendragon
Young Knights: Merlin

The
Glass Swallow

JULIA GOLDING

Frost Wolf

www.juliagolding.co.uk

First published by Oxford University Press 2010

This edition 2014
© Julia Golding 2010
Map © Julia Golding 2010
The moral rights of the author have been asserted

ISBN: 978-1-910426-00-5

For Lucy

Shard 1
Iron Grey

C aught out in the storm, Rain ran for home, fleeing the barrage of droplets hammering rings in the dirty puddles. Her normal route down Smith Alley had become a quagmire.

'Blast all weather-sayers,' she muttered, hovering on the edge of the muddy walkway, wondering if she could make it across. If she did, it would be at the expense of her new stockings and leather boots. She should have taken no notice of the local weather-woman who had promised a fine day.

Thunder crackled, urging caution. Deciding to wait out the worst under an overhanging roof, Rain retreated to huddle against the wall, sheltering her basket from the downpour. Shivering a little in the chill breeze, she pulled her shawl around her head and closed her eyes, listening to the raindrops hitting the roof above.

A cart rumbled past, the owner huddled under an improvised cloak of canvas, his grizzled face staring determinedly out from under the peak of his hood.

'Want a lift, little mistress?' the old man called.

'No, thank you,' Rain answered, giving him a smile. 'I'll wait it out here in the dry.'

'Suit yourself. Spearthrower weather this,' he grumbled as he clicked the horse into movement again.

'Yes, it's cruel enough.'

'Good day to you.'

'Good day.'

The cart jolted away, dousing the walls of the alley with dirty water, the backwash slopping on Rain's skirt, wetting the navy-blue swallows she had embroidered on the hem. She grimaced, cursing herself softly for not jumping out of the way in time. The wagon turned the corner and she was alone again. From the look of the skies, it seemed likely she might be trapped here for a while yet. Rain seized the chance to dream, letting her thoughts trickle back to the past like the water running away down the gutter.

According to her father, she had begun life in such a storm. Born on the first day of March in the third year of the reign of King Ramil and Queen Taoshira, she emerged into the grey morning of the world. As the midwife cut the cord, the heavens opened, rain pouring from the eaves over the bedroom window like a waterfall. The flowering vine that clambered up the brickwork and peeked into the room stirred and twitched under the onslaught, orange trumpet petals bobbing a fanfare. Flushed red with outrage, the newborn mewed and protested as she took her first unwilling breath, fists waving blindly. Her mother, roused by the cry, lifted her head from the pillow and reached out to take the child.

'Little Rain,' Sunbeam murmured, snuggling the baby to her breast, choosing a name suiting the moment of birth, as was the custom in the families belonging to the glassmakers' guild.

Torrent took his wife's hand in his scarred fist, smoothing his fingers over her palm. He caressed her with the same light touch he used for his finished masterpieces as they cooled after exposure to the furnace. Torrent and Sunbeam had waited so long for their family and he could hardly believe it had finally happened.

'She's a miracle, Sunbeam,' he said hoarsely. 'Perfect. And she'll be the first of many, you'll see. She'll have brothers and sisters to play with. She'll never be alone.'

But he was wrong. There were to be no more children. Before the year was out, fever swept the land and Sunbeam Glassmaker was among those who died, leaving Torrent with a baby to tend and a business to manage.

'You must marry again, for the child's sake,' his neighbours advised the silent man as he toiled over his workbench, rolling, spinning, and blowing the molten gather, twisting it with pincers into anguished shapes.

Rain's father merely shook his head and returned to creating droplet-shaped bubbles, the only tears he allowed himself to shed. As he finished each one, he suspended it over his daughter's cradle. He carried on until the ceiling in her bedroom was covered with them. When the setting sun shone obliquely through the window, the teardrops caught the light, scattering rainbows across her room. Finally, his grieving at the furnace done, he sat beside Rain's cot and admired the effect.

'I'll fetch you the moon and stars, Rain,' he crooned to the baby. 'But for now, here's your mother's sunbeams. You and I must carry on.'

As she had grown, the teardrop bedroom had stayed with Rain, a sanctuary in her busy home. It had become the place where she dreamed and made her plans. Now she had reached fifteen, and her father had risen to the head of his craft, his workshop on the outskirts of Tigral a place of pilgrimage for those who wished to collect the finest glassware. There was rarely a quiet moment. Young men fought to become his apprentices; he could have filled his house three times over with pupils had the guild rules allowed. Rain thought the five who lodged there at the moment were more than enough, their voices loud in the kitchen, boots clattering on the stairs at all hours.

And feeding them required many trips to and fro from the market, even when the weather was like this. Rain wriggled her toes in her damp boots, amused by her ability to blame the apprentices for everything.

The clouds were beginning to break up, the intensity of the storm fading. Despite the damp, cold conditions, Rain felt strangely content, set apart by the weather which was keeping others indoors. She so rarely got any peace at home. Orders for her father's products had flooded in ever since Torrent developed an expertise in the making of stained-glass windows; all acknowledged him as the leading exponent of the art. To walk into a room lit by a Torrent window was to step inside a miracle, they said, and Rain agreed. Little wonder that the Queen herself had chosen him to make the stained glass for the temple being built in the palace complex.

Rain shaded her eyes to look over the rooftops of Tigral to the throne room at the summit of the hill, the new temple just beyond. The tempest had tarnished the gold pavilions and stripped the fruit trees of their leaves—yet another gloomy day after weeks of rain. It had truly been a dismal harvest and without the wise government of Prime Minister Melletin the land would have been facing a winter of starvation. As it was, though the city would avoid real suffering, everyone would be expected to tighten their belts and obey the rationing laws. Commissions such as the Queen's were hard to come by in these difficult days. Hopefully, the job should see the forge through the bad times until conditions improved. Rain knew they would do better than many others and was grateful for the Queen's generosity, as the monarch funded public works out of her private purse.

Slowly, the rain eased off and weak sunshine filtered through the iron-grey clouds. Seizing her chance, Rain edged her way down the alley, jumping from doorstep to doorstep to avoid the worst of the filthy water. Raising her woollen skirt and cotton petticoat above her shins out of the wet earned her a whistle from Mil Blackfire, one of the smith's boys.

'Want to come and dry off by our fire, Mistress Rain?' he called. 'I've a nice spot for you just here.' He patted his knee as he lounged against the anvil.

'Save it for Cora!' Rain replied, rolling her eyes at his antics. Mil was courting her friend—and half the girls in the district if rumours were to be believed. 'She won't be pleased to hear you've been inviting me in.'

Mil gave her a cocky smile. 'We could keep it just between us two. Come on, Rain, you're half drowned.'

Rain leapt to the next step with a flounce. 'Give over, Mil. Not now, not ever. Anyway, I don't believe in having that kind of secret from my friend.'

As his attempts at flirtation were pure habit rather than seriously meant, Mil gave up with a good-humoured laugh. Soon the regular chink of hammer on metal broadcast that he'd returned to his work.

But the exchange reminded Rain that she did have one secret—one that risked her whole world if it came out.

'Rain, my love! Are you soaked?' Her father had been anxiously waiting for her return. He strode out of the workshop, a big man with capable hands and a curly thatch of grey-streaked hair, face craggy with lines. Whisking the basket from her grip, he smoothly steered her to the furnace. Work paused as the apprentices stopped to watch the pair.

Her father tutted. 'Look at you: you're like a cat that's taken a tumble down the well.' He brushed her straggling locks off her forehead and kissed her brow. He smiled into her blue eyes. He often told her that he counted himself fortunate to be able to look into a patch of summer sky each time he saw them.

Used to his fussing over her, Rain submitted to him peeling off her wet shawl to hang in a warm spot so it could return from muddy pink to its normal rose colour.

'I took shelter for a while,' she told him, dragging her fingers through her wet hair in the absence of a comb. She twisted it up out of the way and fastened it in place with a pearl-headed pin. 'Smith Alley has turned into a swamp.'

'Aye, the blacksmiths' guild said they were going to see to the drainage but they never do what they promise. Sit down, sit down. Nettle, fetch Mistress Rain some tea.'

The youngest apprentice, a lean youth, all bony knees and elbows, hurried off to the kitchen.

'I'm not that wet.'

'Love, you're dripping on the floor.'

She scuffed at the puddle she was making with the toe of her grimy boot, making her swallow hem dance. 'But I got the beef. Last bit to be had in Tigral.'

'I'm sure we'll all be grateful for that come suppertime, but for now I just want to get my girl dry.'

7

Nettle came back with a steaming cup. 'Here you are, Mistress Rain: you get that down you and you'll feel better.'

She smiled up at the young man, who was only a year or two older than her and the sweetest of the current crop of apprentices. 'Thank you, Master Nettle.'

He blushed and stammered something incomprehensible as he backed away.

Torrent nudged his daughter. 'Stop it,' he whispered. 'What?'

'Smiling at him. The poor boy's in love with you—half of them are, you know. He's quite handy until you come along and then he's all fingers and thumbs. I can't do anything with them when you're in the workshop. I'm thinking of banning you from being in here, least when the fires are lit.'

Rain laughed. But was it true? She glanced round at the apprentices, trying not to make it too obvious that she was studying them. They had returned to their tasks but every so often they would sneak a look at their master and his daughter. A number of tools clattered to the floor as a plague of clumsiness swept over them.

'They don't fancy me—they just fancy the idea of marrying the master's only child,' she hissed back, well aware of the realities of life in a guild craft.

Torrent didn't laugh as she expected. Indeed, her comment made him a little glum—a strange mood for her usually cheerful father. Something must have happened to upset him. He knelt at her feet to ease off her boots, his tough leather apron reluctantly folding in the middle.

'That might be so, love, but it doesn't stop you being the prettiest glassmaker's daughter in Tigral.'

She prodded him in the stomach with her foot. 'I'm almost the only glassmaker's daughter, Papa, in case you've forgotten. You wouldn't count Master Blizzard's Ember because she's only three.'

'I'd forgotten that little mite. Well then, you're the second prettiest—'

He didn't finish because Rain had jabbed him harder as punishment for his teasing.

'Where's your respect for an old man?' he gasped, threatening to tickle the sole of her foot.

'Show me an old man, and I'll respect him,' she replied smartly. 'You're still in your prime, Papa.'

He shook his head sadly, releasing her foot and standing up. 'Not so, love.' He tousled her damp hair. 'When you've finished your tea, I've left something in your room for you to see.'

He didn't say any more—didn't need to.

She took a sip and nodded. 'All right, Papa. I'll go up immediately.'

The glass teardrops tinkled gently in the breeze through the open window. Rain rubbed her hair dry and quickly changed into a gown, a fine woollen weave the colour of a red sunset. She laced it up at the sides as she took a seat at the desk to unroll the scroll her father had left there. This was their secret. While her father, the master glassblower, provided the skill to colour the glass to the exact shade required and solder them in their lead frame, it was his daughter who had the vision to create the designs that had proved so successful. It was fortunate that the guild had never got wind of this fact. As a bastion of old-fashioned ideas, withstanding as many of the reforms introduced by King Ramil as they could, the guild-masters did not allow women to practise the art of glassmaking. Despite his recognized gifts, her father would be thrown out of the guild, forbidden to work in Tigral, if anyone outside the family discovered their secret. But to work together was important to both of them; they made a perfect team, the creativity of one prompting the other to new heights of achievement, something the guild failed even to consider possible.

Yet, thought Rain, taking note of the suggested alterations to her original design, she had allowed herself a little rebellious gesture against the guild rules. Inspired by Queen Taoshira's custom of taking a creature to represent an individual's personality, Rain included her own sign, that of the swallow, in every window. A raindrop would have been too clear a statement, so she had chosen the bird that returned each year to Tigral around her birthday as her signature. If you looked carefully, the forked tail and curved wings wove their way into each Torrent creation, either as the bird itself, or more commonly, in the repeated shapes in foliage and sky. The guild-masters were praising her work without knowing it.

The parchment crackled as she weighted it flat with some smooth stones. In this design for the temple, the swallow sailed above the child-goddess's head, her playmate in a spring field. Happily, the Queen had found no fault with it, but had requested a dragonfly to be added, hovering over the pool at the child's feet. Rain picked up her charcoal and began to sketch the new element, already seeing the colours in her mind, turquoise blue and black, a fine web for the wings in specially blown glass that would trap the bubbles to represent the mesh.

An hour later, her father knocked discreetly on her door.

'May I come in?'

'Of course.' Rain sat back from her work, pleased with herself. 'What do you think?' Absent-mindedly, she toyed with her necklace of silver-glass teardrops her father had crafted for her.

Torrent bent over, his hand resting on the curls that scattered down his daughter's back. Now dry, her hair had returned to its mahogany colour, a deep reddish brown that shone like polished wood.

'Magnificent.'

'Yes, I'm pleased with it. Can you make the glass for the dragonfly wings as I've suggested?'

He scratched his chin. 'With a little experimentation.'

'You'll enjoy the challenge.'

11

'You know me well, love.' He let his hand linger on her shoulder. 'You're my world, you know that, Raindrop, don't you?'

Alerted by his sombre tone, Rain turned her head to look up at him. He was staring out of the window, the setting sun bronzing his face with golden light.

'What's the matter, Papa? You've been acting strangely ever since I came home.'

'I've asked your cousins to come to supper tonight.'

Rain wrinkled her nose. 'Shadow and Timber? I can see why you're feeling gloomy.' Neither of them relished the company of the two young relatives, both aggressive businessmen making a name for themselves in the guild as glass traders. Torrent had only used their services because they were family. All they talked about was the price of raw materials, the strength of the market in Kandar and Gerfal, or the evil of import duties; they had no creative soul or appreciation of the beauty of the goods they handled. If you made a joke in Shadow's presence, it was five minutes before he got the punchline and his laughter was creaky and dutiful. Timber was quicker-witted, but he only laughed when someone else was the target of the jest.

'Now I'm fifty, the guild has said I have to name my successor in my workshop,' Torrent added.

Rain put together the apparently unconnected remarks.

'You've chosen?' she asked in a small voice. Part of her had known that their life could not continue on its quiet path, but she hadn't realized that change would arrive so suddenly.

'It has to be family or you would not be safe,' he said, in a plea for her to understand.

'I see.'

'Shadow and Timber may leave a lot to be desired as people but they will protect you. I'll make it a condition of my will that you can carry on working if they move in.'

Rain rolled up the design and carefully secured it with twine before handing it to her father.

'That's good.'

'If I die before you're settled, they'll make sure you're looked after, see you well married.'

'I'm not marrying, Papa.'

He gave her a fond smile. 'Of course not yet—you're barely fifteen. But life is fragile—your mother taught me that. I would be a fool not to think of your future.'

'I wish you could leave the forge to me, Papa, then none of this would be necessary. You wouldn't have to worry.'

'I know, but I can't. Rules are rules.'

'The rules should be changed.'

'Maybe they will, but there's no sign yet of the guild-masters coming to their senses any time soon. I've made discreet attempts to influence them in our favour but I'm afraid of saying too much. If they think I'm arguing for women to be allowed to work because of you, they might poke their noses into our affairs and spoil what we have.'

Rain already knew this but it was hard to accept such an injustice just because she'd been born the wrong sex.

'You should have pretended I was a boy, Papa.'

He chuckled and pulled her up into a hug. 'It might have worked while you were a child but no one would believe the little waif I've raised was a fifteen-year-old boy. I'm afraid to shatter your illusions, Raindrop, but I fear you are never going to be what one would call a tall woman.'

'Oh, be quiet, you big bear.' Her lack of height was something which annoyed Rain and amused Torrent.

'Well now, that's no way to treat your father. Remember to show our guests your best manners so they fall in with our plans.'

'I'll try. But you must admit, they have a way of putting your teeth on edge.'

'Cousin Rain, this stew is very wholesome,' complimented Shadow Glasstrader. 'I see that even without a mother's influence you have not failed to attain all the womanly skills needed in a household.'

Biting her lip, Rain gave him a tight smile, hoping for her father's sake he mistook her irritated silence for maidenly shyness.

Shadow leaned back in his chair and folded his thin hands across his rounded belly. In his late twenties, he was already settling to a paunch, which looked odd on his lanky frame. His reddish-brown hair was combed smoothly back from his forehead, framing his pale oval face. He surveyed the room of apprentices with a superior expression. Rain could tell he was preparing himself to deliver another of his little words of wisdom to what he believed were grateful listeners.

'Uncle Torrent, I'm not sure it is quite fitting that my cousin should live without female companionship in a household of men,' he said in a carrying voice, his choice of subject as unwelcome as it was unexpected.

The gentle conversation in the room fell away. The apprentices turned their eyes on their master, sitting at the head of the table with his fork arrested halfway to his mouth. Rain stared at her plate, the gravy smearing the white surface the exact colour of her cousin's hair.

'Come now, Shadow,' intervened his brother, Timber, slopping some more beer into his glass, 'you think too much of what is proper and what's not. You just said Rain was skilled in all womanly crafts; I'm sure the same can be said for all her female virtues. You are getting as narrow as those priests of the old war god, Hollin, always moaning about one thing or another, concentrating on the ceremony rather than the substance.'

Timber winked at Rain. Blessed with better looks than his brother, he appeared to think his wavy brown hair and stylish moustache made him irresistible. To Rain, who cared little for the current fashion, the hair on his upper lip looked like a dead mouse.

'My daughter is above reproach,' growled Torrent. 'I will not have anyone imply otherwise.'

'Of course, uncle,' Shadow backtracked quickly. He and his brother knew they stood to gain much from an association with their uncle's forge; Rain suspected they had agreed to humour the old man as long as was necessary. 'And as I said, my cousin is a very talented cook, even in these days of scarcity.'

Torrent gave a grunt of assent, letting the matter drop, but the damage had been done. Rain now felt conscious of her position in the household as never before and she disliked Shadow even more than usual for stealing her peace of mind. She was just deciding whether she should retire from the table to avoid further criticism, when Timber broached a new topic.

'The word on the exchange, uncle, is that the King is entertaining ambassadors from one of the newly discovered lands to the east, some place called Magharna.' Timber twitched the flared tails of his bronze silk jacket into precise folds on his lap like a lady fussing with her skirts. Shadow was wearing an almost identical one of a bilious shade of green. Another unfortunate fashion the brothers had chosen to follow, thought Rain.

'Never heard of it,' said Torrent, wiping his plate clean with a crust, shirt-sleeves rolled up to his elbows, his only concession to dinner being that he no longer wore his apron.

'I'm not surprised.' Timber turned to Rain like a tutor addressing a pupil in need of instruction. 'You are too young to remember, cousin, but under the old emperor, Fergox Spearthrower, there was not much interest in exploration, only in military conquest. The present King has greatly expanded our knowledge of distant lands, funding numerous voyages of discovery.'

'Best thing King Ramil has done, good for business,' interjected Shadow, speaking through a mouthful. 'He should concentrate on this kind of thing and less on reforms in my view.'

Just as well your view doesn't count for much, thought Rain, who was a firm supporter of the present King and Queen.

'So what are these Magharnans like?' asked Torrent, moving the subject away from a critique of their ruler.

'I've heard that, as a race, they are quite tall, black hair thick and dead straight, skin a burnished colour, like field workers. They dress strangely, elaborate robes over tunics, fine layers of slashed cloth so that they look like walking cobwebs.'

Must be a pain to wash, mused Rain, thinking of the great pile of clothes from her household waiting for the tub in the back kitchen.

'Do they have a king?' Torrent enquired, pushing his plate away.

'They have someone they call the Master at the head of a ruling family. As I understand it, they think of him more like a deity.'

As a follower of the god Hollin, Shadow sniffed his disapproval at such sacrilege.

'But there's more, Uncle Torrent. They are looking for craftsmen to come to their country to work on a summer palace for the Master.' Timber gave a smug smile. 'I put a word or two into the right ears, of course, and luckily the Magharnans had already seen one of your windows in the temple—the one of the Goddess as healer. They were enquiring about you; I would not be surprised if they ask you to send someone from your forge to Magharna to design something similar for them.'

Torrent looked at his daughter. 'They want a designer?'

'Yes. They say they have craftsmen skilled in glass-making, but no designers to match you and no tradition of stained-glass manufacturing.' Timber glanced round the room. 'Surely one or two of your apprentices have learnt something of your skill, enough to satisfy these Magharnans? Just imagine the honour for our guild: the first craft to establish a trade with this country! I know the King is very eager to see us succeed.'

Torrent stood up abruptly and clapped his hands, addressing the apprentices. 'Boys, clear the table and then retire for the night.'

Timber frowned. 'Are you not going to say any more than that? This is great news for us—for your forge.'

Torrent pushed the door open with a bang and strode out, calling over his shoulder. 'Shadow, Timber, come to my study. You too, Rain. There's something we have to discuss.'

* * *

'You did what? You've been letting her dabble in design for years!' Timber paced the room, tugging at the roots of his hair with one frantic fist. 'Do you know what you've done? You've risked everything—your business, your wealth, your own family!'

Torrent stood with his back to the shuttered window, calmly lighting the candlestick on his desk. Rain sat on a stool near the draughtsman bench. Rolls of her sketches were stacked in the pigeonholes behind it, stretching almost to the ceiling—years of her labour. Shadow slumped in an armchair near the fire, his mouth slack with shock.

Her father blew out the taper. 'I don't think you understand, Timber: she does more than dabble. Rain *is* Torrent stained glass. Every single one of them is her vision; I'm merely the one who has the privilege of realizing it for her.'

'I don't believe you.' Timber spun on his heel and loomed over Rain. 'Cousin, what is this foolishness? Tell me my uncle has lost his senses. It must be a joke.'

Rain did not meet his eyes but ran a finger over the ribbon tying the scroll containing her first design, a wheatsheaf for a local baker.

'I'm not joking,' said Torrent.

'By Hollin, I wish you were!' Timber slammed a hand down on the bench by Rain's arm. 'It must stop immediately, you hear. You can't risk the family like this. You'll ruin us as glass traders if this comes out!'

Anyone would think I'd committed murder, not created something beautiful and unique, thought Rain, focusing on the black hairs that flourished on her cousin's forearm like a little forest.

'Rain is not going to stop,' Torrent replied calmly. 'She is a brilliant artist. It would be a crime to prevent her using her talent.'

'It's a crime to let her continue.'

'No, it merely breaks a rule—a rule that should've been challenged long ago.'

Timber paled. 'You're not thinking of bringing this out into the open, surely?'

Torrent shifted uncomfortably. 'Perhaps if I were a more courageous man, I would, but I cannot do that to Rain. More likely than not, we'd be thrown out of the guild with no means of earning a living. I would prefer it if we were simply left in peace to continue working as we have. No one has been harmed.'

'I don't believe you!' Timber was off again, ranting as he strode. 'You say no one has been harmed but you fail to recognize that you've endangered our entire family by your flagrant disregard of guild rules. And why? Because you wish to spoil your daughter. You've let her have her way in this household for too long.'

Shadow chose this moment to add his weight on his brother's side of the argument. 'Indeed, uncle, I fear you've done our cousin a great disservice, taken her from the station into which she was born and tried to make her into the son you never had.'

Torrent's anger grew now the attacks had turned on

Rain, his hands shaking as he tried to hold on to his temper. 'I do not need a son; I have Rain.'

'Rain is a girl, destined for marriage and family— that's if any decent man will have her now,' said Shadow piously.

'It would be an honour for any suitor to marry my daughter.'

'Not if you've been cast out of the guild and are reduced to begging in the streets because of her,' interjected Timber.

'It won't come to that.'

'It might. What if one of the apprentices informs the guild-masters?'

'They don't know it is her work; we're very careful.'

'But you are taking a senseless risk!'

'There is nothing senseless about it. Look at the accounts, Timber. The stained glass is the most profitable part of my business; without her we would be just a mediocre forge.'

Rain doubted that very much, but it warmed her to hear her father's defence.

'What are you going to do now, uncle?' asked Timber sarcastically. 'The Magharnan interest in your designer is likely to place you under intense scrutiny. It will be a miracle if the truth does not come out.'

'Why should it? Unless one of you takes it upon yourself to reveal our secret, we can carry on as before. I had hoped by confiding in you like this, by naming you both as my successors, you will protect Rain as you would the rest of my business.'

His declaration deflated the cousins' indignation like a pin in a pig's bladder balloon.

'You've named us as your successors?' repeated Timber.

Torrent gave a jerky nod. 'I intend to, if you agree to let Rain continue working.'

The two men exchanged a look.

'You are thinking of retiring?' asked Timber.

'No, not just yet, but I will take you on as junior partners until I do so if that is your wish. When I'm gone, the forge will be left to you both equally, with the exception of a generous provision to be made for Rain's dowry, if she has not already married by then.'

'Perhaps one of us should marry her,' mused Shadow, 'keep the money in the family.'

Rain snapped the charcoal pencil she had been toying with.

'That will not be necessary,' replied Torrent curtly. 'I wish her to marry for love, not as a business arrangement.'

Timber stroked his moustache. 'Of course. How very enlightened of you, uncle.' He gave Rain an overly warm grin. 'Hers would be a heart worth winning.'

He's changed his tune quickly, thought Rain. *One moment calling me a disgrace, the next a prize. I'm not so easily fooled.*

'Then I can rely on you both to keep our secret?' pushed Torrent, wanting their promise before the interview ended.

'Certainly,' agreed Shadow.

22

'Indeed. But what's to be done about the contract with the Magharnans?' enquired Timber, frowning. 'No one will believe that you say you wish to turn it down. Questions will be asked.'

Torrent put an arm around his daughter's shoulders, aware that she had not said anything during the whole discussion, which was unlike her.

'We'll worry about that when we have to. I've not been asked yet.'

'You will be.'

'Then we will find a way round the problem as we always do. Right, my love?'

Rain nodded, resting her head against her father's side. 'Yes, Papa.'

Shard 2
Flint Blue

'I tell you, Peri, the bird is sickening for something.' Helgis tugged the back of his brother's sleeveless leather jacket to get his attention, his small round face and dark eyes bleak with anxiety. 'She's off her food and her feathers look dull. You've always told me that's a bad sign.'

Peri kept his eyes on the distant falcon, flying over the crag. The ground under his boots squelched as he readied himself to swing the lure, but he paid no heed to the discomfort of wet feet.

'I'll take a look at her when I've finished here,' he promised, his voice as calm and melodious as always. There was something about him—his air of being utterly centred—that appealed to all creatures, especially winged ones. Even Helgis's anxiety eased listening to his brother's words. 'Now stand back: I need room.'

'Please, don't take too long. I'm really worried about her.'

'I know—and it's natural. Goldie's your first bird. We all worry too much about our first.'

Helgis sighed, realizing his brother was not going to come with him until he was good and ready. He often complained that Peri was as immovable as the peak of Mount Bandor; even now, as he stood ankle-deep in the mud, his shoulder-skimming black hair tied back with a leather thong, his long limbs relaxed, there was no budging him until he was finished. Yet Peri had a sure hand with the birds that kept even the tricky ones, like the falcon he was now flying, obedient to his will. Helgis wished he had even a fraction of his patience.

Peri caught his brother's envious look and smiled inwardly. He knew his little brother thought him always the capable one. Helgis had announced only the night before that he wanted to be exactly like Peri when he grew up, much to the amusement of the rest of the family. They all anticipated that Helgis's hot temper might not allow it. But Peri loved his little brother dearly and hoped he could live up to the high opinion Helgis held of him.

'You'd best move to a safe distance,' Peri said gently.

'I'll get out of your way then.' Helgis jumped from tussock to tussock to reach the shelter of a rock. 'I'm clear.'

Peri slowly began to spin the lure above his head, the piece of rabbit meat tied to the end humming in the wind to tempt the falcon on the wing. He put aside the problem of Helgis's sparrowhawk for later attention, concentrating on the task at hand. Would the bird respond? The crotchety falcon had been almost impossible to train so as a last resort had been given to him to straighten out. Peri guessed a previous handler had mistreated the creature or failed to be consistent with his rewards; it had developed an unpredictable and malevolent streak, as likely to dive for the trainer as the meat lure.

'Come on, beauty,' he urged the hunter. He was the bird's last chance: if it didn't respond to him, then it would be destroyed, a thought which made Peri want to rage at the unfairness of life. The only birds of prey the Magharnan Master allowed near his capital, Rolvint, were those under the control of the falconers.

With a contemptuous loop over the crag, the peregrine flaunted its superb flying skills. It skimmed along the ridge, teasingly suggesting that it planned to continue on until it was out of sight. Then, finally, as if sensing that even Peri's patience was running out, it turned and rocketed towards the lure, as fast as an arrow from a longbow. It made a perfect grab for the meat, landing it on the grass.

Now the test: could the handler separate it from the lure? If the falcon ate the kill, it would never do as a hunter. It had to be trained to let go of what it had captured. Peri moved closer, slipping off his jacket, then threw it over the lure, making it seem to the falcon that it had 'disappeared'. He then cast a small chunk of meat within easy reach. Would the falcon let go of the prize it still gripped but could not see, in favour of the reward that was very visible on the ground a pace away? The falcon raised its ebony eyes, its expression one of resentment, but then hopped off the lure to pluck the titbit from the grass. Next Peri held out his gauntleted hand with another larger piece of meat. Rogue gave him a cold look but flapped up to snatch this reward too, allowing Peri to secure the bird in place by the jesses attached to its legs. Back under the falconer's control, Rogue was too busy eating his treat to worry that Peri was putting away the much larger feast on the end of the lure.

'Phew!' exclaimed Helgis, jumping out from behind his refuge. 'I never thought I'd see Rogue follow orders.'

Usually unruffled by anything that happened on the training grounds, Peri could not disguise his delight. 'I didn't think I'd live to see it either. He's been the most difficult bird I've ever had to train.'

Helgis hooted. 'Oi, Rogue, you scrawny old thing! You owe Peri, you know. Without him, you'd be cat's meat.'

The raptor looked up from its meal, fixing the twelve-year-old boy with a disdainful glare.

'I don't think he's grateful,' noted Helgis.

'No, it's not in his nature,' agreed Peri.

'About Goldie—'

'I'm coming, I'm coming, sprout. Just let me hood Rogue and we'll head back to the barracks.'

Peri subdued the falcon with a tiny leather hood, allowing it to keep its reward in its talons. He was comfortable with Rogue's weight on his arm; like the rest of his family, he almost felt undressed unless he had one of his birds along for the ride. He headed back to where he had left his horse in the shelter of an oak tree; Helgis's pony grazed alongside. Peri had expected to see an escort of at least a couple of other lads from the compound, but Helgis had apparently made the journey alone.

'Does our father know you've come to find me?' Peri asked shrewdly.

'Not exactly.' Helgis mounted then waited while his brother put the falcon in its travelling basket.

'So you're beyond the compound without permission and on your own?'

'You could say that.'

'Hmm.' It was not Peri's way to scold his younger brother, preferring the boy to reach his own conclusions about the recklessness of his actions.

'But you're out here alone,' Helgis argued.

Peri raised a brow, his dark brown eyes solemn.

'Yes, I know you are trained to defend yourself— and you've the falcon as well—but it's broad daylight: it's hardly likely that the bandits would pick on me, is it?'

Peri clicked his horse into motion. The gelding began a smooth trot back down the mountain road, picking a safe route through the potholes and fallen stones.

'I mean, I'm just a boy. I suppose they might have wanted Apple.' Helgis patted the piebald pony as she gamely tried to keep up with the long legs of Peri's chestnut. 'I know people are desperate—but we're close to Rolvint—bandits don't come here, do they?'

Nutmeg splashed across a stream. Peri hadn't wanted to chance the rotting bridge. He waited on the far bank for Helgis and Apple to reach them.

'The Master's guards no longer patrol out here, Helgis,' he explained, gesturing to the appalling state of the highway. 'There's no money to pay for enough of them. A group of pilgrims from the coast was attacked on this very spot only last week. Three of them died. The rest walked to the capital barefooted and wearing only their shirts.'

Helgis grimaced. 'That's terrible—attacking pilgrims, I mean. Isn't anyone safe?'

Peri knew his point was now made and waited for Helgis to realize. It didn't take long.

'So I'm not safe either, am I?' Helgis shuddered and urged Apple into a faster trot. 'Let's get home, Peri.'

The falcon men's barracks were situated beyond the city walls in the graveyard district. Their role as carers for birds of prey made them unclean to other Magharnans so they occupied this ground with others of their class, the refuse collectors, dog handlers, butchers and undertakers—anyone who handled the dead, or creatures that killed. Peri always thought it strange that while the higher classes were quite happy to consume the carcasses caught by the hunting birds and prepared by the butchers, they despised those who did the work to bring the food to their table. Where did the nobles and merchants think the fine meats covered in rich sauces came from if not from the ugliness of the slaughterhouse or the bloody reality of the hunt? He was thankful he did not have to live with such hypocrisy at his home.

The barracks themselves were basic but comfortable, as far removed from the extravagant buildings of the city-within-the-walls as you could get. His home's thick stonework, low slate roof, and stubby corners made it appear like a common earthworm squirming below the soaring butterfly architecture of the palaces, temples, and squares of Rolvint. The designers had attempted to make the city appear worthy of its god-ruler; nothing low or base was allowed inside; fountains must spring in the market places, trees blossom in the streets, houses be full of light and air. Arches and fretwork abounded, making the city from a distance look as if it was worked from lace. Raised with the prejudices of his outcast class, Peri had come to distrust the appearance, thinking such artistry wasted when people in the surrounding countryside could not travel on sound roads or even rely on the law enforcers to do their job. He suspected it was all a fine icing on a very stale cake.

Hefting the saddle off his sturdy Nutmeg, he shook his head at his own thoughts. He would have to be careful. It might be safe to think such things in private, but if he dared voice them he would be in trouble. The Master hated dissent.

Helgis had already broken the news of Rogue's success when Peri ventured into the communal kitchen.

His father was cooking at the open hearth in the centre while his mother helped his younger siblings with their schoolwork on a table under an open window. Other people were gathered in the spacious single storey building, each group occupying their allotted place, together yet separate for the evening family time. The bird handlers used three trestle tables set up on the eastern side of the fireplace; butchers congregated to the west. The hunters lounged around tables arranged in a sociable square, their tools and weapons hung on the southern wall behind them. To the north, in what should have been the darkest corner, the refuse-collectors assembled, their patch brightened by a collection of odds-and-ends gathered in the course of their work: mismatched drapes, cracked china, and battered copper pans polished to a shine. The scavenger families all slept elsewhere in huts scattered around the compound, but most preferred to spend their waking hours in this room where there was warmth and company.

Peri's parents looked up and stopped what they were doing to congratulate him.

'My boy,' smiled Katia Falconer, kissing his cheek proudly.

'Have some stew,' growled his father, shoving a bowl in his hands. A man of few words, everyone understood that Hern meant this as approval and reward, feeding his son just as he would treat one of his falcons when they'd behaved well.

'I'd best see to Goldie first,' said Peri.

'Nonsense,' his mother replied, patting the bench, 'that bird will wait ten minutes. Helgis is worrying unnecessarily.'

Peri's brother frowned, not wishing to gainsay his mother, knowing how handy his father was with a wooden spoon administered to the top of a cheeky boy's head. 'Am not,' he muttered.

Hern let this pass; he had already dealt out to Helgis a week's long punishment of extra chores for going to the mountain pass without permission. 'Any trouble?' he asked Peri, returning to his cauldron.

He shook his head and sat down. 'All quiet. But I saw no patrols either. You would've thought they'd increase the guard on the mountain passes now they know there are bandits out there.'

His youngest sister, a girl of four called Rosie, crawled on to his lap.

'Leave your brother alone,' called his mother as she marked sums drawn on a slate.

'It's all right, Ma, she's no trouble.' Peri stroked his sister's head, her dark eyes glowing with adoration. Awkwardly he ate the stew, taking care not to drop any on her, which was made all the more difficult by her wriggling.

'Well done, Bel.' His mother kissed her eldest daughter for getting all her sums right. She ushered Bel away to eat before returning to her subject. 'I don't understand it. They're spending money in the city on that new palace as if there is no tomorrow, while all around us things are falling apart.'

She did not dare say any more in this public space, but Peri and his parents thought it was a criminal waste what the nobles were doing when the harvests had been so bad this year. Merchants had begun hoarding grain and the poor could no longer afford to buy it. The rich were living as extravagantly as usual, indeed to even greater excess as if they were afraid that if they stopped, they too would starve.

'I meant to say, Pa: the bridge to the pass needs serious work. Don't use it if you go out that way.' Peri ruffled Rosie's hair and put her to one side. 'I'll come and say goodnight,' he promised, 'but for now I have a sick bird to see.'

Rosie stuck her thumb in her mouth and nodded solemnly.

Helgis danced along beside Peri as he made his way to the mews. It was Peri's favourite place in the barracks, a long, specially designed building where the birds could rest in comfort on their perches, in groups or alone as suited their species. Rogue was already back in his niche, his flint-blue feathers gleaming like polished steel as he roosted on his ledge, next door to Bel's merlin.

'Obedience tired you out?' murmured Peri, stroking the bird lightly, savouring the rapid beat of the tiny heart under the pale breast feathers.

Goldie was lodged a few niches along. As Helgis had said, she did not look her usual bright self, her ribbed stomach feathers yellowed, her dark brown coat flat and dull. Peri lifted her from her perch and sniffed the top of her head, alert for the smell of sickness. The bird nestled closer, strange behaviour for the usually proud sparrowhawk.

'Not eating, you say?' he asked.

'No.' Helgis showed him the untouched food bowl.

Peri wrinkled his nose: there was an unpleasant tang in the niche, the ground below the perch soiled. He crumbled apart a casting expelled from her crop, finding fur and bone inside the hard pellet. 'Did you clean her out this morning?'

'Of course,' bristled Helgis. 'She was really stinky.'

'What was the last thing she ate?'

'A rabbit, caught on Jettan Kirn's estate.'

'I think Goldie's got a mild case of food poisoning. I can only guess that the rabbit was not fit for her to eat.'

Helgis nodded. 'It was slow to move. She had no trouble snatching it.'

'The jettan has had a poor harvest. His gamekeepers must have been laying out poison for the animals that eat his crops.'

'He should have said!' Helgis exploded with outrage. 'He shouldn't call in the falcon men if he's using poison.'

Peri shrugged. 'It happens. Someone like the jettan doesn't consider the feelings of those under him when he gives his orders. He probably just told his estate manager to use every means available to salvage his harvest.'

'But still—' Helgis looked ready to knock on the jettan's door himself and give him a piece of his mind—a fatal step for any of the lowly falcon men with one from the highest class. Jettan Kirn was the Master's chief adviser, the sort who would not think a month of baths enough to cleanse himself for breathing the same air as a scavenger.

Peri put a hand on his brother's shoulder. 'Let it go, Helgis. Goldie will recover. I have a purgative I can give her. In a day or two she'll be back to normal. All we can do is warn the others not to let their birds feed on the jettan's estate.'

'It's not fair.'

'No, it's not.' Peri could understand the anger that was driving his brother. Few things were worse for a falcon man than to have one of his birds harmed in the course of doing its duty. He too remembered his feelings of frustration when he realized for the first time just how society was weighted against people of his class. With the Master at the top of the pile, backed by the jettans, it was a very long way down to his level: first there were the courtiers, called the drummers, and priests; then wealers who handled the money; codifiers who administered the law; warriors; purveyors, artificers, and farmers; servants and labourers; and at the bottom, the bondsmen. Finally, after this accounting of classes-within-the-walls, came his people and the other scavengers. There was no chance to rise up through the ranks: you were born to your class and remained in it until death. But the unfairness did not stop there: a jettan could injure a man from a lower class and no charge would be brought against him; but should a bondsman or a scavenger even look at a noble wrongly then he was liable to the severest of punishments: a flogging or imprisonment. While capital punishment was relatively rare, it was not unknown for someone from a higher class to demand it for a lower class offender even when the offence was relatively mild. A tailor had been imprisoned only the month before for failing to complete a jettan's wedding garment on time, regardless of the fact that the unfortunate man had fallen ill a week before the marriage took place.

Peri distracted himself from his bad mood by preparing the medicine from the stocks in the mews storeroom and feeding it to the sparrowhawk. He had trained himself to deal with his strong emotions by focusing on the task at hand, putting aside the negative feelings. It had led to people believing him to be different from the rest of his family, thinking he lacked the temper they exhibited—a still pond, as his mother described him. This was far from the truth. If Peri had chosen an image for himself, he would have said he was more like a river concealing powerful currents. To be the best falcon man he could, he had long since decided that the birds he looked after had to be protected from any overspill of temper; they flourished or flagged depending on the atmosphere in which they were raised. He owed it to them to maintain his control.

Goldie really wasn't too bad, Peri decided, only a little off colour; he was confident she would bounce back quickly. Crooning softly, he restored her to her perch and shut her up for the night.

On his way back to the kitchen, the bell rang at the barrack gate. Peri groaned. As no person from the city would venture into the compound with those they considered unclean, the scavengers had to answer the summons and go to them. Being nearest to the gate, Peri set off to open it, waving away one of his neighbours who had poked his head out of the communal kitchen.

'I'll get it.'

Peri opened the postern gate and stepped outside on to the muddy highway. Across the road, the pale oval slabs that marked the tombs in the cemetery stretched into the distance, gleaming in the moonlight like fallen petals. As expected, he was greeted by the sight of a deputation from the city: a servant from one of the jettan families by the look of his blue slashed tunic, accompanied by four muscular bondsmen, protection against the dangers beyond the walls.

'Falcon man?' asked the servant.

'Yes, sir.' Peri bowed low as required, feeling weary of the ceremonies he had to observe when meeting a superior.

'I serve the great jettan, Kirn the Magnificent, strong arm of the realm, chief of works to the Master.'

'Indeed.' Peri stifled a yawn. Great: a message from his least favourite jettan. It had been a long day and he did not feel up to listening to the long list of titles and declarations of greatness that accompanied any interview with any retainer to a jettan. All of them adopted fantastical claims for their employers—magnificent, benevolent, ingenious, enlightened—it was a wonder there were enough praise-words in the Magharnan dictionary to go round.

'My lord requires a falcon man to hunt the crows that infest the building site of the new summer palace. You must send one of your number to the royal district tomorrow at dawn. The work must be completed before the jettan arrives to oversee progress on the building at ten in the morning.' The little man paused, waiting for a response.

'It is our honour,' replied Peri insincerely. He was hardly going to say anything else with four strong men alert for the least sign of disrespect from a low-life such as him.

'Good. See that it is done.'

'I doubt it can be done with only one visit. The crows will flee then return once our hunting birds are gone.'

'Make as many trips as is necessary, scavenger.'

'Yes, sir.'

The servant turned with a flounce of his blue costume and scurried back to the city. Shutting the gate with a tired smile, Peri wondered what offence the lackey had committed to be given this, the lowliest of tasks: talking to him.

'What was that about?' Hern asked as Peri entered the kitchen.

'Jettan Kirn's servant.' He raised his voice so that all the families could hear. 'Anyone volunteer to rid the summer palace of crows tomorrow at dawn?'

There was a long silence before people returned to their meals, avoiding Peri's gaze.

'Thought not,' he muttered. He slumped down on the bench next to his sister, Bel. 'I suppose it'll have to be me.'

Bel grimaced. 'The ritual bath shouldn't be too bad, Peri.'

'It is at that time of day—water isn't heated and the bath-house attendants scrub you raw. Still, someone has to do it.'

'Which bird will you take?' Bel twirled the end of her black plait, dusting it over her knuckles absent-mindedly.

'He wants the job done by mid morning: it'll have to be Fletch.'

'Poor old Peri,' commiserated Bel. 'But you're the best of us—you'll manage where others wouldn't.'

'I'd just prefer it if it wasn't a jettan asking.'

'Wouldn't we all.' Bel rubbed her eyes. 'I'm ready to turn in. Have you forgotten to say goodnight to Rosie?'

'You're right. I expect she'll have fallen asleep by now.'

'No, she won't. You're her hero. She'll be propping up her eyelids, desperate for you to come and give her a kiss.'

Peri scooped up his sister under his arm, heading

towards the family's lodgings. 'Let's go then. Can't keep her waiting any longer.'

The ritual bath was as unpleasant as he anticipated. Forced to strip off everything that he was wearing, he stood in the bath-house by the city gates shivering as a sleepy attendant attacked him with a scrubbing brush. The water was freezing, the bristles unforgiving. Sensing his master's discomfort, the goshawk, Fletch, shrieked from his basket, making the attendant jump with consternation.

'It can't get out?' he asked fearfully.

'No,' replied Peri, 'he can't.'

Next the attendant handed him a black robe, simple sandals, and a rope belt. His own clothes were to be kept for his return.

'You are purified, falcon man,' the attendant announced.

I felt pretty pure before I set foot in here, thought Peri.

Ushered past a suspicious gate warden, Peri began the long walk to the palace district. Rolvint had been founded on a bend in the River Rol; the richest houses were built on the steep bank, enjoying the protection of the cliffs. The new summer palace was some distance from the gates in a corner of the extensive parklands belonging to the Master. It would take Peri at least half an hour to reach the building site. He carried Fletch on his arm, having left the travelling basket back at the bath-house. The hawk was content to ride, head hidden in a hood, claws firmly planted on Peri's leather gauntlet. Man and bird walked at peace with each other, having the streets almost to themselves. The few people up this early stepped out of their path, not wanting to risk the bother of a ritual bath should they inadvertently brush against one of the scavenger class.

A toddler stumbled out of a purveyor's shop doorway—a bakery judging by the delicious smells coming from inside. The child's ball rolled across the street and stopped against Peri's feet.

'Mine!' she squeaked, before noticing Fletch. 'Big bird.' She chuckled with delight and stretched up to pat the strange creature.

Peri smiled and nudged the ball towards her with his toe. 'Yes, he is, isn't he? Best not touch him though: he can get a bit cranky.'

The child's mother ran from the house and snatched her daughter from the ground before she could retrieve the ball. The child shrieked and beat her legs angrily.

'No touch! Dirty man; dirty ball!' the mother scolded. She banged the door of the house, leaving the ball unclaimed on the road. No one would want it now he had made it unclean.

With a resigned sigh, Peri bent down and picked it up. 'Think Rosie would like this?' he asked Fletch. 'I thought so.' He pocketed the ball and carried on down the street.

He reached the building site a little after dawn.

'You're late,' grumbled the bondsman left on watch to let him enter the enclosure.

Peri decided not to reply. The fact that he'd had to wait for the baths to open had not been considered when this job was handed out last night.

'Crows are making a real mess,' the bondsman continued. 'The master-masons won't touch anything they've crapped on, so Muggins has to clean up the whole time. Waste of my blinking time.'

Peri began to relax: it was clear that the grouchy bondsman moaned about everything, not just his time keeping, so it no longer seemed personal.

'Filthy critters nest up in the elm trees. Can't cut them down because the jettan says they're special. Look like any other blinking tree to me, not that anyone asks me nothing. Your bird get rid of them?' The old bondsman's rheumy eyes flickered nervously to the goshawk.

'Yes.'

'About blinking time.' The bondsman conducted him into the forecourt of the palace. The white stone walls were already up, pierced by scores of empty arched windows, insubstantial like a dandelion seed head—one puff and parts of the building would float away, thought Peri.

'Don't talk much, do you?' grunted the bondsman.

'No.'

'Suit yourself. The crows hang around here too, sitting on those ledges. Got to get rid of them because the jettan is expecting some foreign muckety-muck to come and do the glass for them and we can't expect a foreigner to touch our crow-crap, can we?' The bondsman chuckled. 'Ruddy madness: kitting out an expedition to some heathen land. Cost a fortune, they say. Bringing back glassmakers and fancy woodworkers to do the finishing work when there're queues at the soup kitchens and people going hungry. Jettan Kirn thinks to impress the Master with his original design, bull's blood!'

'What's your name, sir?' Peri asked, intrigued by this outspoken man.

'Muggins.'

'No, really.'

The old man gave a lopsided grin, a couple of teeth missing. 'Mikel. And you?'

'They call me Peri.'

'Daft name.'

'It's short for peregrine. Somehow, my birth name didn't stick. No one uses it now.'

'So you moulted it and got yourself a nickname?'

Peri nodded, surveying the crows' nests high in the leafy elm. 'You could put it like that.'

Mikel hooked his thumbs in his leather belt. 'You're all right for one of them scavengers.'

'You're all right for one of them bondsmen,' replied Peri, tugging the falconer's knot on the jesses to release Fletch for the hunt.

Shard 3
Blood Red

The Magharnan ambassador came to see Torrent's workshop the day after the discussion with Rain's cousins. His arrival was heralded by no less a person than the Prime Minister Melletin.

'Master Glassmaker, you do not mind this intrusion?' asked Melletin jovially, striding into the forge. In his mid forties, the Prime Minister still carried himself like a fighter, his arms brawny and hands calloused in contrast to his fine clothing of belted silken tunic and loose trousers of forest green. His wiry red hair was constrained by a smart velvet cap and feather; his beard close-clipped to his chin. He never stood on ceremony and was frequently to be glimpsed around the capital, keeping in touch with the traders, farmers, and craftsmen.

From her sunny corner by the window which she shared with the family cat, Rain snapped the thread on the shirt she was mending, tidying her work away. It wasn't every day that one of the most notable people in the land came calling. As a close friend of the King,

Melletin had shared Ramil's struggle out of the slave pits to seize control of Holt from its ruthless emperor, Fergox Spearthrower, and served him in government ever since.

'Of course not, my lord. You do me a great honour.' Torrent bowed, followed by all his apprentices. Rain stood and dipped a curtsey though she doubted anyone could see her.

Three people followed the prime minister into the workshop: a stately looking man with a cobweb scarlet cloak, a woman dressed in a feminine version of the same attire, and lastly, an energetic lady with long dark hair and mischievous eyes in a tunic and loose trousers like Melletin's only in sizzling orange. She wasted no second taking in everyone and everything, including Rain, with her shrewd gaze.

'May I introduce our guests, Ambassador Lintir and his wife, Jettana Mina, and of course my own wife, Yelena,' said Melletin.

Rain studied the latter with particular interest: Yelena was as famous as her husband, having served for many years as foreign minister, and another ally of the King and Queen. She had been an impressive fighter during the rebellion, but after bearing four children, her activities had toned down slightly. She now only bested her husband in every other sword match.

'Please,' Torrent ushered his guests in. 'Nettle, Unis, bring our guests some chairs.'

Melletin waved the offer away. 'We won't be staying long. Ambassador, as you've seen up at the temple,

Master Torrent is without doubt the most gifted glass-maker in our land.'

The ambassador looked down his long beaklike nose at the craftsman. 'He designed the windows?' he asked, using the Common tongue but with an unfamiliar accent that broadened and flattened the vowels.

'Well, yes, I—' began Torrent.

Melletin held up a hand. 'I'm very sorry, Master Torrent, but the ambassador is prevented by the customs of his country from talking directly to someone of a different class. To him it is as if you speak in a tongue he cannot understand.'

Even if he can speak the language? How silly, thought Rain. She then noticed with amusement that Foreign Minister Yelena had raised a disgusted eyebrow, but fortunately for diplomatic relations she refrained from passing comment on the traditions of other nations.

Torrent flushed. 'Well, in that case, perhaps you could tell the visitor that my workshop is indeed responsible for the windows he saw.'

Melletin began the laborious process of acting as translator between the two, repeating everything Torrent said about the process of making the stained glass. The ambassador's wife stood back, her attention wandering as she eyed the stunning collection of blown glass on display.

'How perfect,' she exclaimed, running her finger over a vase. 'Such a shame it would not survive the journey home.'

As Yelena joined her to admire the pieces on the

shelf, Rain's cat got up from his spot on the windowsill and stretched luxuriously. Jumping down and rubbing on Rain's ankles, he went off in search of new people to pet. Scraping himself against Yelena's legs earned him a rub of his head, venturing to touch the ambassadress produced a shriek.

'Get it away from me!' the woman shouted, leaping back against the shelf. The vase she had admired wobbled and tumbled to the floor, smashing into hundreds of shards. The Magharnan paid no heed, flailing with her skirts to shoo the animal away. Yelena rushed to steady the rocking shelf; Rain darted into the fray and scooped up the startled cat, cradling him to her chest.

The ambassador hurried to his wife's side. 'What happened, my dear?'

She held out a hand. 'Keep away—I'm unclean—that carrion-eater contaminated me!'

The ambassador shuddered. 'Water! Fetch water for my wife!'

Bemused, Nettle ran to obey.

'What's wrong, your excellency?' asked Melletin, glancing at Rain, thinking perhaps she had been the culprit.

'The cat,' spluttered the ambassador. 'We cannot touch hunting beasts or those that eat that which is already dead.'

Rain buried her face in the sweet smelling coat of the family tabby. It was remarkable that any culture could deprive itself of the pleasure of stroking such soft fur.

'I'm sorry for the mistake. I will send my men ahead in future to make sure all such creatures are cleared from the houses you visit.' Melletin gave Rain a commiserating smile. 'Young lady, perhaps you could make the unfortunate offender disappear?'

She bit her lip to hide a grin and whisked the cat away to the kitchen where she shut him in with a piece of dried fish. When she returned to the workshop, she found the ambassadress's servants bathing her ankles and a new robe replacing the old, which had been flung into a corner for disposal.

'We will pay for the breakage, Master Torrent,' Yelena said sweetly, 'as it was our lack of foresight that caused the accident.'

'Thank you, my lady.' Rain's father looked quite harassed by all that had happened, his hair up on end where he had run his fingers through it.

The ambassador had calmed now he understood that no insult had been meant to his wife. 'Please tell Master Torrent that I wish him to send one of his best men from this workshop to survey the summer place in Rolvint and design windows suiting its exceptional location. Speed is essential as it must be completed by mid-year's day. We are prepared to pay six thousand of your gold rams for his services.'

Six thousand! Rain almost swooned at the sum stated: it was as much as the workshop earned in a year.

Torrent pulled at the collar of his shirt. 'That is very generous.'

'Tell him that his man can travel with my delegation.

We are returning next week, taking passage from a port in Kandar. The entire journey takes around a month and we can expect to arrive back in Rolvint before the beginning of winter. That will give him six months to complete the commission.'

'Please ask the ambassador how many windows and of what size.'

'Sixteen, and each of a size to match those in Queen Taoshira's temple.'

Torrent shook his head. 'It can't be done so quickly.'

'It must be done,' the ambassador addressed Melletin. 'The Master demands it. All we require are the designs. I have hundreds of glassworkers to put on this task once the plans are agreed.'

The prime minister turned to his craftsman. 'Master Torrent, this would be a wonderful beginning for our trading relationship. All of us will be in your debt.'

'Can you not just order him to do it?' asked the ambassador disdainfully.

'Things don't work like that round here,' replied Melletin, a glint of humour in his eye. 'I don't want to spark off a riot.'

'At least, not again,' added Yelena, taking her husband's arm and patting it. 'You gave that up eighteen years ago.'

The pressure in the room for Torrent to agree was immense; Melletin had no need of orders when a dutiful citizen wanted to please him and his King.

'I will send someone,' Torrent agreed reluctantly. 'I realize the journey is long, sir, but is it safe?'

'Tell the craftsman that his man will be well protected, travelling with my guard at all times,' the ambassador said stiffly. 'I have many rich goods to bring back with me; I will take no risks.'

'Is that acceptable, Master Torrent?' asked Melletin.

He nodded. 'Yes, thank you, sir.'

A week after the Magharnans' visit, the agreement had been sealed by contract and an instalment of a thousand gold rams paid. Torrent stacked the money on his desk, head in his hands.

'What do I do, Rain?' he asked his daughter. 'Do you think any of our apprentices are up to the task?'

They both knew the answer: no.

He handed her the personal letter from King Ramil, congratulating Torrent for being the first craftsman to begin trading with the new ally.

'*Much rides on your endeavours,*' the King had written. '*All of us rely on you to give our goods and services the highest reputation in Magharna.*'

Rain's resolve had been building since the visit of the ambassador. The answer was obvious: the designs for the Queen's temple were complete now; all that remained was for her father to make them.

'I'll go, Papa.'

'That's impossible, Rain. The guild would never allow it.'

'The guild need not know. I can accompany someone we trust, let them take the credit for the work.'

Torrent pushed over a pile of coins. 'We don't need this, you know.'

'But our country does. You've read the King's letter. And besides, I'd be travelling with the ambassador's party; he promised it would be safe. I'd like to do it.'

She could see that he was still far from convinced. She had to come up with some more arguments, even if they weren't strictly true.

'I'm a little bored with Tigral, Papa, and I'm ready to see new countries. Didn't you travel as a journeyman at my age?'

'That's different: it's part of a glassmaker's training.'

'So this can be part of mine. Think of all the new ideas I'll discover, new patterns: we can start a fashion for Magharnan ware when I come back.'

He took her hand and pulled her closer. 'So you're fed up with your old father?'

'No! But that doesn't mean I don't also want to take the chances I'm given.' She had started the conversation arguing against her own inclination, but now, as she imagined the new places and people she would see, excitement unfurled inside her. 'These Magharnans are so different from us: their capital city must be fascinating.'

'I don't know—'

'Who can we trust to go with me?'

'Are you sure?'

'Very. A little adventure before I settle down to the rest of my life in Tigral.'

He stood up to pace his study. 'It will have to be one

of the cousins, I suppose. But how can you travel with him on your own?'

'She'll have to marry one of us,' said Timber.

Rain swivelled round quickly to see Timber and Shadow in the doorway. She had been so absorbed by her discussion with her father that she had not noticed their arrival, but, predictably, they'd rushed over as soon as they heard about the delivery of the Magharnan gold.

'She's too young,' protested Torrent.

'A formal betrothal then. That should quiet the malicious tongues. We can dissolve it on our return if our lovely cousin should still be averse to the match.'

Timber was talking as if she was going to be tied to both of them.

'Which one of you will it be?' she asked, her spine creeping at the thought.

The two cousins shared a look between them.

'Fancy a jaunt to Magharna, brother?' Timber enquired.

How nice to be so wanted, Rain thought sourly.

'But the business—there's so much to do,' protested Shadow.

'Come now, you know I'll handle that. I need you to forge these new trading links for us; you're far better than me at all that.' Smoothly, Timber flattered Shadow into doing his will. Used to controlling his weaker brother, he had obviously decided he could spare himself the bother of a journey and marriage while still enjoying the benefits of the prestige and wealth. 'In the vanguard of a new market. Exploration and riches. I would love to go myself, of course, but I have to think what is best for our trading relationships.'

'Me? You think I can do this?'

'Undoubtedly. You're the best man for the job.'

Shadow smoothed his tunic over his rounded stomach and coughed self-importantly. 'Cousin, would you do me the very great honour of entering into a betrothal with me?'

He was the opposite of everything she had dreamed of in a man. She looked to her father for confirmation.

'Your offer is most kind, Shadow,' replied Torrent. 'I will have the papers drawn up immediately. But you must promise that you will treat this as a temporary measure. My daughter must be free to marry as she wishes when she is ready.'

'Of course, that is very clear. I do this merely to protect my cousin's reputation.' Shadow kissed Rain's fingertips. 'And that of our forge.'

A month later, Rain found herself aboard a Magharnan ship bound eastwards across the vast Portic Ocean. The journey to the coast had been long but uneventful: the roads in Kandar among the best in the empire. The ambassador's vessel amazed her from the first: many masts, snowy white sails, built for speed. Yet she also felt a little unsafe; the ship did not reassure her with a great weight of ballast and sturdy hull as was common among the Holtish trading vessels. When she mentioned this to Shadow, he had given her one of his patronizing looks and begun a lecture on shipbuilding, praising the elegant lines of the square-rigged vessel with its raked masts. He was swiftly becoming a convert to all things Magharnan. She didn't ask him anything again, just prayed that they would not run into any foul weather.

At first she was excited by the experience of being on board a ship at sea, studying the routines of the sailors, the changing light on the blue-grey ocean, the dolphins that leapt from the water alongside the ship and the occasional sighting of a whale. After a time, loneliness set in. She had no one to talk to. The Magharnans kept themselves to themselves, following strict procedures as to whom they could address. The captain acted as intermediary but he only spoke to Shadow, expecting him to relay everything to his betrothed. He began teaching Shadow the basics of the Magharnan language, explaining that, due to the insular nature of his country, very few of his compatriots knew any Common. Rain listened in on the lessons, practising in private; not that she had much occasion to use her new skill. She decided that the Magharnan capital, Rolvint, must be a very quiet city with no everyday conversation between different types of people being allowed. She thought of her own home, how she freely talked to a noble if he or she came to the shop, and how she chatted to the beggars that haunted certain corners. She felt homesick and out of her depth.

One morning a week into the voyage, she was taking a turn on the deck when she almost ran into the ambassador's wife. Tall, her long black hair as straight as a ruler, her skin bronzed, the jettana made a strange, unyielding contrast to her cobweb robes of green and gold, like a giant redwood poking out of a leafy forest canopy. This stately personage was promenading, sheltered from the elements by a canopy held by four servants, though Rain secretly doubted that anything could topple her.

Rain curtseyed. 'My lady,' she said in Magharnan.

The tedium of a day on board ship must have got to the jettana too because for the first time on the voyage she stopped to acknowledge the existence of the foreigner. She turned to her senior servant, one whom the others referred to as a 'drummer', who acted as her connection to those of lower classes.

'Paulis, enquire of the young woman how she fares this day,' she said in Common.

Rain bit her tongue as she waited patiently for the serious-faced Paulis to relay the question.

'I am very well, thank her ladyship for asking.'

'Tell her I admire her husband's work greatly. His designs for the temple in Tigral were so beautiful; I, who have seen many marvels, was astonished by his accomplishments. Our Master will be delighted.'

'My *betrothed* will be pleased to hear of her ladyship's high opinion of his craft.'

The jettana gave her a perplexed look. 'She is not yet married to the glassmaker?'

'Our betrothal is very recent,' Rain explained. 'I am but fifteen and my father wishes me to wait before I get married. I have accompanied my cousin on this voyage as his helper, to care for him as he works and see if we will suit.'

'How strange. But the Holtish customs are not ours.' Comforted by this thought, the ambassadress began walking again. 'Tell the girl that I hope she will choose to complete the ceremony in Rolvint. It would be better thus. And I would give the couple a gift if they did so. One of my song birds perhaps.'

The woman's servants fluttered their slashed sleeves and muttered excitedly amongst themselves, noting the great favour shown the craftsman and his wife-to-be.

'Please convey my thanks to the lady,' Rain replied, 'but our plan is to return to our families in Tigral before we marry.'

The ambassadress paraded away. 'The girl will have a long wait. There is much work to be done.'

I can wait for ever, thought Rain, watching the little entourage move off.

As the ship neared Magharna, Rain spent more time on deck watching the coastline passing to starboard, listening to the sailors chatting to each other in their native language. She could pick out a few sentences now, but still she was barred from understanding much that happened around her, which added to her frustration.

First signs that they were close to their destination were the outlying islands, arriving like heralds running before royalty. The isles were rugged outcrops of volcanic rock, home to colonies of seabirds and seals but no people as far as she could see. Her artist's eye savoured the luminous quality of light which turned the sea pearl blue in the shallows when sun broke through the grey covering of cloud. Occasionally, she glimpsed fishing boats trawling the ocean for their catch, but it was nothing like the busy seaways that marked the approach to Tigral. She wondered with whom the locals traded. Shadow had informed her that Magharna was a spacious peninsula at the northern extremity of a vast and little known continent. He had been pressing the captain for details but as far as he could gather Magharna was so big that it was self-sufficient in most goods and minerals. It was only in recent years that the Master had decided that there was benefit in looking beyond his borders, hence the warm reception given to the first envoys from Holt and the exchange of ambassadors.

As Rain followed the progress of a pod of porpoises, Shadow arrived at her shoulder.

'My sweet, I've been informed by the captain that we should make port this evening.'

Rain shuddered at the endearment. 'I will go below and pack our things.'

He detained her, taking her arm. 'Don't hurry away, cousin. You've been avoiding me all voyage, I think.'

Rain attempted a smile, sure it was a pitiable failure. 'Not really, Shadow. I didn't want to get in the way.'

'No, you've not been in my way.' He patted her like a good dog. 'In fact, I've been impressed. You've carried out your duties, been quiet and demure, just as a guild wife should be. I'm very pleased with you.'

Rain felt like spitting. 'Thank you, cousin.'

'We might want to give this marriage thing serious consideration,' he continued, more pleased with himself than her, she guessed. 'You obviously have talent but will always need a man to shield you.' He tucked his thumbs in his belt, feet planted apart. 'I am prepared to be that man.'

She resisted rolling her eyes. 'You are too kind. But I'd prefer to leave things as you agreed with my father.'

'Well, well, give it some thought. And Rain?'

'Yes.'

'Don't forget to fold my shirts so they do not get rumpled in my trunk.'

And he thought she would marry him! 'Of course, cousin.'

Rain escaped as quickly as possible. She should have known: her attempt to put some distance between herself and Shadow, keeping a low profile, had only endeared her to him. He wanted a servant for a wife: someone who made him comfortable, saw to his needs. She would have done better being difficult. Still, there would be time to put him right when they reached Rolvint.

* * *

The Magharnan ship passed the lighthouse at the entrance to the harbour of Port Bremis as the sun began to set, the last shafts striking the snow-covered peaks of the mountains behind the town so they seemed on fire. A brazier burned at the top of the lighthouse, dark shadows flitting in front as the keepers stoked the blaze. The white-painted houses on the quayside glowed in the twilight, intensifying the shadows that sprawled between them. Most of the dwellings were boxlike, practical buildings, suited to a maritime location, but the customs hall was a different matter entirely: a soaring edifice made up of layers of arched balconies, places for the ship owners to keep watch for their cargoes.

Rain waited beside Shadow as the ambassador and his wife disembarked first, greeted by an effusive harbour master who led them to the best accommodation the port had to offer.

'We stay here the night,' Shadow informed Rain. 'Our escort to the capital leaves at dawn. It will take us all day to reach Rolvint.'

Rain nodded, hugging her bundle to her chest. Besides her own clothes, it also contained the robe discarded by the ambassadress in the workshop. Rain had brought it with her, not liking to waste such a beautiful garment.

Their turn to leave finally came.

'This way, my dear,' called Shadow cheerfully as the

captain beckoned them to the gangway. The two men shook hands, but as on the voyage, the seaman did not acknowledge Rain's presence. Being small, she was used to people overlooking her, but to be completely invisible was a new and unwelcome experience.

'Thank you for looking after us on the journey,' she said in a loud voice as she passed the captain, using the Magharnan she had picked up from his lessons.

Shadow tutted. 'Don't embarrass the gentleman, Rain. You know he can't speak to you. In his country, he is far superior to an unwed girl with no profession, so he must address you first, and then only in emergencies or with permission of a jettan.' He turned to the captain. 'Forgive my betrothed's presumption: she finds it hard to adapt to your customs.' He then hurried Rain down the plank. 'I hope you will remember your place, cousin. I have been happy with your behaviour so far; I trust that will not change.'

If he speaks to me again like that I'm going to strangle him. Rain struggled for control over her temper. She couldn't survive six months of living in a bubble with only Shadow to talk to. There had to be some exceptions to the Magharnan law, someone who would befriend her, surely?

Perhaps there wasn't. Perhaps this was going to be her life until they returned to Tigral.

She glared at Shadow as he strode ahead of her, his annoying sleek hair, his smug expression. If he'd been even the least bit pleasant, she might have managed, but every interaction with him only served to deepen her dislike.

Remember why you're here, she told herself. *You're here to help Papa. This will be good for his business if you can make a success of it. Soon you'll be so busy creating your designs. You won't have time for Shadow to annoy you, or to feel lonely.*

At least, that was her hope.

Horses were provided for the journey over the mountain pass. Rain eyed hers with trepidation. As a city dweller, she had only ever sat on the most placid hacks on her few excursions from Tigral; the mount chosen for her looked to have far more spirit.

'Splendid,' beamed Shadow, patting his piebald gelding. 'See in what esteem they hold me, my dear, providing a horse of such breeding.'

Rain bit her tongue, knowing better than to remind him that it was her work they valued.

'I'm not sure I can handle mine,' Rain admitted. She was not afraid to own up to her shortcomings.

Shadow frowned. 'I hope you won't disgrace me by snubbing the mare they have selected. I am sure the drummer would not err and will have judged your needs better than you can. He, after all, knows the road we are going to take.'

'But he doesn't know that I'm a novice when it comes to riding,' Rain pointed out.

'Stop grumbling and get on,' snapped Shadow,

showing that his approbation of her behaviour was of very short duration once challenged in any way.

Was there a more annoying man in the world? wondered Rain as she swung up into her saddle. *There can't be.*

The horse frisked and side-stepped.

'Easy now, lady,' Rain said, patting her neck. 'You and I have a long way to go and we'd best be friends.'

Beside her, Shadow put a foot in his stirrup then hopped several times before he was able to get his leg up and over the horse's flank, earning the snickers of the mounted escort.

What a hero! thought Rain. *If I really was engaged, I'd be embarrassed to be seen in public with him.*

The cavalcade set off. The ambassador and his wife rode at the front, surrounded by their personal guard. Rain found herself to the rear of the column with only two men behind her. Her horse would go no faster and she had no skill to bend it to her wishes. At least in this position she was not forced to hear Shadow as he extolled his virtues to anyone who would listen. It appeared that the guard considered him of a class worthy of their recognition and they deigned to talk to him. They must have regretted their condescension after ten miles of Shadow going on about the fascinating business deals he had put together with the people of the Blue Crescent Islands, far to the west. Even the most polite would have switched their attention away when he began explaining the intricacies of letters of credit and deep discounts.

As the morning passed, Rain had plenty of time to

take in the landscape around her. The road was surprisingly bad. She wondered if the ambassador had purposely taken them by a back route to avoid notice because this couldn't possibly be the main route from a major port to the capital. King Ramil would exile any commissioner who let the surface of a Holtish road reach this level of disintegration. When attention could be spared from the potholes, she bathed her gaze in the soft greens of the hillside, the random hummocks of stone, the woods losing their autumn livery to black-branched nakedness. The trail wound up into the mountains, following a ridge giving spectacular views down into the valleys either side. In one narrow gully, she spotted the mouth of a mine shaft sunk into the rock, slag heaps slipping down the slope, but it looked abandoned.

Late in the afternoon, as the shadows stretched across the road, the cavalcade funnelled into a narrow gorge, a castle-like crag rising to the right, steep slope to the left. White sheep moved between the fallen rocks, grazing on the meagre vegetation.

Living off such a land would be a harsh existence with bitter winters and only a few crops and sheep between the inhabitants and starvation, but there was also something elemental about seeing the bones of the land peeping through the thin skin of turf. She was getting new ideas for her designs already, a window that combined the moss green of the land with the grey of the rock. Perhaps if she got the colours right, she would be able to capture the pearly blue light she had seen on the ocean?

And there—perfect! A falcon corkscrewed in the sky above. That would go in the window too: the creature in harmony with the wild land it ruled from on high.

A scream rent the air. Confused, Rain looked to the bird, wondering if it was a falcon cry she had heard.

'Take cover!' shouted the rear guard.

Cover? Cover from what? And where?

Before she could react, her mare whinnied in pain and bolted across the open ground. Thrown backwards, Rain reached wildly behind her to grip on to the saddle and her hand brushed the feathers of an arrow planted in the horse's flank. With a toss of her head, the mare ripped the reins from her rider's fingers. Rain felt herself slide. She grabbed her saddlebag to stop herself falling but to no avail. The strap holding the leather sack snapped and Rain went flying. With a painful thump, she ended up on her back on the grass, still holding the bag, but the horse was fast disappearing back the way they had come.

Overhead the falcon circled once then sped off eastwards. Rain knew she had to move but she was stunned by the fall, her hip throbbing where she had made contact with a stone. Lucky it hadn't been her head.

The clash of weapons brought the urgency of her situation back to her. Rolling on to her knees, she crawled to the shelter of a large rock and peeped out at what was happening on the road. The guard around the ambassador, thinned by the volley of arrows, fought at close-quarters with scores of hooded men.

Dressed in the green of the hillside, more and more rose up from the grass, overwhelming the escort with their numbers. The bandits concentrated their attack on liberating the baggage train from the column, killing anyone who got in their way. She picked up a stone, meaning to bombard their attackers, but she was too far away. Bile rising in her throat, Rain watched helplessly as Shadow was cut down as he tried to protect his belongings from a pair of thieves. Once he tumbled from his horse, they took his mount, loading it with loot, not sparing a glance for their victim. Next to fall was the ambassador, an arrow in his throat. His wife's screams reverberated in the gully before she too went down, a shaft sticking from her back.

'Oh no, oh no,' moaned Rain, rocking herself in horror. Nothing in her life had prepared her for this crude outburst of violence in broad daylight on a foreign road. She covered her head with her hands, fist still clutching the stone, praying she would just disappear, leave this scene of blood and go home.

What seemed hours later, the noise of fighting ceased, replaced by the shouts of men arguing over spoils, cursing each other or laughing.

Maybe they'll just go, she told herself. She couldn't deal with the fact that everyone she had been with for the last few weeks was probably dead. She refused to even think about it.

A man shouted behind her. A fist grabbed her hair and pulled her up. Rain screamed and swung round to face a bald man with a thin black beard, letting the stone fly in a wild throw. It glanced off his cheek and he shook her as he continued to yell in her face, but she couldn't understand what he was saying. He dragged her towards the road, snatching her bag from the ground. The other bandits looked up from their job of stripping the dead and hooted.

'Caught yourself a warrior, Morg?' jeered one.

Rain shuddered—she didn't understand many words of Magharnan but she grasped that she was being discussed.

'I told you there was someone spying on us,' Rain's captor retorted. 'I could feel it in my bones. I'm taking her to the captain.'

Morg thrust Rain into the presence of the leader of the bandit army. A big man with stubbly hair, the crown of his head covered with a black skull cap, arms bare and leather jerkin blood-splattered, he was making himself at home on the thoroughbred horse so recently ridden by the ambassador. At war with the state that had booted him out to a life of banditry, the bandit leader was not averse to enjoying the luxuries his old persecutors had once owned.

'Krital, look what I found,' Morg shouted. 'She was watching us from over there.' He jerked his head toward the rocks where Rain had sheltered.

Rain was shaking so hard she wouldn't have been able to stand if the bandit hadn't been gripping her arm.

The leader eyed the girl curiously. 'Who is she?'

Morg shrugged. 'I dunno. She doesn't seem to understand Magharnan. Can I keep her?'

'Where from, girl?' The bandit asked the question in the few words of Common he'd picked up in Port Bremis. Rain's eyes flew to his face as she realized she could understand him.

'Holt,' she whispered. Her gaze strayed to the bodies of the guard piled around them. The bandits paid them no heed, far more interested in the spoils than the dead.

'Never heard of it. On own?'

'I'm with my cousin.' She put her hand to her mouth and bit hard to stop herself screaming: she had just spotted Shadow. His body lay only a short distance from where she stood. His clothes were covered in blood and he was very still so she had to give up any hope that he had survived. 'Why did you have to kill everyone?' The horrified question slipped out before she could stop herself.

Krital shrugged as if the answer was obvious. 'We kill when men fight back. You going fight?'

She shook her head quickly.

He gave her a ghastly smile. 'I thought not.'

The bandit who held her arm lost interest in the conversation he didn't understand and decided to explore the contents of her bag instead. He up-ended it, tipping her few clothes, papers, and charcoal out on the road. Toeing through it, he grunted in disgust. He then tugged her necklace off, spilling the teardrops into the dirt when he realized they were only glass.

'Nothing of worth,' he complained to the leader.

Krital hadn't taken his eyes off the little foreigner,

intrigued by her colouring: she would make someone an exotic pet slave. 'I'll buy her off you,' he said coolly, not wanting his man to see how much he wanted the girl as that would raise the price. 'You don't really need another bondswoman, true?'

Morg pushed Rain to her knees and indicated that she should gather her belongings together. In a daze, she fumbled to collect the beads and put them in the pack with the rest of her things. 'All right, I'll swap. You can never have enough horses.'

Krital frowned. Even he had limits to what he was prepared to give for her. 'Not this one. You can have that one over there.' He pointed to Shadow's piebald.

Morg wasn't really bothered which one he got. 'Thanks. She's yours then. But I don't think you'll get much work out of her.'

'The dealers pay for novelties and you have to admit they'll never have seen hair like hers. There are jettan families who will pay well for a housegirl they can boast about to their neighbours, true?'

'Yeah, true.' But Morg had lost interest, busy examining his horse.

Krital dismounted and approached Rain. She moved back a step before realizing there was nowhere to go. Krital pulled the ribbon off the end of her braid and shook it out. 'Look, it's like a chestnut's tail: beautiful.' He gave Morg a mocking bow. 'I'm more than pleased with my bargain.' He picked Rain up by the waist and placed her on the ambassador's horse. 'Let's go, little one.'

Shard 4
Sky Blue

P eri arrived too late to be of any use to the victims of the bandits. He watched from the upper slopes of the crag as the thieves stripped the bodies of all valuables. There were more outlaws each day, men who, having lost their jobs, were thrown out of the cities with no way of making a living for themselves and their families. From his vantage point high over the road, Peri recognized the big man who had made himself leader of this irregular army: Krital, famous for his wrestler's build and crafty mind. He was the magnet bringing the others to hunt on the road to the capital. Peri decided to wait until the bandits cleared out, then he would go and see if there were any survivors.

Rogue circled round the battlefield, his hunting instincts sent wild by the sight of blood on the ground. Glancing upwards, Peri feared that his falcon might give away his position. He drew the lure out of his backpack and cast it on the grass, hoping he could recapture the bird before anyone noticed it. Rogue

ɔr it, plunging from the sky to pounce
meat, allowing Peri to hood him.
,' he murmured soothingly. 'What's down
for you.'

ne looked back to the road, the situation had
for the worse. A girl had survived the attack
as being haggled over by Krital and another
she looked tiny, smaller than his sister, Bel.
le Peri was not going to risk himself for dead
dies, he drew the line at watching them harm the
,irl. But there were too many bandits for him to stand
a chance against them; he would have to wait until
they broke up to return to their hideout.

Krital took off on his horse with the girl in front of
him. He was heading on his own towards the capital,
which meant he would have to follow the road round
the hill to cross the river in the next valley. That gave
Peri an idea: if he could get to the bridge first, he could
waylay the bandit leader. With only the two of them,
he might even have an advantage as he had Rogue
with him.

Peri scrambled down the far slope, holding Rogue
clear of the tumbling stones. He ran for Nutmeg and
leapt into the saddle, urging the gelding into a canter.
He steered with his knees as he loosened the dagger
from his saddle pack. Rogue screeched—though
hooded, he could sense that his master was disturbed.

'Hush now, we don't want them to know we're
ahead of them,' said Peri soothingly.

They clattered across the ford. Peri slid off Nutmeg

and urged the horse to go on out of sight round the bend. There was a patch of grass there that he often grazed so Peri had no fear that he would wander too far.

'Right, my beauty, time for you to earn your keep.' Peri took the hood off the falcon. Rogue mantled his wings, a loose feather flying as he tried to escape, but his master had a firm hold on his jesses. 'That's perfect. Look as mean as you can, my crotchety friend.' Shaking his head at his own foolish bravery for the sake of a stranger, Peri took a stance on the bank by the ford. He guessed that Krital would know that the bridge was in a terrible state and not wish to risk it laden down with spoils and a prisoner. Peri didn't have to wait long before he heard hooves on the road. A stallion trotted around the bend, going slowly due to the uneven surface. He glimpsed a pale face surrounded by a mass of auburn curls; Krital's muscular forearm was bound across the girl's chest to keep her in place.

'Hold!' Peri held up the falcon. Rogue flapped his wings and screeched.

Krital reined his horse to a standstill, fetlock-deep in the ford. 'Master Scavenger, what do you want?'

'Release the girl.'

Krital laughed. 'Why?'

Peri let Rogue go. The bird pushed off from the gauntlet, flew low to skim Krital's head, the down-draught of wings fluttering the girl's hair. The bandit ducked. Peri took the rope from his belt and began to swing the lure in lazy loops over his head.

'What are you doing?' Krital watched the lure with suspicion.

'Showing what will happen to your eyes if you do not do as I ask. It is illegal to take innocent people as bondsmen.'

'And I care so much about the law?' laughed Krital, but his gaze was glued to the revolving lure. 'Besides, she's not Magharnan, so she's fair game, true? You're a scavenger like me: you should understand.'

'Not true, and I'm nothing like you,' Peri replied quietly. He gave a shrill whistle and Rogue exploded out of the sky to snatch the meat. The falcon landed it on the ground and gave a shriek of triumph. 'Think what my bird could do to your face, bandit.'

'You can't scare me with that,' Krital said derisively, taking his hand off the girl to reach for his sword. 'You'll have to fight me if you want her. I've a trader who'll pay good money for something a bit different.'

Peri didn't move an inch. 'So be it.' He held out his gauntlet. 'Rogue!'

The bird fluttered up to Peri's arm, dragging the lure with him.

Taking advantage of the distraction, the girl suddenly threw herself from the saddle, landing backwards in the river with a splash. The bundle she was clutching went flying. Scrambling to her feet, she ran for the bridge, fleeing both men, her only thought to get to cover and hide. Krital cursed, knowing that the wooden planks would not take the weight of his horse. He dismounted and ran after her, his long strides eating up the distance she had managed to put between them.

'Get back here, girl, or I'll beat you within an inch of your life!' he yelled, making a lunge for her but coming away with a fistful of shawl.

Peri had to think fast. He did not fancy his chances in a fight with Krital; he had to distract him.

'Go!' He released Rogue, directing him towards the stallion. Smelling the blood on the ambassador's saddle, the falcon swooped, claws extended. Spooked, the horse reared and bolted, heading back down the path.

Krital caught the girl in the middle of the bridge and shook her till her teeth rattled. The bridge groaned, a plank dropped into the stream and was quickly swept away by the current. The structure shuddered and slumped, water now running over the centre.

'Krital—look to your horse!' called Peri.

The bandit spun round to see his prize disappearing down the road. He swore, having to choose between the girl and the stallion.

'I'll get you for this, scavenger!' he shouted. With another curse, he released the girl and ran off in pursuit, leaping the broken section of bridge. The prisoner crumpled to her knees, hugging a post as if fearing he would return to drag her away.

'It's all right now. He's gone,' Peri called, holding out a hand to her. He didn't want to step on the bridge in case his weight caused it to collapse but he had to get her off before the whole thing ended up floating downstream.

She raised a pair of shocked blue eyes to him, round with fear. The words Peri meant to speak froze on his tongue. He'd never seen anything like her. In Magharna, everyone had straight black hair and dark eyes; she looked like one of the fey people from children's tales, hardly human, with her wild curls and strange-coloured irises.

He swallowed. 'Really, it's all right.' He dropped his arm, suddenly doubting himself in front of such a perfect creature. Perhaps she did not want to talk to a scavenger, maybe she thought he'd make her unclean? Annoyed by the thought, he strode to the river and salvaged her bundle which was caught on a fallen branch. 'Here. We've got to go. Krital might be back any moment.'

She still didn't react.

He could feel his anger building but he refused to let it show. The foolish girl was going to drown if she stayed where she was. He pointed in the direction Krital had gone. 'Do you want him to catch you again?' He made his tone neutral.

She shook her head. So at least she understood him.

'Then come on.' With a whistle, Peri summoned Rogue from a nearby tree and crooned praise to the falcon as he replaced the hood.

Rain made herself let go of the wooden post. She had passed beyond terror and was now numb. She'd fallen out of the clutches of one bandit and into the power of this strange young man with his cruel hunting falcon. What was he going to do with her? At least with Krital she had understood the man's moods and intentions; this stranger's calmness, even facing down a bandit twice his size, disguised his emotions from her. His face was made up of angles and planes like cut glass crystal: high cheek bones, hawkish nose, stubborn jaw. He seemed as hard and polished as the bird he carried. Perhaps it would be better not to know what he was going to do.

Gathering her courage, she stood up and walked off the bridge, her slight weight making no impression on the creaking structure. The falconer did not try and take her hand again, just beckoned her to follow him, speaking too quickly for her to understand his rapid Magharnan. Knowing she didn't really have a choice, she trailed after him down the road to where a stocky chestnut horse grazed under a tree. The young man busied himself placing the falcon in a travelling basket while she huddled against the trunk, shivering from cold and shock. She felt very far away from what was happening, as if watching herself from a great height. He was talking to her now, opening the canvas bundle and pulling out the first change of clothes he came across. He threw it towards her and gestured to her to put it on.

'W-why?' she stuttered through chattering teeth, wishing she had learnt more than very basic Magharnan.

'You'll catch your death of cold if you don't get out of those wet things,' he explained, his tone a touch impatient. 'But hurry, mistress, your admirer will be back at any moment and we must be gone.'

She couldn't follow half of what he said: something about death and a threat that she'd be caught again. Feeling horribly powerless, she picked up the dry clothes. He turned his back while she changed. She only realized as her fingers caught on the slashed material that he had handed her the jettana's robe. She was going to be sick: the woman was dead, lying on the road not a mile away with her cousin, left for the scavenging crows.

Rain rushed behind a tree and retched until her stomach hurt. Tears poured down her face; her nose was running. She felt so miserable, she wanted to die.

'Easy now, fey lady.' The young man's voice was strangely soothing, even if his words were unfamiliar. His hand rested lightly on her shoulder blades, rubbing in a circular motion.

Rain swiped her wrist across her mouth and stood up straight. Wordlessly, he took a step back and handed her a waterskin to rinse the taste away.

'Thank you,' she said huskily, tears still sliding down her face.

'Come now. We'd best get you to the capital. At least you'll be safe there.'

She nodded, understanding most of what he had just said.

He boosted her up to sit on the horse's back, then took a seat in front of her so she could hold on to his waist.

'I'm sorry you have to touch me,' he said.

Rain didn't care: just then it felt wonderful to cling on to someone warm and kind.

'You can take a ritual bath at the main gate so that you'll be purified.'

Rain didn't follow what he was saying, something about baths. She did feel dirty after the attack, but was now worried that she must smell really bad to him.

'I want a bath,' she replied in her stilted Magharnan.

'I expect you do, being forced to share a saddle with an outlaw and now me.'

Again, he was speaking too quickly for her to follow. She decided not to say anything.

'You must belong to one of the jettan households,' he continued, gesturing to her robe. 'What are you? A drummer? A wealer's daughter?'

He appeared to be asking about her identity.

'I am Rain Glassmaker.'

'Ah, an artificer. I wouldn't have guessed: your robe is too fine for that. Or perhaps your family is one of the very wealthy ones? I've been told they live like the jettans. They won't like the fact that you've been in contact with a scavenger, will they?'

He'd lost her again. She expected him to reply with his name in response to hers, not this long speech full of words she didn't understand. She tried again.

'I am Rain Glassmaker. Who are you?'

'Peri Falconer.' He made a slight dip of a bow in the saddle. 'Pleased to meet you, my lady.'

This she did comprehend as it had been in Shadow's first lesson.

'Please to meet you, Peri Falconer.'

Peri smiled at her carefully spoken polite words. Of course her kind manner would only last as long as she needed him; as soon as they were back in Rolvint she wouldn't even look at him. Then he remembered something Krital had said.

'You are not Magharnan? You certainly don't look it.'

'No. I origin from Holt. My betrothed glassmaker for summer palace.'

He grimaced: another useless craftsman being paid extortionate amounts to decorate one of the Master's many houses while ordinary people went hungry. But he'd never even heard of Holt, let alone met people from there.

Wait a moment: what was that about a betrothed?

'Your man: where is he?'

Rain shuddered. 'Dead on road. With the ambassador and his wife.'

It was worse than Peri feared. He had suspected that the cavalcade had been a particularly rich one, but he hadn't thought it belonged to a member of the government. This would be terrible news for the people of the capital, proving how little control the Master now had over lands beyond the city gates if

80

even ambassadors were cut down within a few hours of home. Peri spurred Nutmeg on.

'You must ask for the artificers to protect you when you get to Rolvint,' he said. 'They'll take you in for your betrothed's sake.'

Having passed through so many shocks today, Rain felt reluctant to leave the safety she had found with this birdman for an even more uncertain future.

'Can I no stay with you until go home?'

He gave a bitter laugh. 'You have a funny sense of humour, artificer. There's no place for the likes of you in the graveyard district.'

Rain loosened her arms from his waist. He was rejecting her, didn't want anything to do with her now he had done his duty and rescued her.

'You are right. No place for me here.'

It sunk in for the first time that she truly was on her own. Her mind reeled with the enormity of her situation. She had no money and no Shadow to pretend to be the designer while she worked. How would she be able to afford the journey back to Holt? Had the ambassador even had time to tell the Master he had engaged a foreign glassmaker's services? The people who had brought her here were dead; it seemed likely that no one still alive in Magharna would take any responsibility to see to her welfare.

Rain closed her eyes, resting her forehead on Peri's stiff back. Then again, at least she had her life. How could she be so selfish, worrying about the future when her cousin went unburied? She would survive and find a way back to Holt; she had to, for her father's sake if for no other reason.

'Here we are, my lady, the gates of Rolvint.' Peri slowed Nutmeg to a stop. 'The baths are on your left, though I expect you know that.' He felt the girl slide off from behind him and drop to the ground. He'd forgotten how tiny she was; her head barely reached his knee as he remained in the saddle.

'No, I do not know,' she said, not looking at him but at the imposing gateway. 'Not been here before.'

'But I thought . . . ' Peri quickly reviewed their conversation. He'd assumed she was travelling with a Magharnan craftsman as part of the ambassador's entourage but another possibility struck him. 'When did you arrive in my country?'

'Yesterday.' She gave a little hiccup of laughter that sounded more like a sob. 'I do not like it very much.'

What bad luck: to tie herself to a Magharnan visiting her country, travel back to his home, only to lose him. Still, she wore jettan clothes and had been under the protection of the ambassador—an extraordinary honour for a foreigner. Her betrothed must have been one of the jettan's most valued men to allow a non-Magharnan wife in his party. The city would look after her. She would only be at a disadvantage if it were known she had any link to a scavenger. Peri tried to ignore a niggling feeling that all was not right with the little stranger.

He felt in his pocket and flipped her a brass coin. 'Here: this will pay for the bath. Then ask for your betrothed's family: I'm sure they'll take you in when they hear what has happened to him.'

Rain shook her head hopelessly. He was talking too fast again. She looked at the strange disc in her palm: it had a hole in the centre.

'What is it?'

'Money,' Peri repeated slowly, frowning. 'For bath.' He pointed to the building.

'You want me to have bath now?'

'Yes.'

She must reek really badly if he thought that she had to bathe before doing anything else. Surely she should be reporting the bandit attack to someone?

'Go on. That way.' Peri passed her bundle.

'All right. Thank you.' Rain walked in a daze to the bath-house door and handed over her coin. She did not have to say anything. The woman on duty took one look at her escort and ushered her in. Half an hour later, scrubbed raw and shivering with cold, Rain emerged on to the street. Her falconer had gone.

Peri rode back to the barracks with a deep-seated sense of unease. It wasn't only that he'd witnessed the bloody aftermath of the bandits' attack, shocking as it had been, nor the fact that he had made an enemy of Krital, dangerous though that may prove in the future. The root of his discomfort was his doubt over leaving the girl alone. He told himself that she would be all right, that the city had special measures to look after people such as her, but part of him felt as if he'd just led a lamb into a wolf den and abandoned her. Something about her guileless blue eyes made him fear for her in the tough streets of the capital.

Helgis bobbed up in the stable to help him unsaddle Nutmeg.

'Goldie's doing much better, thanks to you,' his brother chattered away, brushing the lower reaches of the horse.

'Good.'

'Much happen today?'

'Some.'

Helgis threw the currycomb back in the bucket. 'What?'

'I met a girl—'

Helgis sniggered.

Peri gave him a quelling look. 'She survived a bandit attack.'

'Oh. Was she hurt?'

'Not hurt. In shock I think.'

'What did you do with her?'

'Took her to the city.'

Helgis shrugged. 'Well, that's that then. You did what you could.'

His father entered the stable, leading his own horse, loaded down with the fruits of his hunt over on the marshes to the north of the city. 'What's all this, Peri? Who did you meet?'

'It was another bandit attack, Pa, much more serious this time. They killed an ambassador and his escort. Krital led them.'

His father gave a melancholy whistle. 'It's getting completely out of hand, Peri. It's like they're waging war on us. You're not to go up on the mountain passes again, not until the government stamps out the bandit threat.'

Peri heartily agreed with his father's order, not least because he did not want to cross paths with Krital any time soon.

'I helped this girl—I think she was the only survivor. Took her to the baths.'

'Who was she?'

'That's the odd thing: she said she was from Holt. Does that mean anything to you?'

Hern's brow wrinkled in thought. 'Now you come to mention it, I did hear a rumour that Ambassador Lintir had gone on an embassy to a new trading partner over the Portic Ocean. He was going to bring back some fancy foreign craftsmen to work on that palace. His kinsman, Jettan Kirn, is overseeing the works and wanted something special.'

'So the craftsmen were outsiders? The ambassador wasn't travelling with his own people?'

'I think so. But it's not really our area, is it? I only hear the rumours at third or fourth hand.'

Peri groaned and rested his head on Nutmeg's flank. 'I've made a mistake, Pa.' An old conversation had come rushing back to him; Mikel had mentioned the foreign craftsmen but Peri had forgotten all about that until this moment.

'What you? My perfect son do something wrong? Surely not?' Hern teased him, rubbing Peri's neck to relieve the tension.

'The girl I told you about, she said she was travelling with her betrothed in the ambassador's cavalcade. I assumed that he had to be Magharnan because when have you heard of foreigners being allowed as part of an ambassador's party?'

Hern shook his head. 'Never.'

'Her Magharnan is very weak. She couldn't explain herself well.' And she had probably not understood half of what he had said, he now realized. 'I left her, telling her to go to her betrothed's family.'

'I see.' Hern began to unload his horse, passing the catch to Helgis who was keeping very silent during Peri's confession. 'What do you think you can do about it? You're not responsible for her bad luck.'

'No, I suppose not.'

'We're scavengers, in no position to help anyone else. Once she found out about us, she wouldn't thank you for making her unclean to any other Magharnan.'

Peri grimaced. 'She did seem a bit bemused that I was so insistent that she bathed. But you should have seen her, Pa: she's very young and tiny with it. People in her country must be only half grown compared to us.'

'You always do want to take the wounded creatures under your wing, don't you, Peri?'

'Not all of them: only those that drop into my path, so to speak.'

'Like this girl.'

'Well, yes.'

'I'll ask around tomorrow. I have a friend among the butchers who makes deliveries about the city. He might be able to find out what happened to her. After all, she's a foreigner, bound to be noticed. I imagine she'll be taken special care of because of that.'

'Thank you. If I could find out that she was looked after, I'd not worry so much.'

His father left for the butchers' sector of the compound, carrying his catch on a pole balanced on his shoulder. Helgis swung himself up on the stable door as Peri forked a fresh bed of straw for the horses.

'So what's she like, this foreigner? Did she have two heads? Six fingers? Breathe fire?'

Peri gave a half-hearted chuckle. 'No, nothing like that. I think she must come from a race related to the fey people: she comes up to here,' he tapped his chest, 'and has long curly hair the colour of Nutmeg's coat, and blue eyes.'

Helgis almost fell off the door. 'Blue eyes? Could she see with them? She wasn't blind or anything?'

'No, they seemed to work perfectly well. Strange— like bits of sky, or a forget-me-not.'

Helgis snorted. 'You'll be spouting poetry next, Peri.'

His brother just shook his head and continued to spread the straw.

Shard 5
Clear Glass

H e'd left her. The stupid falconer had just gone, without a word of goodbye or hint what she should do next. How could he do that to her when he knew she was a foreigner in a strange city?

Anger revived Rain's spirits, far better than the dull shock of the past few hours. No one in Tigral would treat a visitor like this! Common courtesy would demand that you open your home to the traveller.

If she saw him again, she would be tempted to slap him for his neglect. Energized by her rage, Rain turned on her heel and strode back to the bath-house.

'I want to say about a crime,' she announced, trying to make herself understood to the woman in charge. 'I say about an attack. Bandits.'

'What's new, love?' the portly woman said with an indifferent shrug. 'Been a raid each week for months now. But if you must, take your tale to the guard house at the gate.' She pointed across the street to a prisonlike building with bars on the window.

Rain marched to the guard house before her nerve failed her and rapped on the door.

'Come!' called a gruff voice.

Rain entered, finding herself in a darkened room that smelt of stale beer and unwashed humans, which she thought odd considering the bath-house was so close. A man sat with his feet up on a table, his blue uniform with its slashed sleeves unbuttoned at the waist so that his belly hung over his belt. He examined her with vague but friendly interest.

'Where are you from, darling?' he asked. 'Not seen the likes of you before.' He put his feet on the floor and brushed some crumbs off the table. 'Sit down. Tell me your tale.' He seemed relaxed, in no hurry to hear the report of a crime.

Rain took the bench opposite him, twisting her fingers in her lap. 'Thank you, sir. My name is Rain Glassmaker. I come from Holt, a long way from your country. I travel with ambassador. He is dead. Bandits attack.'

'What! An attack on an ambassador?' The guard shot to his feet and lunged for a bell rope; he pulled it three times, summoning more help. 'Where?'

Relieved that her report was being taken seriously, Rain pointed westwards.

'On road from the port. All killed.'

Two men came into the room, buckling on their swords.

'Was everything taken?' The guard scribbled a message down on a piece of paper.

Rain frowned, puzzling her way through his words. 'Yes, people killed, baggage stolen.'

'And you: how did you escape?'

Rain rubbed her hand over her eyes, wondering if her limited Magharnan would stretch to explaining.

'Man called Krital took me. A man with a bird helped me.' She feared she wasn't making much sense.

The guard turned to his colleagues. 'Take a party out to the mountain pass and check the girl's story. You'll need wagons to transport the bodies and to bring back any survivors. Be quick: it sounds like a jet-tan was involved.'

The men left hurriedly, leaving Rain alone with the guard again. Standing in front of her with his arms folded, he inspected her from head to toe.

'You look surprisingly unscathed for your ordeal, mistress.'

Rain frowned. 'Sorry, I do not understand.'

He gestured to her appearance.

'Ah, I see. Falcon man, he made I go bath.'

The guard relaxed his stance, his suspicions quieted. 'Good. Then you are purified and can enter the city. I'll escort you to your people.'

'What people?'

The guard hitched his belt, making his tummy wobble. 'You must know someone in Rolvint?'

She shook her head. 'I be in Magharna one day only.'

He whistled. 'Well, well: that is a bit of a problem.

91

You see, we all have places in our city. I can't just let you wander off on your own.' He clicked his fingers. 'I know, I'll take you to the vagrants' office.'

She did not know the word. 'What office?'

'The office that deals with people with no home.'

'I have a home—in Tigral, in my country.'

He smiled patiently at her as if she were a touch simple. 'But not here, you don't, love. Come along. They'll look after you.'

Rain wondered how many people she would be handed on to before someone realized she was tired, hungry and thirsty, still experiencing cold waves of shock whenever she thought of the attack. Resigned to struggling on, she trooped after the guard, watching as he despatched a boy with his message informing his superiors of the bandit raid, then following him to a second building further up the street. This was about as welcoming as the guard house: ugly crude furniture, stone floor, and grey walls. A long line of people sat on the benches, their expressions desperate. The guard ignored them and walked straight to the head of the queue to where three men sat behind a desk loaded with papers.

'Found you a stray,' the guard announced jovially. 'A foreigner, would you believe it?' He waved to Rain who stood beside him, knotting her fingers in the holes in her robe. 'She's a funny looking thing.'

The man in the middle, a sullen individual with white streaked hair, stared down his nose at her.

'She'll have to wait her turn,' he pronounced.

'Fair enough. I'll leave her with you then.'

'You do that, officer.'

The guard briefly rested his hand on Rain's shoulder. 'You'll be all right now, darling. These men will look after you.' He wrinkled his brow. 'Not sure exactly what they do with vagrants, but I know they see to those in need. Just tell them what you told me and something will be done for you.'

'Thank you,' Rain said dully, counting the number of people in the queue. It did not take a genius to realize that she'd be lucky to be seen today. But there was obviously a system; as a stranger who didn't understand Magharnan ways, she would have to give it a chance to help her.

'That's the spirit. Oh, and welcome to Rolvint.' With a benign smile, the guard made his way back to his post, happy in the knowledge that he'd done his best for the little stranger.

Rain took a seat at the far end of the line. There weren't enough benches so she was forced to sit on the floor. No one spoke. Rain wondered if that was because they were all from different classes, forbidden to speak to each other, or because they were too depressed to make the effort. She passed the time listening to the interviews at the table. The three men asked the same questions over and over: profession, reason for losing employment, reason why relatives would not support the vagrant, and so on. Rain rehearsed her own answers.

At the conclusion of each interrogation, the person

was given a coloured stick. Rain wondered what the different colours meant: the blue was met with smiles of relief, the yellow, looks of despair. One man was given nothing but escorted from the building by a burly guard who held him by the scruff of the neck.

'What will happen to him?' Rain whispered to the person sitting next to her, a thin woman with straggly hair and scarred hands.

'Thrown out of the city,' she replied. 'Nothing for it but to join the bandits, if they don't kill him first.'

'I see.' Rain tried to still her fingers which she had been knotting and unknotting in her lap until they ached.

'He was probably a purveyor.'

Rain gave her a blank look.

'He sold things in a shop or market,' the woman explained. 'There's no work for them these days with so many businesses struggling to get by. No one has any money for anything.'

'And if there is no work, they throw you out?'

'Of course. Can't have people with no place in Rolvint.'

'What do you do?'

'I'm a cook. My master can't afford me any longer, had to let me go. Served him for ten years and this is where it has brought me.'

'There is always work for cooks, surely?'

'We'll see.' The woman folded her arms, signalling an end to the discussion.

As Rain had not lost a job but just needed to explain

her situation, she decided she must be in the wrong place. She tried to attract the attention of the men at the desk and finally caught the eye of the one nearest her—the junior clerk.

'Yes?' he asked.

She cautiously approached. 'Am I in right office?'

He raised an eyebrow.

'I need help go home, not job.'

The clerk turned to the white-haired senior official, an incredulous smile on his lips. 'Sir, she doesn't think she needs a job. She thinks we hand out free tickets to return people to their homes.'

The man did not crack a smile. 'Everyone works in Rolvint,' he said, not even bothering to look up at her. 'There are no free rides: you earn them. Sit down, girl, or I'll have you thrown out of the city.'

Rain quickly returned to her seat, scared of finding herself back on the bandit-infested roads again. More people joined the queue below Rain and by nightfall she was near the front. Afraid she would lose her place if she went in search of a privy or a drink of water, she tried to ignore her body's needs.

The cook exited with a blue stick, a smile back on her drawn face.

'Next!' called the senior official. He looked up. 'Oh yes, the foreigner who doesn't want to work. Do you speak Magharnan?'

'A little,' admitted Rain standing before the desk.

He tutted. 'Not enough I warrant to hold down a proper job. What is your profession?'

'I came with my betrothed. We are glassmakers. We came here with Ambassador Lintir but Jettan killed. On road.'

The official was not interested in her story. He had rules to apply and was not going to budge from following them even by a foreign presence in the system. 'Where is your man?'

'I think . . . I think he is dead too. With ambassador.' She wanted to say so much more—about the commission, the contract, her need to return home, but could not find the words.

He tutted again, making it sound as if this were her fault. 'He was a glassmaker; so what are you? You look very young. How old?'

'Fifteen.'

'Ah, that's better. You do not break the law by not having a profession then. Until you reach eighteen, it is thought reasonable to be unassigned.' He scanned a list. 'We have a space in the retraining facility for servants.'

'I want to be with glassmakers. My betrothed had a contract—'

He cut her off. 'But that died with him. Ambassador Lintir's grieving family will not want to be disturbed at this time and our glassmakers will doubtless be pleased to find the commission will now come to them.'

The third clerk snorted. 'Jobs for Magharnans, not outsiders, as it should be. You won't find a welcome there, lass.'

'We do not need another glassmaker—too many of

them,' said the senior official coldly. 'Yellow, do you think, gentlemen?' He looked to his colleagues. 'Strictly speaking, seeing that she is foreign, we have no reason to assist her, but the Master would want us to show charity.'

The junior clerk reached for a pile of sticks in front of him. 'Yes, she's too young to be made an outlaw and not skilled enough for a blue employment permit: it'll have to be yellow.'

He held out the stick for Rain to take.

'What do I do with this?' she asked, realizing with a hollow feeling that this was all the help they were going to give her.

'Take it to the matron at the House of the Indigent on Harrow Street. Move along.'

Rain found herself on the pavement outside the office. Stupid men, stupid system: why would no one listen to her? All she needed was help to get home. She'd pay them back eventually. But it appeared that the Magharnans were just not interested in solutions outside their normal methods. She looked down at the yellow stick: she was left with only one option if she wanted shelter.

After a bewildering time asking directions from curious bystanders, Rain found the right door on Harrow Street and knocked. It opened a crack.

'Too late: we don't take anyone after sunset.' A hand pointed to a large sign on the wall that listed the rules of the house.

Rain held out the yellow stick to the unseen

gatekeeper. 'I was told to come here. They gave me this.'

'Come back tomorrow.' The door snapped shut.

Rain couldn't believe it: after waiting for hours, she wasn't going to be let in and it was already dark. Rolvint had to be the most unfriendly city ever! She wondered briefly if she should try and find the falcon man. He'd mentioned that he lived somewhere called the graveyard district—but she did not relish the idea of going to a cemetery now. It sounded scary. But then, sleeping rough in a strange city was frightening too.

She had no choice. Not being able to speak the language was a handicap: she couldn't explain herself, didn't know whom to trust, had no understanding of how the city worked. All she could do was find a safe corner and bed down, hoping that the House of the Indigent would let her in at dawn.

The streets were nearly deserted when she turned to seek a place for the night. The district looked poor, home to the lowest workers in the city with one-roomed houses and badly maintained streets. The smell was foul: rubbish lay in piles on any patch of unclaimed land. Rats flitted among the scraps, discouraging her from lingering. She walked on into an area of larger houses, their richer inhabitants signalled by the ornamentation around the doors and windows. She found a darkened house that had a deep porch with a pillar to hide behind. She crammed herself into the small space and wrapped her arms around her knees. Nervous, she could not sleep, but spent the hours listening to every sound: the voices in a neighbouring house, a drunken man singing on his way home, the wind in the tree that shaded the street corner. She was freezing: Rolvint had a harsher climate than Tigral; summers hotter, winters colder. The night felt damp and chill. Unable to stop her shivers, she hunched miserably in her haven, praying that no one would spot her and turf her out. In the small hours, sleep finally claimed her.

She awoke next morning when a bucket of water was upended over her head.

'Get off my doorstep!' screeched a servant, shaking her fist at the vagrant. 'Now I'll have to scrub it clean before my master can go outside.'

Gulping with shock, Rain scrambled to her feet, the yellow stick still clutched in her fist.

'Get lost! Scat!' yelled the woman, prodding her with a broom as if she was a dangerous beast she feared to touch.

Rain wiped the water from her eyes, still disorientated by this rude awakening. The servant took a step back.

'You're a fey?' the woman asked, clutching at her throat in fright.

Rain did not understand the question but knew it was well past time to leave.

'Sorry, fey lady,' the servant whispered, circling her breast. 'Please, do not make the milk go sour because I threw water at you. I always leave a dish out for your folk and follow the old customs.'

Rain shook her head, annoyed by her inability to follow what people were saying to her.

The woman dashed inside, muttering to herself. With a sigh, Rain started off back towards the House of the Indigent only to hear a voice calling behind her.

'A moment, fey lady.'

She turned. The servant thrust a round of bread in her hand. 'Here, take this. It's fresh. Don't punish my house for my thoughtless actions, please!'

Rain's stomach grumbled: she'd not eaten since before the bandit attack. 'Thank you.'

The servant's generosity lifted her spirits a little. Rain still felt tired, but with a drink from a street corner fountain, she was ready to meet the new day. Until she had sorted out a way home, she would see what the Magharnan system could do for her. At least it didn't appear that she would starve. And there *had* to be a way for her to earn enough for the passage to Tigral; she just had to find it.

The door to the House of the Indigent stood open this morning. Rain passed over her yellow stick and was admitted with no more delays. It was a stern-looking building, stone whitewashed, grass clipped, even the shrubs were teased into regimented geometric shapes. A grumpy girl in a grey dress and apron showed her the way to the office where yet another queue waited. Resigned now to Rolvint bureaucracy, Rain joined the end of the line.

'Name?' asked the matron behind the desk, looking over a pair of steel-rimmed spectacles at Rain.

Rain gave her replies as she had the day before.

'In my house, you must always say "thank the Master" every time you answer a question as from now on you owe everything to him.'

Rain resisted a comment on the absurdity of such a practice, guessing it would get her expelled from the room quicker than a slippery eel through a fisherman's fingers.

'I will try to remember, mistress.'

The woman sat back for a moment, considering her latest charge. 'Your appearance is odd. What did you do to your hair?'

'It is not strange where I come from,' Rain explained patiently, then remembered to add 'thank the Master'.

The woman was singularly unimpressed to hear Rain was a foreigner, seeing that fact only as a problem for her institution.

'You'll have to keep your hair covered. Your employers won't like it. What with your eyes, the superstitious will be afraid of you and that won't do. Keep them lowered at all times.' The matron ran her finger down a list in front of her. 'I have a training position available in the kitchens that feed the builders working on the summer palace. Basic duties: cleaning, carrying water. You'll report to the cook each morning at seven and return here for curfew at seven in the evening.'

'What is the pay?' asked Rain, thinking of the cost of her journey home.

The woman snorted. 'Pay? You are being given food and shelter by the Master's generosity—that is your pay.'

'Is there any way of earning money?' Rain persisted.

'Not till you are qualified.'

Rain didn't know that word. 'Qualified?'

'It takes three years for a cook. By the time you are eighteen, you can hope for a small salary. Until then, you are reliant on us.'

There was clearly no point in arguing; she would have to look for another solution to her dilemma of getting home. Rain thanked the woman. 'When do I start?'

'Today. We have no idle hands in the House of Indigent. I will send someone with you to show you the way. First, you should change into our uniform. You cannot go around Rolvint dressed like a jettana. You are one of the lowest classes—not as low as a scavenger, of course, but still, you should not insult your betters by aping their ways.'

'I'm sorry but I don't understand what you just said.'

The woman rolled her eyes, having no patience with a foreigner and assuming Rain was slow-witted. 'Change your clothes then work: is that clear enough?'

Rain nodded. 'Yes, as clear as plain glass.'

The matron raised an imperious brow.

'Thank the Master,' added Rain reluctantly.

Shard 6
Crow Black

O ver the cold months that followed, Peri often wondered what had happened to the little foreigner he had prematurely abandoned at the bath house. His enquiries via his father came to nothing. None of the glassmaker families knew of a girl from Holt; there was no discussion among the jettan class of the visitor. Peri had assumed that, as Rain was the first person from her country to visit the capital since the Holtish embassy the previous year, she would be treated as special. She should have been made a guest of one of the ambassador's relatives, seeing that it had been Lintir who had brought her to Rolvint, but no one had heard anything. It was as if she had dropped off the face of the earth.

'Perhaps she was a fey like you first thought,' suggested Helgis one day when he caught his brother scanning the crowds outside the city gate waiting for market day to begin. Carters queued, arriving in heavily armed convoys to bring goods from the countryside. A huddle of fishmen stood to one side, baskets of fresh catch adding a tang to the air. Spring had just arrived in Magharna, and the roadsides were lush with new growth. Sunshine glinted on the distant rooftops of the palaces by the river, highlighting their delicate artistry, melting the last of the icicles dripping from the eaves. 'I think she clicked her fingers and disappeared in a puff of smoke, back to join her folk.'

People gave the two scavengers plenty of space as they walked with their birds on their arm through the archway. They were off to deal with the return of the crow problem up at the summer palace.

'If she could have done that, she'd have used her power on Krital, believe me,' said Peri drily. 'No, she's flesh and blood—just a little different.'

'Why do you keep on worrying about her?'

'I suppose I feel responsible. I can't let it go until I know she's all right.'

Helgis scratched his nose. 'I bet she's spent the winter dining off gold plates and sleeping between silk sheets somewhere up in the jettan district.'

'I hope so, but why then is there no word of her?'

Helgis shrugged. 'Perhaps Pa doesn't know the right people to ask? Maybe she'd gone home already. I would if I were her. There's nothing here for her now.'

They reached the building site to find the bondsman, Mikel, on the gates.

'Blooming waste of time,' he grumbled, opening the doors for them. 'Unless you can get rid of every crow in Magharna, what's the point?'

'A very philosophical question, Mikel. And good morning to you too,' smiled Peri.

'Who's the sprout?'

'My brother, Helgis.'

'You as stubborn as him, sprout?'

'Worse,' replied Helgis cheerfully.

'Master save us,' exclaimed Mikel with mock-horror. 'All right, the pair of you, get to it. If you can spare an old man a moment or two, come have breakfast with me when your birdies need resting.'

'Birdies! You hear that, Goldie?' Helgis stroked her feathers lovingly.

'They're no more scavengers than blinking chickens, if you ask me.' Mikel eyed the sparrowhawk with respect. 'Hens eat grubs, don't they?'

Helgis nodded at this undeniable fact.

'So why are these birdies of yours shunned just because they eat bigger prey? I never understood that. And don't get me started on cats. We need more than the ones licensed to the cat men. The whole blooming city is overrun with mice and rats thanks to that stupid rule.'

'I thought you said not to get you started,' commented Peri.

'None of your cheek, falcon man.' Mikel waved them on. 'Get to work, you pair of lazy so-and-sos.'

The crow hunt went well with both Fletch and Goldie working the site. They bagged three and scared away the rest before an hour had passed. Job done for the moment, Peri and Helgis sought Mikel out in his cabin by the gate. He had tea already brewing and a batch of fresh buns waiting. He poured them each a mug and then lifted the lid on the kettle.

'Need some more water if we're going to have a refill.' He picked up an old pan and stood at the door beating it with a wooden spoon.

Helgis raised his eyebrows at Peri. 'What's he doing?'

Peri smiled. 'No idea. Mikel is a law unto himself.'

'Must be if he eats with scavengers.'

Mikel threw the pan on the floor with a clank. 'Here she comes,' he said with satisfaction.

'Who?' asked Helgis.

'My little water-carrier. One of the scullery maids from the kitchen.'

Peri glanced out of the door to see a girl in a grey uniform and white scarf staggering over the uneven ground with a yoke over her shoulders. She didn't look big enough to carry the two large buckets but she managed somehow, head bent to the ground.

'How's my lovely today?' called Mikel cheerfully, using a much kinder tone than was his custom. He went halfway to meet her and plucked the yoke from her back.

Peri couldn't hear any more of the exchange so returned his attention to his breakfast.

Mikel entered, hauling one of the buckets. 'Mind if I ask her in for a bite to eat? They don't give them much where she's from.'

'As long as she doesn't object to us.'

'Oh no, my little friend isn't bothered by all that.' Mikel waved his gnarled hand in a gesture that took in the whole of Rolvint. 'She's not from round here.'

Dipping back outside, Mikel returned, followed by a reluctant water-carrier. She kept behind him shyly.

'You mustn't mind my guests,' Mikel said gruffly, propelling her forward. 'They won't bite. Can't say the same for their birds but they're all hooded and shut up tight in them baskets.'

At the mention of birds, the girl's eyes flew to Peri's face.

'You!' she exclaimed.

'Rain!' Peri got up from his seat and took a step back, feeling as if her gaze had punched him.

'This her then?' asked Helgis, both intrigued and delighted to meet the girl he had heard so much about. He approached the stranger and flicked his hand in front of her face, making Rain flinch. 'You're right: she can see with those blue peepers of hers.'

'Leave her alone, sprout.' Mikel dragged him back by the jacket. 'She gets easily spooked, don't you, lovey?'

Rain was still staring at Peri.

Mikel assessed the pair of them. 'Met before have you?'

'Yes, on the day I arrived,' Rain replied softly, adding, 'thank the Master.'

Mikel clicked his tongue dismissively. 'You know better than that: none of that House of Indigent claptrap round me. You've little to thank the Master for if you ask me, working you to an early grave, he is.'

'But I get punished if I forget.'

'We won't tell, will we, lads?'

Helgis shook his head.

'No. Thought is free as far as I'm concerned,' said Peri. He was pleased to hear that her Magharnan was much more fluent now, her words coming easily.

Mikel scratched his head as he looked from Peri to Rain, running in his mind the conversations they had had previously. 'Don't tell me, Rain, that he was the idiot who dumped you at the gates?'

She nodded.

'I thought I liked you, falcon man,' Mikel said stiffly, 'but I can't believe you left her high and dry. What were you thinking, pig-brain?'

'That the city would look after her?' Peri offered, though he knew it made for a lame excuse.

Mikel snorted. 'Dream on, scavenger. The city's been working her to the bone and given her nothing in return. The House of the Indigent is nothing but slavery with a charitable name, if you ask me—which no one does, of course.' Mikel went off into his usual litany of grumbles as he poured Rain a cup, selecting the best one he owned from the shelf and scrupulously checking that it was clean before filling it.

'Are you all right?' Peri asked, his insides twisting with guilt. She didn't look well: her eyes had shadows under them and she had lost weight—not that there had been much of that to start with.

'I am as you see,' Rain replied with dignity, taking the cup from Mikel. Peri noted that she gave her smiles freely to the old doorkeeper but spent none on him.

'Why didn't anyone look after you? The ambassador's family should have stepped in.'

Her eyes slid across him to the doorway. He could feel her unspoken question as to why he hadn't done so himself. She seemed loath to let her gaze land on his face. If it had been anyone else in Rolvint, Peri would have said she was doing so because he was a scavenger; with Rain, he guessed it was more complicated. She probably felt very angry with him for what had happened on that first day.

'I have to explain why I left you.' Peri wished she'd just look at him. 'I assumed your betrothed was a Magharnan. You must know by now that a scavenger would not be welcomed in the city, even if he had helped a kinswoman. I thought I was doing you a favour leaving you as I did.'

Rain gave a tight smile directed somewhere over his right shoulder. 'That's all right, falcon man. I survived.'

'But the ambassador—'

'Is dead. No one in Rolvint owes me anything. I'm lucky to have my job.' Her tone was bleak, the speech rehearsed.

Peri rubbed the back of his neck, feeling her distress. The girl seemed so tired, defeated by her circumstances. He had let this be done to her.

Helgis meanwhile was indulging his curiosity about the stranger. Having proved his theory about her sight, he had circled around her and discovered her hair only imperfectly hidden under the scarf. He touched a curl lightly, making her jump.

'Helgis!' Peri tugged his brother to take a seat beside him. 'Forgive my savage of a brother. He's only twelve and not yet learnt his manners.'

'It's nothing,' she said in a low voice. 'I've known worse.'

Peri swallowed hard. He knew what she meant: the dormitories of the House of the Indigent were rough places by all accounts. Someone who stood out as being a little different would be in for serious bullying. Now that he examined her for the evidence, he noticed that the backs of her hands and forearms were bruised. His heart dropped down to his boots: he'd been partly responsible for this too. Perhaps he should have taken her home with him as she had wanted. At least in the barracks there would have been his family to look after her. He had been a fool.

Rain tried to ignore the black-robed falcon man but he seemed to fill the room with his calm reasonableness. He'd expected her to be welcomed by the jettans. He had a sound answer for everything he'd done, or not done. He'd apologized but he didn't really regret his actions; he was too calm, too smooth for someone racked with guilt. He represented everything she hated about Rolvint: its adherence to silly rules of association, its lack of care for a stranger.

It didn't help that he was still the most attractive Magharnan she'd met. She had thought him kind, but that had been short-lived. She preferred the gruff old bondsman; at least he didn't drop her at the first opportunity.

She turned to Mikel. 'Thank you for breakfast. In fact, it's my birthday today. Now you've made it special.'

His eyes twinkled at her. 'What! A stale old bun! We can do better than that.' He patted his pockets and drew out a penny. 'Here, lovey, buy yourself a ribbon with that.'

Rain held the coin as if it were priceless. 'Thank you. But would you mind if I saved it?'

'You can do what you want with it: it's your penny now. What are you saving for?'

'To go home.'

'Ah.' He shifted uncomfortably. 'And how much have you got so far?'

She gave him a tremulous smile. 'One Rolvint penny. But it's a beginning. My father always said that every journey starts with just one step.'

'True enough.'

'I know that if he doesn't hear from me soon, he might come looking for me; but I can't count on that. I've got to make my own plans.'

'Sensible girl.'

'Have you thought of applying to the government to pay for your return?' It was Master Calm-and-Reasonable again.

Rain gave a short laugh. 'What do you think I've been doing the last few months, falcon man? The first thing I did was ask the matron at the House of the Indigent to make an approach on my behalf.'

'And did she?'

'Oh yes. She has no more desire for my presence cluttering up her halls than I have to be there. She petitioned the foreign ministry but was told that as I merely accompanied the craftsman and was not the one bidden to do the work on the palace myself, the Magharnan Master had no further responsibility to me. In short, it was my bad luck to be a victim of your bandits and I had to be grateful that I hadn't been left to starve.' She gave him a brittle smile. 'They did mention that they had buried my kinsman at their own expense. So generous of them, don't you think?'

'How much do you need to get home?'

'I'm not sure. It's a long voyage and I don't think ships make the journey unless chartered to do so.'

'Chartering doesn't come cheap. You're talking thousands of gold signets.'

Rain knew full well that her own efforts to pay for her passage were pretty futile and she was unlikely to see a silver jettal, let alone a signet, in exchange for her work, but she would not just give up. She shrugged. 'Oh well, I'd better keep on economizing on the hair ribbons then.'

'Rain! Rain! Get your lazy carcass back here!' yelled a woman outside.

'My summons.' Rain rose from her seat by the fire and dipped a curtsey to Mikel. 'Thank you for breakfast.'

The old bondsman passed her another bun. 'Here, keep that for later.'

'You are the kindest man.' Rain reached up and kissed him on the cheek.

Mikel blushed and held his hand over the spot reverently as if to preserve her touch. 'Get along with you.'

Rain nodded slightly to the falcon men in farewell, but did not look at them. She had had it drummed into her that she should not turn her unearthly blue eyes on ordinary Magharnans so it had now become habit. Besides, she did not want to see Peri: he was too big, too calm, too good looking . . .

Now where had that traitorous thought come from? She had to stop it before she got herself in more hot water. She had already been reprimanded for numerous infractions of Magharnan customs; to be caught hankering after one of the scavengers would probably have her thrown out of the city.

He wasn't handsome. He was arrogant. Too tall. Yes, that was it. He was no more good looking than the rear end of a donkey . . .

Who was she trying to fool?

'Rain, you will take no break at midday since you've been frittering away the morning with that dirty bondsman by the gates.' The cook waved a rolling pin at her as she entered the shabby, low-ceilinged kitchen. It smelt of boiled cabbage and the tables were none too clean. By chance, it had turned out that Rain's new mistress was the very woman who had sat in front of her in the employment office. The claim to prior acquaintance had not helped. Rain suspected it had worked against her as the cook felt ashamed she had been seen there by someone else.

'Yes, Mistress Hundle.'

'Wash yourself thoroughly. I will not have the artisans' food rendered unfit for them because you have been gossiping with the lower classes.'

'Yes, mistress.'

The cook turned to address the gathered servants, tapping a metal bowl to get their attention. 'A glassmaker will be on site today. Since the attempt to bring in foreign craftsmen failed last year, Jettan Kirn has appointed one of ours to design the windows. You will treat him with utmost respect.'

Rain clenched her fists. That was supposed to have been her job. She'd spent long enough on the site to have thought up patterns for all the empty window niches as a means of filling her lonely hours. In her mind's eye, she could already see the summer palace as a blaze of colour: flowers, skies, wild animals, trees, all delicately picked out in a lacework design to complement the airy architecture.

'If you are fortunate enough to come across the glassmaker during your duties, you are to stand to one side and curtsey. Rain, keep your eyes lowered.'

'Yes, mistress.'

'And for the Master's sake, do something about your hair. I can see it tumbling down your back.'

Rain tried to bundle it all under her scarf but Helgis's exploration earlier had undone her braid. She would have to start again.

'Now, stop all looking at me like a herd of mindless cows. Get back to work!'

Rain couldn't help watching for the designer as she went about her tasks. Given the unpleasant job of heaving buckets of water from the well, she made many tottering journeys across the site. She knew that Mikel was keeping an eye on her from the gate, making sure she wasn't bothered by any of the labourers, but there was no sign of the falcon men. They'd probably left before the ordinary workers had reported for duty. Towards noon, a party arrived on horseback, flanked by six guards dressed in blue livery. Rain recognized Jettan Kirn, the overseer of the works, a thin man with receding hair and an expression of permanent disgust. She'd been told he was the most important man in Magharna after the Master. Kirn's footsteps were dogged by a smartly dressed drummer, employed to be his intermediary with the lower classes. Next to the jettan was a stout man with brawny arms. He had the look of a glassmaker, down to the scarred hands of one who worked at a forge. Rain felt a pang of homesickness. He reminded her of her father—the same stature and air of competence. The bucket slopped, dampening the hem of her gown, as she stumbled out of their way.

'Now, Master Glassmaker, Jettan Kirn would like you to explain your preliminary sketches to him,' said the servant.

The man began his description, relating how he planned to fill the windows with images taken from Magharnan history, portraits of famous Masters, images of decisive battles.

All wrong, thought Rain. They would ruin the building, being completely out of harmony with the vision of summer lightness created by the architect. The palace needed beauty with a touch of fantasy.

'That sounds very satisfactory,' said the jettan. 'I expect work to begin immediately.'

'Tell your master that I will have my best apprentices dedicated to the task working day and night,' replied the craftsman.

'I will leave him to his work then.' The jettan gave the glassmaker a nod and strode from the site, his work for the day complete. The designer wiped his brow and gave a huff of relief, thankful for passing the test. He looked up and saw Rain waiting by the side of the plank walkway over the rough ground.

'Here, girl, bring me some water.' He beckoned her closer.

Rain presented him with the dipper she carried at her belt for use of the builders when they required a drink.

The glassmaker took a long, deep draught and smacked his lips. 'That's better. Thirsty work, dealing with a jettan.' He held out the dipper. As Rain reached to take it back, she glanced up, giving the glassmaker a glimpse of her eyes. He kept hold of the scoop, not letting her tug it from his grip. 'Wait a moment, I've heard of you.' He scratched his nose trying to remember. 'You're that girl from Holt. A few months back someone was asking around for you, but I said I'd never seen you.'

Rain felt a leap of hope. 'Who, sir?'

He relinquished his hold on the dipper. 'Oh, some scavenger. I couldn't understand why that lot would be interested in a foreigner. You came to Magharna with the Holtish glassmaker, didn't you?'

'Yes, sir.' So it hadn't been someone from home; she'd been foolish to let herself even think this.

He rolled his shoulders, easing the tension. 'Sorry for your loss, but I can't say that I was sad that the work stayed with us Magharnans. Still, do you know anything about Holtish glassmaking?'

Rain could have laughed: what did she know? Only everything.

'I grew up in my father's forge, sir. I have picked up a few bits here and there.'

'Do you know what your kinsman had in mind for the palace?'

Rain glanced towards the kitchen, wondering if she would be reprimanded for talking so freely to the craftsman. 'I think he would have made the windows

117

with a variety of summer themes—fruit and flowers, that sort of thing.'

The glassmaker shook his head. 'Just as well then. That would never have done for the Master.' He gave her another inspection. 'In the House of the Indigent, are you?'

'As you see, sir.' She wondered for a moment if he was going to offer her the hospitality of one craftsman to another. That is what would have happened in Tigral.

'Good. I'm glad to see the Master is looking after you.'

Her heart sank. 'He has been most kind,' she lied.

He reached in a bag hanging from his shoulder to draw out a scroll, already dismissing her from his thoughts.

'Sir?'

'What?'

'If anyone from Holt should ask after me, will you tell them where I am to be found?'

He looked puzzled. 'Why would they ask me?'

'I think my family would expect me to be lodged with the glassmakers.'

He didn't take the hint. 'All right, I'll tell them. Now leave me in peace: I've work to do.'

Shard 7
Flame Gold

One evening late in March, Hern returned from a hunting trip on a jettan's estate.

'Another merchant convoy's been attacked,' he announced to the family as everyone gathered in the shared kitchen for supper.

Shaking his head, Peri finished oiling his gauntlet and started on Helgis's glove.

'Any survivors?' asked Katia, checking that Rosie wasn't in earshot. The little girl was playing ball with some other scavenger children by the open door, untouched by the troubles that worried their elders.

'None. Word has it that they carried a cargo of gold for Wealer Damset.' Hern poured himself a mug of beer, took a gulp and wiped the foam from his top lip. 'There will be lots of worried people up in the city tonight.'

'Why?' Helgis scrawled absent-mindedly on a slate, drawing the mountain pass. 'It wasn't their stuff that was stolen, was it?'

'Not directly. But Damset runs the biggest house of

coinage; his money underpins our whole currency. If he goes down, so do many of the people who borrow from him,' Hern explained.

Helgis grinned. 'So what? A few rich men lose out: sounds like good news to me.'

'We'll see.'

Peri checked the stitching on the gauntlet carefully, ensuring there were no loose threads to catch on a raptor's claws. Remarkably for Helgis, it was in a sound condition, unlike the Magharnan state. That had been fragile ever since the run of bad harvests and huge losses to the bandits. This latest attack was cutting off the blood supply to the heart of an already wounded patient; there was only so much trauma Magharna could withstand.

'What do you think we should do, Pa?' Peri asked quietly.

Hern sat down next to his oldest son and lowered his voice. 'I think we should make preparations for the worst. Your mother and I, along with the other families, have been stockpiling supplies for some time now, but we'll have to think how we'll react if law and order breaks down in the city-within-the-walls. I wouldn't put it past the rich merchants to think they can walk in here and take our stuff if they are in need.'

'So, what? An armed guard?'

'Yes. All of us capable of defending the compound will have to take our turn.'

'Starting when?'

Hern took a breath. 'About now, I'd say.' He stood up, climbing on a bench. 'My friends!'

The chatter quickly died away as the scavengers gathered in the four sections of the room turned in their seats to look up at Hern.

'We've been expecting trouble for some months, haven't we?' There were rumbles of agreement. 'It's time to take precautions. The city's on a knife edge and there's no guarantee the problems won't spread down here. If you agree, I propose we choose someone to organize our defenders and another to control our stores to see us through the bad times to come.'

A woman at the far end of the room stood on her chair. 'We trust you, Hern. My vote is to put you in charge of our defence.'

Her suggestion was seconded by many in the room.

'I'd be honoured, Kentara.' Hern shifted uneasily. 'But what about supplies? Will you take that on?'

She shrugged, hands on hips. 'If you think I'd do a good job.'

'It's right that a butcher does it,' agreed Katia, standing beside her husband. 'You're the best woman for the position.'

Kentara grinned. 'All right. At least between us, we won't run short of meat, eh?'

There was a ripple of laughter in the room, lightening the mood despite the seriousness of the occasion. Peri found it hard to join in. The scavengers wouldn't be able to save everyone, their resources just didn't stretch that far, but he hoped to make the case for some exceptions. He wondered what would happen to those he knew in the city, to Mikel and to Rain. If things got as bad as his father feared, he would have to do something for them; he couldn't hide in safety knowing they were suffering.

Rain encountered the first sign of the approaching crisis on her way to work the next morning. Queues had formed outside a beautiful mansion on a city square, the line snaking round a peacock-shaped fountain and under the arcade of exclusive tailors' shops. The house was decorated with a shield over the door, inscribed with the word 'Damset'. But the mood of the crowd was out of step with the tranquillity of the plaza; the people were talking angrily, the men at the front thumping on the closed gates.

'Let us in!' they shouted.

'No more worthless paper and empty promises: we want gold!' yelled a puce-faced man.

Rain hurried on, arriving just in time at the kitchen for the start of her duties.

'Keep off the streets today, lovey,' Mikel advised her when she went to fill up his kettle. 'There'll be ugly scenes.'

'Why?' She accepted the cup of tea he offered her and took a perch on a stool with a sigh of relief, her feet aching in her ill-fitting clogs.

'Big wealer going down, taking lots of little ones with him. No telling where it will stop.'

'That won't affect us, will it?'

Mikel sneezed into a grubby handkerchief. 'Wish I could get rid of this blooming cold. No one knows. We're travelling in uncharted territory, if you follow me.'

Rain wrinkled her brow. 'I'm not sure I do. Haven't you had problems before in Magharna?'

'Not as bad as this.'

'But can't the Master do something to put things right?' She thought of her own country where King Ramil always seemed to have a plan to deal with any trouble before it developed into a crisis.

'Don't know what the Master will do.' Mikel blew his nose with a hearty trumpet, his eyes streaming. 'Don't know that he thinks about what happens to us ordinary folk. I've never seen him.'

'What, never?' The royal family were always on display in Tigral. It was a rare person who had never managed to see them at some state occasion.

'Few people have. Just a couple of hand-picked jettans. The Master has to be kept from contamination.'

'How strange. Where I come from it is thought to be the king's duty to know as much as he can about what happens to his people.'

'Well, not here.' Mikel tapped his cup. 'Enough doom and gloom. I've some news.'

'More news, you mean?'

'Yes, you impertinent chit.' He teasingly let an impressive silence build. 'The first window is going in today. That glassmaker will be back to oversee its installation.'

'That's . . . that's good.' She was torn between a desire to see what the man had done and chagrin that she had not been the one to do it.

'Bleeding waste of money, if you ask me—'

'But no one does,' finished Rain with a giggle.

'That's just it: no one does.' He winked. 'Wouldn't be in this mess if they did, I can tell you.'

A board protected the glass as the frame was winched into place. Rain had seen this many times back home and it was always a nail-biting moment. She didn't even have to hide her interest: all the servants were hanging around the courtyard for the moment of unveiling so she could mingle inconspicuously with them. Finally, after much adjusting and swearing from the glassmaker, the time arrived. The cover was prised off the frame, revealing a stained-glass window in browns, dark blues, and reds: a battle scene.

'What is it?' Rain asked the cook.

She frowned, pushing her lanky hair off her face. 'Looks like the Battle of Viguria, three centuries ago. Rolvint was founded not long after.'

Rain was disappointed. Though it was beautiful in its own way, she thought the colours were sludgy, the subject matter predictable, the battle without passion.

'Do you like it?' she asked the cook, wondering if her reaction was due to her Holtish tastes.

'It's all right, I suppose,' the cook said grudgingly. 'Not the sort of thing I'd like to look at day and night.'

The crowd dispersed, the unveiling an anticlimax. At least the glassmaker looked pleased; he was probably just relieved to have it in place without damage.

One of the last to leave work that night, Rain couldn't avoid the streets for her journey home. The queues had gone from outside the Damset mansion, but the doors hung open and the pavement was littered with scraps of paper, many of which had been torn into pieces. She snagged one out of the fountain and read the inscription:

I promise to pay the bearer the sum of one thousand gold signets, signed Wealer Damset.

It was paper money. The whole plaza was covered in the stuff which told Rain that for some reason Wealer Damset's signature was no longer worth the parchment it was written on.

She arrived back at the House of the Indigent to find the doors lay open there too. She went in, a nervous flutter in the pit of her stomach. Instead of the usual crowd of grey uniformed inmates, the place was empty. No preparations had been made for the evening meal—there was no food at the hatch where she reported for her ration. The dormitory was silent; the beds stripped. Rain hovered in the doorway, wondering what she should do. Footsteps approached. She turned. Never before had she been so happy to see the matron.

'We're closed,' the matron said sharply. 'You have to go.'

'Go where?'

'I don't know. That's your problem.'

'But what's happened?'

'Wealer Damset dealt with our finances. Now he's gone, there's not a signet left.'

'Gone?'

'Committed suicide. Couldn't stand to lose everything so jumped off the cliff into the river this morning.'

'Poor man!'

'Stupid man!' corrected the matron. 'Look what he's brought us to: it's the end of everything I worked for! I've no job any more, no place to go.'

Rain couldn't imagine the matron sitting in a queue at the employment office.

'Where do we go to get new places?'

The matron gave a slightly hysterical laugh. 'Don't you understand? There are no places. Nothing is working, nothing! The shops aren't accepting any money but gold and there's precious little of that to go round. People are being turned away from their jobs. Rolvint has ground to a halt, all because some idiotic wealer let his valuables be looted. If there's any justice left in Magharna, they will string up his family, then the bandits.'

Rain didn't think that sounded very fair at all but had no wish to argue. 'So I've lost my job?'

The matron picked up a bundle of what looked suspiciously like bedding. 'Catching on, are you? No, you'll not be needed there any more. No one can pay for that extravagance now so there'll be no labourers to feed. Hurry up, I've told you to leave; I want to lock up. I don't want anyone to say I didn't do my duty to the bitter end.'

'And that includes stealing the blankets?'

The matron hissed. 'It's the least they owe me. Get out!'

Rain was relieved to find that her own small collection of belongings was still on the shelf she had been allocated. No one had thought her beads, charcoal, and paper worth stealing. All the other niches were empty. She stumbled out on to the street, tripping on the board listing the rules and regulations that someone had shattered on the step. The matron followed her, locking the door to the House of the Indigent with jerky movements before scurrying off into the city. In the few short minutes Rain had been inside, things had changed on the streets. She could now hear angry voices coming from nearby, the sound of breaking glass and screams. There was no sign of any law enforcers but perhaps they too had decided, like the matron, that they were not going to get paid so were no longer fulfilling their duties.

Perhaps they were the ones breaking the windows?

I've been here before, Rain told herself, trying to stave off panic. *One step at a time: first I need to find shelter for the night.*

She quickly reviewed her options. She only had one real friend in the city, but that meant crossing the rich districts again to reach him. There was nothing for it: she would have to take the risk.

The beautiful, elegant streets were given over to a running battle. One house of coinage was on fire, the people taking off with bags of gold signets and silver jettals rather than attempt to control the blaze. The owner stood outside, screaming at them to stop, but his cries went unheeded. Rain ducked down an alley, hoping to avoid the scene entirely, only to find her path thick with choking smoke. She pulled off her scarf and wrapped it over her face. Couldn't they see that if no one put out the fire, the whole district would go up in flames? Didn't they care?

The answer was clearly 'not'.

In the next street, she found a huddle of people pelting a purveyor with paper money.

'Here, take it,' they shouted at him while a chain of men removed the bronze statues from his display cases.

He wept and pleaded but the looters were determined.

'Fair exchange!' they chanted. 'Fair exchange!'

At first, Rain was terrified that the crowd would attack her, but she soon realized that no one was interested in a foreigner. Rolvint had turned into a frantic free-for-all: shops being emptied, houses of coinage looted, mansions belonging to the rich sacked. There was plenty of violence—fights over spoils, arguments between householders and rioters, drunken brawls—but she managed to slip through unscathed to arrive outside the site of the summer palace. As it was still a shell, the rioters had not thought to come here yet.

She hammered on the gate. 'Open up, Mikel, open up!'

There was silence from inside.

'It's me—Rain.'

She heard a hacking cough and then the entrance scraped open a fraction.

'Get in quick,' Mikel said hoarsely. 'Best if they think no one's here.'

She darted inside and watched as he chained the gate. He was bent over and wheezing, his face flushed.

'You're ill,' she said.

'My cold's turned out to be a bit of a fever,' admitted Mikel.

'You must go back to bed. If you let me, I'll stay and look after you.'

He shuffled back to his cabin. 'Looks like you'll have no choice. I won't let you back out there for all the money in Rolvint.'

'There's hardly any of that and what there is, is worthless,' Rain remarked, going on to describe the scenes just a few streets away, how the paper money had been discarded and the precious coinage looted. 'I don't understand how your Master can allow it. Things have changed so quickly—it was all right this morning and now places are on fire, people stealing things. I wouldn't be surprised if someone gets killed: it's madness.'

Mikel collapsed on to his thin pallet, his narrow ribcage heaving in another bout of coughing. 'Then you stay with old Mikel,' he said when he'd got his breath. 'I may be a stubborn cuss but at least I'm not crazy.'

'No, you're not. You're the best man in Magharna.'

He laughed at that and lay still, following her with his eyes as she pottered around his cabin making him a little soup from the scraps of vegetables she'd got him from the kitchen earlier in the day.

'Your father must miss you,' he said after some minutes of silence had passed.

'And I him.'

'I had a daughter once.'

'Oh yes?' Rain realized she knew very little about her friend's past. 'What was her name?'

'Mikela, of course.' His wheezy laugh petered out into coughing.

'And your wife?'

'We weren't married. Bondsmen aren't allowed. No point anyway. Your owners send you where they like, split you up just for the fun of it.'

'No one would be that cruel!'

'You want to bet on it?'

She grimaced, considering what she knew about Magharna. 'I suppose not.'

'Wise girl.'

'What about Mikela?'

'She was left with me, worked in the kitchens like you do. Died in an accident on another site: wall fell on her. She didn't suffer. Gone just like that she was.' He snapped his fingers.

'I'm sorry. How old was she?'

'Twenty. My world died with her.'

'That's awful.'

'But then you came. Mikela would've liked you.'

Rain wondered what she could say to comfort him, but words were inadequate. 'And if she was anything like her father, I'm sure we would've been friends.'

'You mustn't worry about what's going to happen. I'll see you are all right,' promised Mikel, folding his hands on his chest to rest.

Rain thanked him and then helped him drink his soup before having some herself. It was kind of him to say so, but she feared that he would need someone to look after him before he could offer protection to others. Sitting by the fire in their quiet enclave while the city burned and rioted around them, she made her plans. Her first step was to break into the kitchen. The looters had not yet considered it worthy of their attention with so many richer places to rob so she was able to take from the stores. She chose carefully, selecting items that would not spoil and that could be hidden in the cabin. She had already decided that safety lay in looking poorer than everyone else. She took several trips to transport her findings across to Mikel's home, and here her yoke and buckets came in useful. Once she had enough for a few weeks, she set about hiding the bulk of it. This was no easy task: the cabin was a simple building. In the end she found places under the floorboards. Knowing that the food would be vulnerable to rats, she buried it all in cooking pots with lids, also liberated from the communal kitchen. Her job done, she stirred Mikel's fire and sat down with a cup of Magharnan tea, a pale yellow leaf that smelt of cinnamon, thinking how precious it was at a time when she could not guarantee replacing it. How strange to be reduced to looting. Though she did not want to count herself as one of the rioters romping through the streets, she knew she wasn't much different from them. In a crisis, it was everyone for themselves—or at least everyone for those they loved.

She smoothed the old man's white-shot black hair off his brow, pleased to note that his fever was not too bad, his breathing less laboured. She'd make sure he was all right, she vowed; he was her only responsibility now.

The rioters came as she had anticipated late the following day. Mikel was still sleeping when they battered on the gates and ordered them to be opened. Grabbing a lantern, Rain approached the entrance.

'What do you want?' she asked. 'There's little left in here.'

'Get these doors open or we'll bash them in,' shouted a man on the far side.

Gingerly, Rain unlocked the gate and stood back to let the group of ten men enter. They were a motley bunch: some wearing the livery of servants of the jet-tan families, others the leather aprons of blacksmiths. It seemed that the distinction between classes had collapsed along with the Magharnan state. The leader, a short, square-built man who carried a spear, hauled her from the shadows, using her own lantern to illuminate her face.

'You hiding something here, girl?' He shook her, dislodging her scarf. 'I've seen you about: you're that foreigner. Fey blood some think. Is it true?'

'It might be.' Rain fixed him with her blazing blue gaze, willing him to be just a little scared of her.

He relinquished her arm but kept hold of the lantern. 'Well then, keep out of our way and we'll keep out of yours.'

She nodded, not trusting his momentary wariness to last. 'There's not much here to take, but help yourself.' She swept a mocking arm to the building site.

The men split up, raiding building stores and the kitchen. Rain hovered in the door of Mikel's cabin, determined to stop them entering if they should approach. She watched as they heaped piles of loot by the gate but they must have been disappointed with their haul because they soon took to vandalism, crudely punishing the building for failing their greed. One younger man scrawled obscenities on the white walls of the palace; another took a rock and, before Rain could move to prevent it, heaved it through the stained-glass window. Shards speared to the ground, a fallen rainbow. Following an impulse she could not quell, she ran forward, hands cupped as if to catch the pieces, but it was futile.

'Why did you do that?' she asked the looter, aghast at the stupidity of his actions. 'It was worth nothing to you and now you've ruined something beautiful!'

He threw a second stone, taking out a panel he had missed. 'Shove off!'

Rain felt her anger rising. 'This is my home. Stop messing it up!'

'What!' he scoffed. 'A little thing like you laying claim to the summer palace!'

She curled her fists. 'I'm not saying I own it; I'm telling you I live here. You wouldn't want strangers coming in and wrecking your house, would you?'

He tossed a third rock indecisively in his palm. 'Good try, darling, but I'm not buying it. This belongs to the Master and I'm damned if I won't have some fun with it. He owes us for letting things get so bad.' He launched the missile, destroying the last section that hung in the frame.

Outraged, Rain stomped back to the cabin.

'What's happening?' Mikel asked weakly, raising his head from the pillow.

'We have visitors,' she replied curtly.

Mikel attempted to swing his legs out of the bed.

Rain made a move to stop him. 'Stay there in the warm. I don't think they'll come in here, but if they do, I'll make them think twice.'

He evidently didn't find her words reassuring but pulled himself upright and donned a tunic over his undershirt.

'I don't want you anywhere near bad men like that, Rain,' he said, breaking into a fit of coughing.

'I suppose we can threaten them with your cold,' she said wryly, steering him to the fire.

He was having none of it. He shook off her hand and pulled a staff out from behind the door.

'Keep out of sight,' he ordered.

'Too late: they've seen me already.' He glowered at her. 'I had to let them in before they broke the gate down. The rumour's spread that I've something called fey blood so they're a tiny bit scared of me, enough to leave me alone.'

'That's good. Best protection you could hope for.' He peeked out of the door, checking on the progress of the looters. The entry looked like a storm-racked beach, littered with debris thrown high on the strand. 'I'll be having that.' He snagged an axe from among the piles of tools, testing its weight with a swing on the chopping block by his door.

'What is a fey person?' Rain asked. She did her own bit of reclamation, taking a kitchen knife that was sticking out of a bundle and tucking it in her belt.

'They are the folk that legend says live in the hill-sides. Whole kingdoms they have, deep in the earth. Smaller than us Magharnans,' his eyes twinkled at her diminutive stature, 'but they pop out and lure ordinary mortals into their traps. The stories say that if you go on one of their adventures, you are changed for ever: food tastes like ash, the finest sights are pale and uninteresting, all because your appetite has been spoiled by the indescribable riches of the Fey. All non-sense.'

'Sounds good to me.' Already her mind was imagining new designs for windows depicting the folktales about fey people, capturing the visions that they were said to offer. 'I could really work with that.' She then remembered she had no outlet for her talent and frowned. 'Those looters broke the window.'

'Muttonheads,' murmured Mikel, not too bothered by the news. 'But if it hadn't been them, someone else would've done it.'

'I suppose so.'

The looters had finished with the buildings and headed back for the gates. Rain and Mikel stood in front of the cabin, blocking the doorway.

'What's in there?' the leader asked, pointing inside.

Before Mikel could answer, Rain stepped forward. 'It's the entrance to my kingdom, mortal. Do you care to see?'

Mikel coughed, though it could have been a laugh.

The leader peered over her shoulder, glimpsing only the bare cabin and its simple furniture, a pallet bed and a straw mattress. 'Don't look like no kingdom to me.'

'That's because we fey folk hide our riches.' She

tugged a curl over her shoulder, playing with it to emphasize its uncanny corkscrew spring compared to the dead straight locks of the Magharnans. 'Come and find out for yourself.'

The looter shook his head and backed away. 'Oh no, mistress, I'm not falling for any of your tricks. I'm not putting a foot in there.'

'Suit yourself,' she said sweetly.

Grumbling, the men gathered their spoils and headed out of the gateway. Mikel followed them and banged the doors shut.

Relieved to have got away with her ploy, Rain trailed behind him to ensure he was all right. 'You need a sign,' she said. '*Nothing left in here* or others will come calling.'

'Humph! I can't write,' Mikel replied, adding another chain to the existing lock.

'I can—I learnt a little from the cook—and I've charcoal and paper.'

'What? In your kingdom?' He smiled. 'You can spin a good tale, lovey.'

Rain returned to the cabin and quickly scrawled a notice. 'Wasn't a tale, Mikel. I did hide our riches in here.'

The old bondsman looked doubtful. 'You mean, we've got something left?'

'Quite a lot really. Have a look under the floor-boards.'

He took a peek, spying the rows of cooking pots. 'My wonderful girl! Perhaps you do have fey blood;

you've worked a miracle here! I was worried that we would have to move out to find food.'

'No. We can stay put and hope for better times. Now this is infamous as the entrance to a magical kingdom, I don't think we'll be bothered.'

Shard 8
Blush Pink

Peri had spent the days after the collapse of law and order fretting about the fate of his friends within the walls. Against the advice of his father, he had even ventured in on the first night of rioting to search for Rain and found the House of the Indigent abandoned. He was at a loss where to start looking for her, and hoped that perhaps she would come to find him if she had nowhere to go. Returning to the barracks, he worried when she did not turn up that night, his mind imagining all sorts of horrible fates for a stranger alone in a city in chaos. But before he could resume his search, other, much less welcome, people did come looking for the scavengers' supplies and soon the barracks were under siege. It took a convincing show of force and one nasty scuffle involving rioters and the pack of hunting hounds to dissuade the city dwellers from further attacks.

Once the immediate threat to his home had passed, Peri begged his father and mother for permission to return into the city.

'Why must you find this girl?' his mother asked irritably as she stirred their morning porridge. His father leaned over her shoulder and sprinkled in a little cinnamon and dried apple as he carefully measured out the family ration. 'The city is too dangerous for anyone to go on a foolhardy errand of mercy.'

'I just have to,' Peri said, sharpening the sword he'd been allocated as part of the barrack guard. 'I feel responsible.'

'She isn't our business.'

'Come on, Ma, how would you feel if Bel or Rosie were in her shoes, a foreigner alone in a city gone mad?'

Katia pursed her lips. 'I wouldn't have let them go there on their own in the first place.'

'She wasn't supposed to be alone, remember? She's not to blame that everyone she knew was killed by the bandits within hours of landing. It's Magharna's fault she's in the fix she is; we're Magharnans, so why should we not be the ones to help her?'

'The boy has a point,' conceded Hern.

'Anyway, I have another friend, the old bondsman I told you about.' He kept his voice calm, knowing that his mother was more likely to concede if he did not sound too desperate. He had to convince her he had thought this course of action through and anticipated all the pitfalls. 'No one's looking out for him either.'

'What have we got to do with bondsmen? They never give us the time of day under normal circumstances.'

'But Mikel's different. He always talks to Helgis and me, gives us breakfast.'

Katia clanged the spoon against the rim in irritation. 'Oh, get the bowls, will you! I suppose I'll have to cook for two extra tonight.'

Peri smiled and rose to do her bidding.

His mother was right about one thing: it was dangerous to venture inside the walls and certainly not to be done alone. So Peri rode into the city with two young men from the barrack guard as added protection. The eldest, Conal, a shaggy-haired huntsman with an easy smile, held his beagle on a leash; Peri carried Rogue; the third, a lanky-limbed butcher called Sly, had enough knives in his belt to skin and bone a bull. Fortunately no one challenged them: this early in the day, the mobs were still sleeping off their drinking from the previous night and no one else on the streets was looking for trouble.

The change to Rolvint came as a shock to Peri: he saw two unclaimed bodies lying in the gutter, many burnt-out houses, broken windows, shattered doors, fouled drinking troughs. Very few people dared put a foot outside their homes, and if they did it was pure desperation that made them do so. The three riders passed a pinch-faced woman with a child in tow rooting through a pile of refuse. She froze when she saw them. The toddler began to cry. The woman quickly bundled the little girl into her arms and ran back into the roofless shell of the very same bakery Peri had passed a few months before.

'It looks like the end of the world,' muttered Sly, disgusted that they could terrify a woman just by their presence.

'I hope your friends have fared better than them,' muttered Conal, jerking his thumb at the bodies dumped by the roadside. 'Where do you want to start looking?'

Sickened by what he saw, Peri swallowed the bile that had risen in his throat. He had to remain focused if he was to be any use in the search. 'I don't know where my foreigner has got to, but I expect Mikel will still be in his cabin if no one has booted him out yet. Let's try there first.'

They reached the building site to find the gate shut against them and a note written in elegant script claiming that there was nothing left in there to steal.

'Looks like someone's home,' commented Conal.

'But not Mikel. I doubt his penmanship would be this fine, even if he could write,' replied Peri. His anxiety increasing, he banged on the gate. 'Open up!'

A gruff voice called back from the other side:

'Can't you idiots read the sign? You're wasting your time coming in here for stuff. It's all gone, the whole bleeding lot.'

Peri broke into a grin. 'Mikel! Open up, you stubborn old badger: there's a falcon man who wants to make sure you're still in one piece.'

The gate eased open a fraction, and was then thrown wide.

'If it isn't the peregrine himself!' crowed Mikel. 'Come in, come in, lads. Not safe to be out on the streets.'

The three scavengers urged their horses into the building site, dismounted and tethered them under the archway. The beagle trotted obediently at Conal's heels as they made their way over to the cabin.

Peri broke with years of training that had taught him his touch was unclean and put his arm around Mikel's shoulder. 'How've you been?' he asked, studying his friend for signs of suffering.

Mikel's eyes filled with tears at Peri's display of affection but he tried to disguise it with his usual bluff manner. 'Had a blooming cold but I'm over that now. In fact, I've had a nice few days.'

Peri rolled his eyes. 'The city descends into chaos and you are enjoying yourself!'

'Take your pleasures where you can, my friend.' Mikel halted outside the cabin and coughed. 'It's all right, lovey: you can come out now.'

Peri heard the bar on the door being lifted and the creak as it swung open. A nervous face peered out at them.

'Rain! You're here too!' exclaimed Peri, striding to give her a hug before he questioned what he was doing. She was engulfed in the circle of his arms and he felt her give him a slight answering squeeze before pushing him away.

'Master Falconer,' she said primly. She then noticed his companions and dipped a curtsey. 'And company.'

Peri quickly introduced Conal and Sly. They were staring at her with rather more interest than he wished.

'I looked for you at the House of the Indigent that first day but there was no one there,' he explained, catching her hand as if to reassure himself that she wasn't going to vanish again.

'Well, it closed.' She tugged her hand free.

'So I gathered. But don't worry: I've come to rescue you both.'

Rain shrugged. 'I don't think we need saving, do we, Mikel?'

The bondsman laughed. 'Not today, but you never know.'

'Would you like some tea?' Rain asked Peri's companions politely. Her eyes fell on the beagle and her manner transformed. 'What a beautiful dog! I've so missed seeing animals around Rolvint. Does he have a name?' She knelt beside the creature and began scratching his neck, drawing whimpers of ecstasy from the hound.

'I think Sniff has fallen in love,' remarked Conal. 'Doesn't Mistress Rain know that only scavengers touch dogs?'

'Rot!' snorted Rain. 'Only a really stupid person would think there was anything unclean about this dog.'

'You should see him after he's rolled in all the puddles between here and the marshes.'

Rain laughed and stood up. 'Tea?'

Peri struggled with a growing sense of annoyance as he watched Rain charm his friends. The fact that Mikel and she had clearly fended well for themselves without his aid added to his bad mood. Mikel had them laughing with the tale of fey folk that Rain had spun—merriment that Peri did not join in because he was calculating the danger she had been in testing a looter like that.

'So you flashed those big blue eyes of yours and invited him to visit the realm of the Fey?' chuckled Conal. 'I would have loved to have seen his face.'

'He changed his mind pretty quick.' Rain passed round the cups. 'Sorry, I've no sugar to offer. Supplies at this establishment are a little limited at present.'

Pushed beyond what he could bear by her light-hearted manner when he had been having nightmares about her fate, Peri rounded on Mikel. 'You shouldn't have let her go up against a thief like that. What would you have done if he had called her bluff?'

'Er, excuse me, falcon man, I am here, you know.' Rain waved a spoon under his nose, her tone sarcastic. 'I have a brain and decided that it was the best thing to be done in the circumstances. Don't turn on Mikel for something that was my choice.'

'So what would you have done, Rain? They could have taken everything—hurt you—' Peri's mind whirled with the possibilities for disaster.

'But they didn't. Besides, I would've thought of something else if it had gone wrong.'

'Oh yes? A midge like you take on a grown man—many grown men by the sounds of it. You're stupid even to think you're a match for them!'

'Stupid!' Rain stood up, one hand fisted on her hip as she brandished the spoon at him. The other three fell silent, watching the usually unruffled Peri provoke an argument. Conal raised an eyebrow at Sly. Sniff whined and pushed his nose into Rain's hand to comfort her. She stroked his head distractedly. 'How dare you!'

'Yes, stupid. You clearly can't look after yourself. You'll have to come back with us.'

Mikel shook his head, hiding a smile in his tea cup.

'And who made you king? I don't answer to you, scavenger.' Rain's eyes flashed blue fire.

'I'm not listening to this rubbish. Conal, Sly, help Mikel pack; we're taking them with us.' He grabbed a bundle of Rain's clothing from the mattress she had been using.

Rain took a step forward and rapped him on the back with the spoon. He barely noticed her assault.

'Look, you cloth-eared birdman, I'm not going anywhere I don't want.' She kicked his shins for good measure.

'Yes, you are,' he ground out through gritted teeth.

'No, I'm not! There's no point. We're comfortable here; no one's bothered us, have they, Mikel?'

The bondsman was looking fixedly out of the door, refusing to enter into the row.

'That won't last. Fey tales only buy you so much time, Rain. Tell her, Mikel.'

146

'Looks like it might be showery later,' observed the old man to no one in particular. Conal grinned and Sly did not bother to disguise his laugh.

'You can't hide out here for long. And my family is expecting you,' Peri announced as if this was the clinching argument.

'Well, how nice for them.' She threw her weapon on the table and folded her arms stubbornly. 'Don't get me wrong: I'd be delighted to meet your family, Peri, but not tied up and under armed guard—and that's the only way you'll get me to leave here!'

'All right.' Peri gave a nod to his companions. 'I'll see to the first part; you get the stuff.' He pulled some leather jesses from his falconer's bag. 'These will do.'

'What!' Rain's cry of anger made Rogue screech and mantle his wings on his perch by the door. Peri made a grab for her, but she slipped free. 'You wouldn't!'

'Calm down!' Peri said heatedly, shaking the jesses in frustration. 'This shouldn't be necessary if you saw sense. You made your position clear; well, this is mine: I'm not leaving you here.' He lunged again, but she evaded him and ran for the door. He pursued her and the pair of them disappeared into the building site, Rain with only a few paces lead.

Furious at Peri's highhanded treatment of her, Rain dodged the falconer and dived into a gap left between two walls, hoping it would be too narrow for him to follow her. This had been her back-up plan if the rioters came back: to hide in the building site some-where a grown man could not reach.

'Rain, you're wasting my time!' shouted Peri, thumping on the wall in frustration. He could see her huddled out of reach like a wild creature taking refuge in its den. 'We've got to get back.'

'Wonderful. Go back then.'

'You're being childish.'

'I'm not the one threatening to tie someone up!'

'It's for your own good.'

'I decide what's good for me, not you.'

Peri slumped by the entrance to her bolt-hole. 'How would it be if I promise not to restrain you?'

'I'm not going.'

He ran his hands through his long hair. It had escaped from its tie in the scramble over the site and flopped annoyingly over his face. She was scared, he reminded himself; he needed to be tactful.

'Look, Rain, I was just joking. Of course, I'm not going to tie you up. I just want you safe. Come out here and we'll talk.'

'No. You'll jump me, I know you will. You can't bear anyone having their own mind.'

So much for tact.

'Rain Glassmaker, you get out here now and deal with this.'

Silence.

'I'm taking Mikel. He won't make such a fuss. Surely even you realize you can't stay here alone? What's so attractive about here anyway? Is it because we're scavengers? Don't you want to mix with the likes of us?'

'You know that's not the case.' Her voice was less defiant now. He could hear the doubt so he drove home his point.

'Think what's best for Mikel. With us, he'll have people around to look after him and he won't have to worry about you. You must know that he's anxious, wondering what would happen to you if something put him out of action. He might get into a fight to protect you—get hurt. How would you feel if that happened?'

She didn't say anything but he could hear her moving around. He hoped it meant she was coming out.

'I'm sorry I went after you like that in the cabin, but I'm worried too. I've seen what it's like outside. I'd hate to think of you coming to harm when I can protect you.'

'But how will they find me if I leave here?' she asked quietly.

'Who?' Peri didn't understand. 'Someone's searching for you?'

'My father—maybe. I told the glassmaker I'd be here if Papa came asking. I've been gone over half a year and sent no word. He'll come after me—I'm almost sure of it.'

'I see.' Peri rested his head against the wall behind him, trying to imagine what it must be like for her, a foreigner lost in a city in collapse, her one frail link to home a half-built palace that would never now be finished. No wonder she had been so stubbornly attached to the place. To her, it was like the piece of driftwood

149

keeping a shipwrecked sailor afloat. If she let go, she'd sink without trace.

'They broke the glassmaker's window,' Rain added plaintively. 'Why did they do that? I collected the shards. They're beautiful—lovely colours.'

Peri shrugged. 'Fancy windows don't bring food to the table. I never understood why the jettan families went to all that expense when the people were starving.' From the stony silence, he realized he'd made a mistake dismissing her craft. 'I suppose they were all right in their way,' he conceded swiftly. 'I would've let it be myself, not destroyed it.'

'Beautiful things are not a luxury: we need them to remind ourselves that we're more than just bodies wearing clothes,' she said fiercely.

He held up his hands. 'All right, all right: I allow that they do some good for some people. Will you come out now?'

'I don't like you very much at the moment.'

He almost smiled at her grumpy tone but feared she would see and further delay their departure. 'You don't have to like me; you just have to trust me. Do you trust me, Rain?'

She remembered how he had intervened on her behalf with the bandit even before they had met. He might have left her but he had apologized for that and now he had come for her, even if his manner had left much to be desired. She still didn't want to leave here, but his motives for wanting her out were selfless.

'Yes, I trust you,' she said finally.

'Then take my hand.' He held out his palm.

'You've put those leather things away?'

Tucking the jesses in his pocket, he held up his other hand to show her it was empty. 'See, all gone.'

She touched his fingers tentatively, but his grip firmed immediately, not giving her a chance to retreat again.

'Out you come.' He pulled her from the narrow gap until she stood in front of him, her grey gown floured with stone dust. She had a white smudge on her cheek. Cupping her face in his hands, he brushed at it with the pad of his thumb. 'You look like a ghost.'

'Do not!' She rubbed her face with the corner of her sleeve.

'You do.' He kept running his thumb over her skin, marvelling at how smooth it felt, like the softest feathers of a barn owl—a thought he'd best keep to himself as she might not appreciate the comparison. 'Has anyone told you that you have quite a temper?'

She arched a brow. 'My recollection is that it was you who started the argument, so who's the one with the temper?'

He smiled, his thumb coming to rest by the corner of her mouth. 'My family and friends will tell you that I am known for my calmness.'

'Perhaps they just don't know you very well.'

'Perhaps.' Unable to resist, he dipped his head down and stole a kiss, taking them both by surprise. 'Now where did that come from?' he murmured.

151

Rain blushed and pulled away, her fingers touching her lips. 'Why did you do that?'

'Good question. Shall I try it again and see if I can find out?'

'No.' She started heading for the cabin at a fast pace. 'I don't . . . no, thank you.'

Peri followed more slowly, savouring the odd sweetness of the moment. She'd just politely refused another kiss when he had anticipated that she would slap him for his boldness. His little foreigner was a bundle of contradictions, never quite doing what he expected, which made her all the more intriguing.

Shard 9
Plum Purple

Mikel refrained from chuckling as Rain slid back into the cabin. She wasn't meeting his eyes. Fortunately they were alone as the two scavengers were outside loading the horses so she didn't have an audience for her embarrassment.

'Persuaded you, has he?' the old bondsman asked slyly.

'Do you want to go?' Rain pretended to be absorbed in brushing off her dusty skirt.

He shuffled over and put an arm round her. 'I think it best. Those beasts outside—and I'm talking the human variety—will gobble you up if they find you out unprotected and I might not always be here to defend you. I hate to admit it, but I'm not as fit as I once was.'

'So we're just going to give up on this?' She gestured to the summer palace. 'Retreat to the scavengers' barracks?'

'Sounds good to me. We're lucky Peri cares enough to come fetch us.'

She rested her head against his shoulder for a moment. 'How long will the chaos last? Shouldn't something be done? You say we're all right, but there must be other bondsmen, other girls on their own, who aren't so lucky. And what about the children?'

'I know, Rain, but we can't save everyone.'

She eased away and tucked her straggling hair back under her scarf. 'Where I come from, the people would go to the King, demand he take action. What about your Master? What's he doing about all this?'

Mikel spat in the hearth. 'No idea. Never seen him, as I told you.'

Her eyes sparked with a new idea. 'Perhaps he doesn't know what's going on!'

'He only has to look out his palace window to see the place in turmoil.'

'But maybe he's got bad advisers. They might be keeping it all from him. Perhaps there are guards and other soldiers around him that can be used to restore order. He should start by providing safe havens for the most vulnerable—the children and those on their own.'

The old bondsman smiled sadly and shook his head. 'Is that what would happen in your country?'

'Yes—but I doubt King Ramil would allow it to get so bad to start with.'

'I like the sound of it. Perhaps we should go there, lovey.'

'I'd like to but you know we can't. Heaven knows what the road back to the port is like these days.' She clenched her fists, nails grinding in her palm. 'Oh no! My father! He won't understand. He might try and get here—be killed like my cousin!'

'Shh!' Mikel said soothingly. 'Don't claim problems before you know they are yours. Is your father a sensible man?' She nodded stiffly. 'Then he wouldn't just set off without finding out about the route and taking precautions, would he?'

'Yes, you're right.' She made an effort to relax her hands, but she wasn't finished yet. She knew her idea had merit; the roads had to be made safe at the very least. 'How far are we from the Master's palace, Mikel?'

'Oh no, you don't.' The old bondsman pulled his ragged robe from a nail and slung it on. 'We're going to safety—not into the centre of this wasp's nest.'

'It's the people's responsibility to let their rulers know when something's wrong.'

'We're not in Holt now, Rain.' He jerked her shawl off the back of a chair and wrapped it round her before giving her a shove towards the door. 'It's not a little local difficulty we're facing: the whole stinking country's gone down the gutter.'

'All the more reason to make sure the Master knows. We can go on our way to the scavengers' barracks.' It sounded a reasonable plan to her; she couldn't understand why he didn't see it. 'We can turn back if we meet any trouble.'

'There's trouble all right and I'm with her.' Mikel banged the door behind him but thought twice before leaving the latch up. 'No point locking it; someone will only break it down.'

The three scavengers and their animals were waiting in the archway by the gates already mounted. Rogue was stowed in his travelling basket; the dog back on a tight leash.

Peri held out a hand to Rain. 'You can ride with me. Sly said he'd take Mikel.'

'Drew the short straw you mean,' Sly muttered. 'Come on, old man, get yourself up behind me.'

'Pity the poor lad,' Mikel said in an overly loud voice. 'He's got it bad for her and doesn't even know it.'

Both Peri and Rain went red, remembering their shared kiss a moment ago. Rain passed him her bag rather than touch his hand to mount.

Sly laughed and took Mikel's bundle from him. 'Tell me if you want anything else, old man. I doubt we'll be coming back.'

'Amazing,' said Conal, joining in the teasing as he put the remaining food stocks into his saddle bags. 'Peri has the gentlest touch with wild creatures, has them eating out of his hand in no time; and he just went after Rain like an ox on the rampage. I've never seen him so riled.'

'I'm glad I amused you all,' said Peri curtly. 'Now let's get going.'

Rain didn't move immediately, her fingers fumbling as she retied the knot in the scarf that covered her hair. 'There's something I want to do before we leave the city.'

'Here we go.' Mikel rolled his eyes, wondering how long it would take for the little lady to get her way. Maybe she did have fey blood after all?

'As long as it won't take too much time,' said Peri, glancing at the sun. It was nearly noon and the streets would deteriorate as the day progressed.

'I'm not sure how long we need because we're going to pay a call on the Master to ask him to help his people.'

There was silence, then all three scavengers burst into laughter, making Rogue screech.

'You think we'd get within a mile of the Master? Us? Scavengers?' Sly wiped tears from his eyes.

'His Holiness doesn't receive the likes of us,' Conal explained more kindly.

'Well, things have changed. And besides, I'm not one of you. He can't be insulted by my presence as I'm not from one of your classes.'

The embers of his previous temper still hot, Peri's anger flared up once more. Rain was putting her head in the tiger's jaws again with no thought for her own survival. 'You know, I think you should be locked up for your own safety.'

'Perhaps, but only after I've visited this Master of yours. If you won't take me, I'll go on my own and meet up with you later.' She started walking towards the gates.

Without needing Peri's prompt, Conal manoeuvred his horse to block the way, Sniff yipping excitedly at his side.

'Oh, for goodness' sake, stop treating me like a sheep. I've got a brain. I've decided someone needs to do something about the chaos outside and it might as well be me.' She quieted Sniff's barks with a rub on the top of his head. 'If you Magharnans get your way, you'll keep retreating and retreating until the only safe place is your barracks and everyone else can go hang!'

'We've already reached that point, Mistress Rain,' said Conal, refusing to budge.

'All the more reason to take action. Where's your sense of duty to your fellow Magharnans?'

'Our fellow Magharnans, as you call them, think we are unclean and spit if our shadow so much as touches them,' Peri said, stamping down on his seething emotions as he watched her pace off on another reckless tangent from the path he had in mind for her.

'Mikel doesn't. Well, he does spit, but not because of you, it's just that his manners need a little attention.'

'Watch it, lovey,' growled Mikel.

'But it's true—oh, never mind. Look, I'm off to the Master; you can come or not as you wish. And if you try and stop me,' here she gave Peri a hard stare, accurately guessing what he was thinking, 'then I'll wait until I'm free and go anyway. At least if we do it today, we'll get it over with. It might be that your Master's gone—fled the city—but we'll know we tried.'

'I can't believe her—can you?' Peri appealed to his friends.

Sly scratched his chin. 'She does have a point. It wasn't nice seeing those people reduced to searching the rubbish for food.'

'The bodies lying in the street,' added Conal.

Rain nodded and turned to look expectantly at Peri.

'Oh, get on, you infuriating fey menace.' He heaved her roughly up in front of him. 'I've got a bad feeling about this.'

Rain settled herself sideways across his lap, arranging her skirts demurely. 'Well, I haven't.'

'It's your civic duty, falcon man,' Mikel chipped in helpfully.

'It's a civic pain in the behind.' Peri urged his horse forward and out of the gates.

The jettan district was worse than the poorer areas of the city. All the mansions had been ransacked, the destruction spilling out into the elegant squares like entrails from a gutted carcass. There was no sign of anyone, though Peri suspected that there were quite a few eyes watching them from the ruins.

'Where's everyone gone?' Rain asked, her voice quavering. She had little imagined conditions had got so bad so quickly.

'I expect the jettan families have retreated to their country estates where they can defend themselves,' said Peri. 'Seen enough? Want to go back now?'

Rain shook her head. 'We might as well finish this.'

He sighed and clicked his tongue to make Nutmeg

go a little faster. 'You know my mother and father might not forgive you for making me do this. I'm not sure I forgive you.'

She squirmed in his arms, preparing to get down. 'Then go your way, falcon man, and I'll go mine.'

He tightened his grip. 'No you don't: we made a bargain. I'll take you to the Master's palace and when you've seen how futile that is, you'll come home with me with no more complaints.'

'I don't remember promising not to complain.'

He gave a huff of laughter into her hair. 'You're worse than Rogue.'

'Your falcon?'

'He's a contrary beast.'

'But you like him.'

'Yes, I like him.'

As they approached the Master's palace, Rain's hopes plummeted. Built on the high cliffs overlooking the River Rol, the building was separated from the rest of the city by an intricate wrought-iron fence. It was shaped like a barrier of trees as if an enchanter's spell had thrown it up to keep mere mortals away from the one who dwelt inside. Until a few days ago, silver stars had been embedded in iron branches, beautiful leaves that were never shed, but these had been gouged out, leaving gaps like eyeless sockets behind. The gardens beyond were trampled and scattered with litter. Someone had lit a bonfire in the orchard, using the wood from living trees in pointless waste. The upper reaches of the palace were miraculously unmarked, still floating with cobweb delicacy above their heads, walls pierced with eyelets, decorated with carvings; but the lower floors where the vandals had been able to reach were tarnished with mud and smoke. The tracery in the windows had been kicked in; everything that could not be taken had been defaced.

'To come here carried the death penalty,' Peri murmured, equally depressed by the destruction around him. He urged his horse through the open gates.

'I suppose this shoots down my theory that the Master doesn't know. He must have fled.' Rain's resolve was failing; there seemed little she could do here.

Peri brushed a hand over her back in comfort. 'I'm not so sure. We were always taught that the Master *is* Rolvint. If any of that was true, the soul can't leave the body.'

'Maybe he has; maybe that's why it all seems so dead outside, so hopeless.'

Sniff was the only member of their party who seemed unaffected by the sights around them. He was on the trail of many exciting scents, nosing in the debris. Conal summoned him back with a whistle.

'What now, Mistress Rain?' the dog handler asked. They'd reached a semicircular forecourt screened from the garden by a wooden lattice. The flowering vines that had once covered it lay beaten into the earth.

'I . . . I'm not sure.' She looked at Peri. 'Is there any point going inside?'

Peri's curiosity had got the better of him. He didn't feel under immediate threat and knew this chance would never come again. 'We won't know unless we try. I seem to remember someone saying that to me earlier.'

Rain gave him a half smile. 'That person didn't know what she was talking about.'

'I think all of us are making things up as we go along in this situation, sweetheart.'

A tender feeling uncurled inside Rain when she realized what he had said. She wasn't sure Peri had even noticed his casual endearment because he immediately slipped down off Nutmeg, looking around the courtyard to gauge if it was safe for her to dismount.

'Let's leave the horses here.' Peri held out a hand to help her down. 'They're out of sight of the gate so should be safe enough.'

'All the same, I think I should stay behind on guard,' volunteered Sly. 'We don't want to get stuck in the palace with no means of escape.'

Peri nodded. 'We'd appreciate it.'

Mikel dropped to the ground with an oath. 'Look at it!' He swept his hand at the palace. 'Rotten at the core. All show and no substance. No wonder we went down so hard and fast.'

Rain could see what he meant. The buildings looked beautiful from a distance but closer to they reminded her of white-lace fungi that grew on oak trees back in Holt, a frill of deceptive beauty that needed a decaying host to flourish.

'Now we don't know what's going to happen once we go inside,' stressed Peri. 'I want Mikel and Rain to stay behind me; Conal, can you guard our flank?'

'Of course. Sniff should give us warning if there's anyone left.'

Peri noticed that Mikel looked affronted by the suggestion that he needed protection. 'I'm counting on you to defend Rain if it comes to a fight,' he said, holding the old man's eyes for a moment.

It was Rain's turn to be offended. 'I can look after myself, thank you. Just give me a weapon.'

'You are not fighting,' said Peri in a tone that brooked no argument.

Rain clearly hadn't much time for tones. 'I have hands like everyone else. I'll do my share.'

'You will do as you are told or I'll leave you here with Sly!'

Mikel resisted laughing at the irate falconer. 'Rain, I'll feel better if you stick close. My legs are not so good these days; I might need to take your arm.' He swayed, hoping he looked feeble enough to convince her.

Rain turned to him in consternation. 'Oh, of course. Here.' She took his elbow, fearing he was about to keel over.

Mikel winked at Peri. 'Right then, young master, let's get on with it.'

Like the gates, the doors to the palace were off their hinges, lying like drunkards in a gutter. The air in the palace smelt foul: the sweet smell of sandalwood lingered, but now there was a new scent of dried blood and smoke. Peri took Rogue out of his travelling basket and went ahead, holding the hooded falcon aloft on his arm like a torch to guide their way. He felt comforted having the bird's talons at his disposal; the very sight of him should put off most attackers.

'It must've been beautiful,' Rain said, her voice soft as a sigh as she gazed up at the soaring entrance hall. White plaster tentacles snaked from the ceiling. A few had been shattered but most remained, moulded into swirling shapes like branching roots, interlaced in intricate knots.

'They say the hall above has pillars like trees,' explained Peri. 'The palace was built as a forest of wonders, everything decorated to give the illusion that you had wandered into another world. This was supposed to be an underground cavern, entrance to the marvels beyond.'

'How wonderful! I could have made some lovely windows for this place.' Rain ran her fingers over the stonework.

Peri gave her a strange look. 'I thought it was your betrothed who was the glassmaker.'

Rain realized that there was no reason to keep the secret any longer. 'No, it was me.'

'You must come from an unusual country.'

She laughed a little sadly. 'It's just me who's unusual. And my father, for letting me practise my craft.'

They wandered deeper into the palace, moving through rooms that resembled forest clearings, others like hollow trees.

'Why make stone appear like wood?' Rain mused aloud. 'Why not use wood for the building?'

'Ah, but where's the honour in that?' said Peri cynically. 'The point was to do the impossible. In my view, the Master could've just planted a forest and be done with it. Would've saved our taxes.'

Rain shook her head. 'You've no artistic soul, falcon man.'

'Now you understand me.' Peri's smile faded. He stopped in front of her, holding up a hand for quiet.

They stood silently, listening for the sound that had caught Peri's attention. Conal knelt and slipped the leash from Sniff.

'Go get, boy!' he urged the hunting dog.

The hound darted off into the shadows on their right, yipping excitedly, Conal in pursuit.

'Stay here!' warned Peri, rushing after the hunters.

Mikel and Rain exchanged a look, then followed, both determined not to be left behind. The dog led them down a corridor then up a flight of stairs winding round a marble beech trunk until they emerged on a platform built like an ornate tree house. The once shuttered windows had been torn open, giving sweeping views across the River Rol to the line of hills beyond. The floor was strewn with rubbish, the furniture smashed, but in one corner someone had gathered together scraps to build a nest of cloth. Sniff rooted in it for a moment before veering off and barking at a cupboard door, remarkable for the fact that it was still on its hinges. Slipping the leash back on the dog, Conal waited for Peri to join him. The falconer drew his sword and nodded to Conal to throw open the door.

With a yell, a boy burst from his hiding place, a dagger in hand. He took a wild swipe at Peri who was too surprised to react in time. The blade sliced his arm before he had the sense to use the pommel of his sword to knock the boy back. The lad fell on his bottom, the dagger flying off out of reach. Peri quickly swung his blade to rest above the boy's chest.

'Easy there,' he said calmly, ignoring the blood dripping from his wrist to the floor. 'We mean you no harm.'

The boy looked right through him, his lips locked together. He only flinched when Rogue spread his wings and screeched.

'If you promise not to try anything rash, I'll put the sword down and calm my bird. Do we have a deal?'

Still the boy said nothing. Peri looked more closely at him: like all Magharnans, he had long black hair, his eyes the golden brown of brandy in the firelight, and he wore the remnants of fine clothing—very fine clothing. Peri had never seen silk trousers in such a rich shade of plum purple or a gold embroidered tunic decorated with sunbursts. A jettan boy separated from his family, he guessed.

'You've got to move back,' Rain urged Peri, arriving at his side. 'The bird's scaring him.'

'I thought I told you not to follow us.'

'You really want to argue about this now?'

He shook his head and lowered the sword so that the point rested on the ground. 'See, there's nothing to worry about. I'm going to step away and put my bird on a ledge so we can talk without him spooking you. Understand?'

The boy gave no sign he'd even heard.

Rain sighed. 'He's too scared, poor thing. It doesn't help that you're bleeding all over the floor; I'll find something for a bandage.' She went over to the nest of rags to find the cleanest piece of cloth there. The boy's eyes followed her.

Peri retreated cautiously. He wasn't even sure the boy was afraid as Rain thought; if anything, he judged him to be more like a forest creature that had been cornered, liable to attack if he felt he had no other option. He braced himself for another wild swipe at his back.

'See, I'm putting the bird down,' Peri said soothingly, choosing a lamp niche for a temporary perch. 'You've no need to fear: he's hooded so he won't attack you.'

As soon as he nudged Rogue to jump off his gauntlet, the boy exploded into action. He dived away from Conal and the leashed hound, away from Peri and the bird, and sprinted across the room. He tackled Rain, forcing her face down on to the nest of rags. Kneeling on her back, he groped under the cloth and drew out a broken chair leg.

'Leave or I'll kill her,' he shouted, his face twisted in a feral rage. Rain tried to buck him off but he pushed the chair leg into her neck. 'Be still, servant, or I'll hit you.'

'Are you mad?' A red rage tinged Peri's vision; he could see that the boy was hurting Rain. 'She was trying to help you! Get off her!'

'Off, boy, or I'll crown you!' Mikel seized his own bit of wood and swung it threateningly.

'Leave my palace, scavengers! You render me unclean!' The boy yanked at Rain's hair, making her yelp.

That was more than enough for Peri. He leapt for the boy, grabbed the chair leg and ripped it away from him. His momentum knocked the lad off Rain so that he landed with Peri on top of him. The boy gave a squawk as all the air was pushed from his lungs, then thrashed frantically to get free.

'Unclean! Vile! Filth!' he shrieked, pounding his feet uselessly on the floor.

Peri rolled off him and picked him up by the scruff of the neck. 'Shut up! Rain, are you all right?'

She got up shakily, her eyes wide with shock at the unprovoked attack. 'Y-yes.'

'What's the matter with you?' Peri shook the boy. 'Why turn on the very person trying to help you?'

The boy had returned to his silent act.

'He must be a fool to take us all on,' marvelled Conal.

'No, he's just desperate,' said Mikel, lowering his makeshift wooden club.

'He said it was his palace; did you hear him?' Rain

hugged herself as she looked round the ruins of a once fine room.

'Aye, I heard him,' growled Mikel.

Rain frowned, trying to guess the puzzle. 'Who is he?'

'I am the Master,' spat the boy. 'All of you will be executed for daring to speak to me!'

Conal laughed. 'The boy's gone daft.'

Rain kept her eyes on the youngster, noting how he only looked at her, as if all the others were beneath his attention. She'd seen this behaviour in the jettan she had met. 'I don't think so. He believes it.' She took a step closer. 'Are you really the Master?'

He closed his eyes for a moment, blinking back tears, then nodded.

'Where are your servants?' she asked kindly.

More kindly than he deserved, thought Peri, tightening his grip on the boy, still angry with him for being rough with her.

'They all left me,' the boy replied.

'Guards?'

He shrugged, pretending a nonchalance that he couldn't quite carry off.

'So you've been left here on your own for how long?'

'Four days.'

'How did you escape the looters?'

He dipped his eyes to the floor before he could stop himself.

'You've a hiding place?'

'I'm not showing you: it's a secret.'

'Of course. And I don't want to know. I'm just trying to understand what's going on here. You see, I'm not Magharnan.'

'You're not?' His expression flickered with interest before he could conceal it. 'I thought you looked funny.'

She pulled off her scarf, letting him see her mane of curls more clearly. 'I'm from Holt. I came with a glassmaker to work on the summer palace.'

'An outlander?' The boy twisted out of Peri's grip and stood up straight, struggling to regain his dignity. 'I . . . I see. Why did you come to find me?'

'Well, I thought . . . in my country, we take our troubles to our King. I thought you might be able to help your people.'

'I . . . ' The boy looked about him as if hoping his courtiers had miraculously reappeared. 'I would like to but . . . '

'But you need help yourself,' finished Rain. 'You've been let down by those who were supposed to serve you.'

The boy's shoulders sagged a fraction. 'Yes.'

'Are you really the Master?' Mikel asked, putting his weight on the wooden stave.

The boy kept his eyes on Rain and refused to answer.

She took a step closer, ignoring Peri's warning to keep her distance. She held out her hand. She was about the boy's height, their eyes on a level.

'I know you've been told you shouldn't speak to people of other classes—'

The boy frowned. 'I shouldn't be speaking to you either, but I do occasionally say things to my servants so I thought they wouldn't be angry.'

'Who wouldn't be angry?'

'My advisers. Jettan Kirn and the others.'

'Where are your advisers?' She reached for his forearm and slipped her hand down past his wrist to curl her fingers in his.

'I don't know. They've gone.'

'So aren't you angry with them?'

'Yes.'

'Then how better to pay them back than ignore their silly rules?'

'I don't know.' He looked lost, startled by her suggestion.

'Yes, you do know. These men are the only people who've bothered to come and find you. Surely you can speak to them? You're the Master: isn't it up to you to decide?'

The boy took a deep breath like a diver preparing to jump from a cliff. He turned to Mikel. 'Yes, bondsman, I really am the Master. My father died last year and I was appointed his successor.'

'They kept that quiet,' grumbled Mikel. He looked faintly stunned to be talking to the boy he had been taught was nothing less than a god.

'They always do. We're all one, according to the priests, one Master with different faces.'

'But you're just a boy!' Conal spluttered. 'I thought . . . I don't know what I thought, but it wasn't this!'

Peri found he was less shocked than he expected. His disillusionment with the rigid class system and the rapidity of the collapse of the state had prepared him for the revelation that the Master was only human after all—and a vulnerable one at that. How could they blame a boy for what was so clearly well out of his control before he was even born?

A bell rang down in the distant courtyard—a harsh sound, like someone beating on an old pan lid.

'Do you hear that?' the boy asked Rain, gripping her hand as he turned to her for reassurance.

'I do. What's happening, Peri?'

The falconer retrieved Rogue from his perch. 'I guess that's Sly warning us that we can expect company. We'd better leave.'

'What do we do about him?' asked Conal, jerking his head at the Master.

'Take him with us, of course,' answered Rain before anyone else could reply. 'You can't stay here, Master; surely you can see that?'

The boy glanced at the hostile faces of his lowliest subjects, then back at Rain, her eyes alive with concern for him. 'You think it best?'

'Definitely.' She squeezed his hand reassuringly.

'They have food?'

'We have food,' promised Peri.

'Then yes.' Mind made up, the boy rustled through the rags and pulled out a bundle. 'I'll come.'

Shard 10
Silver Grey

The disturbance that prompted Sly to clash together the cooking pot lids proved to be a large group of looters approaching from the gates. They were carrying weapons and towing empty handcarts in anticipation of making off with anything they could find.

Assessing that they only had a minute to spare before the invaders reached the courtyard, Peri quickly lifted the boy on to Conal's horse.

'Who's this?' asked Sly.

'The Master,' Peri replied.

'You're joking, right?'

'No, I'm deadly serious. Hurry.' Peri realized that the main approach was impossible with so many after easy pickings. Horses were too valuable to let pass. 'Is there another way out?' he asked the boy.

The Master nodded and tugged a chain out from around his neck. On the end hung a gold pentagonal disc.

'This is the key to a gate on the river side of the

palace. It goes down to my private landing stage. There's a barge there.' His face took on a stubborn cast. 'That's if the jettan families left it when they fled.'

'It's better than trying to ride three valuable horses through that lot,' said Conal, jerking his head at the approaching crowd. 'If there's no barge, we can always wait down there until they've gone.'

There was no time for further debate. The double-mounted horses trotted swiftly away from the looters, following a path that wound through the gardens. Once they emerged from the cover of the trellis fence, they heard a shout behind. The looters had seen them. Peri urged Nutmeg to pick up his pace. Anxiety spiking, Rain clung on to his waist like a limpet.

'Don't worry, sweetheart: I won't let them catch us,' Peri said confidently.

She wished she felt so certain; instead she pressed her head to his back and closed her eyes, accepting that she had no control over what would happen next. With the boy's directions they reached the gate without losing their way in the gardens. Peri handed the reins to Rain and slipped off. When he reached the ground, the boy tossed him the key. The gate was a smaller version of the ones leading from the city, the pentagon crafted to fill a leaf-shaped keyhole near the handle. He pressed it into place, finding it fitted snugly in the mechanism, and opened the gate with hardly a sound. Wasting no time, Conal and Sly urged their horses through the portal. Peri took Nutmeg's bridle and guided him safely over the narrow threshold so he could lock the gate behind them. When he mounted, the other two horses were already out of sight— welcome news as their pursuers had not given up. He could see people running through the trees headed in their direction, and the fence, though tall, would not stop a really determined man from scaling it. Peri remounted and dug his heels in. Nutmeg clattered down the steep gravel path, hooves struggling to find purchase on the sliding surface. Peri dared not make him go any faster for fear of taking a spill. Rain's grip was painfully tight around his waist but he said nothing, understanding she was terrified and unaware that she was hurting him.

The path wound to and fro down the river cliff until it levelled out on a wooden landing stage floating in the river. The platform was huge, built for state ceremonies and capable of harbouring many vessels. All the moorings were empty, bar one. A gold painted barge remained tethered in the central berth, the celebratory flags hanging limply from the striped awning that protected the throne in its centre.

Peri tapped Rain's hand. 'You can let go,' he murmured, relaxing a little now the immediate danger had passed.

'Oh, sorry.'

'You've probably given me bruises. I didn't realize how strong you are.'

She rubbed the heel of her palm over his stomach in a quick gesture of apology before slipping off Nutmeg.

'Oh, don't stop: I was enjoying that.'

'Don't push your luck, falcon man: I'm not that sorry,' she said tartly.

Biting back her own smile, Rain joined the boy as he stood gazing at his barge. 'How do you sail it?' she asked.

'I can't imagine why they left it. They've taken everything else.' The boy shook his head in disbelief.

'They probably left the blooming thing because they couldn't move it.' Mikel kicked at the rope tying it to the bank. 'I can't see no oars.'

'It doesn't have oars. My bondsmen use long poles to push it along.' The boy searched the dock as if expecting them to materialize out of thin air.

'Can't see no poles neither,' grumbled Mikel. 'We're stuck. Blinking stupid idea to come down here in the first place.'

Sly, who had been watching the path up to the garden gate, gave a shout:

'Peri, we've got company!' He drew his sword. 'They've climbed the fence.'

Peri quickly calculated their chances. They were cornered unless they could escape by river. Perhaps they could fight off the looters but he didn't want to risk Rain, Mikel, and the boy getting hurt.

'Put the horses on the barge,' he ordered Conal as he ran to take up a defensive position with Sly where the path opened on to the landing stage. 'We'll let the river take us out of here. Mikel, see if you can find something we can use to steer that thing.'

Shifting the wide gangplank lying on the deck into place, Rain helped Conal guide the nervous horses on to the barge. Fortunately, it was built for transporting large groups of courtiers so had plenty of room on the wide flat stage in front of the throne. The boy stood watching, not making a move to help.

Rain was left holding Nutmeg and Sly's mount as Conal went back for the last.

'Master, I could really do with your help here,' she called.

The boy stirred, surprised by the request. 'You need me to work?'

Mikel gave him a shove in the small of his back as he passed by. 'She needs you to help save your own blinking skin, young 'un.'

The boy was too amazed by the manner in which they were speaking to him to do anything but obey. He took one set of reins from Rain and stroked Nutmeg's nose soothingly.

'I've never touched a horse like this before,' he admitted.

'I bet you've never been allowed to do many things,' said Rain. 'Horses are wonderful, aren't they?'

'Yes, they are.'

The barge rocked as the final horse stepped on board. Rain twisted round anxiously as sounds of a scuffle broke out behind her. Sly and Peri were fighting now, driving back the first of the looters.

'Get that barge moving!' yelled Peri.

Mikel untied the ropes and shoved off from the

landing stage using a plank he had ripped up to propel them out into the current. Conal pushed off at the front.

'We can't leave them!' protested Rain.

'We're not. They'll catch up.' Mikel slotted the plank awkwardly into a V-shaped steering column at the stern of the vessel, letting it trail in the water as an improvised rudder.

When Peri and Sly judged the barge had gained enough distance from the bank, they abandoned their station and sprinted down the landing stage. Rain watched in horror as the gap widened between barge and land. They wouldn't reach them in time—and they already had looters on their tail.

She gripped Mikel's arm. 'Go back! They won't make it!'

'I can't. The river's got us now. Let's just hope the lads can swim.'

Together, Peri and Sly reached the verge of the landing stage and leapt. They landed on the deck but nearly tumbled back into the water as the barge rocked dangerously. Peri grabbed hold of Mikel as Sly grasped Conal's shirt, all just missing a bath in the Rol. Behind them, men poured on to the bank, yelling insults and hurling anything they could lay their hands on. Rain dragged the boy down behind the throne, covering his head with her arms as missiles pinged around them like a hail storm.

'You would think the horses were theirs,' muttered Conal, shielding Sniff from a stone cast in their direction.

'So they're not after me?' asked the boy in a voice that couldn't quite hide his fear.

''Fraid not, your holiness,' said Mikel. 'Boys are two a penny, horses mean gold.' He swore colourfully as a piece of wood spun through the air and slapped his arm.

'Oh.' The Master slumped against the side of the barge and smiled at Rain—the first she'd seen on his face. 'That's . . . that's a relief.'

The looters gave up throwing things once the barge had drifted into mid stream. The Rol flowed faster than it appeared on the surface, a great sheet of silver-grey satin winding round the low cliffs, once-beautiful mansions on their crest like a diamond tiara. The other side of the river was taken up with farmland which looked peaceful compared to the chaos that ruled the city. Rain could even see a farmer scattering seed in his field, his back to the problems across the Rol. Protected today by half a mile of river, Rain wondered how long it would be before the trouble found its way across to blight the farmer's land too.

Rain turned her attention back to the most recent problem they had harvested from the palace. 'Do you have a name?' she asked the boy as they sat side by side at the foot of the throne.

'I'm the Master,' he replied automatically.

'We realize that. But before you became him, what did you call yourself?'

'They called me Master-in-waiting.'

Rain wasn't ready to give up yet. 'Surely your mother didn't name you that?'

The boy's tawny eyes shifted to a puzzled expression. 'My mother? I never saw her. The jettans and priests were responsible for my upbringing.'

In Rain's opinion, they'd done a terrible job: giving him no life beyond the role prescribed for him then dumping him at the first sign of trouble.

'It might be easier if you have a name of your own,' she suggested gently. 'People might find it odd to come face to face with someone they think is a god only to find he's a boy.'

'But I am of the heavens,' the boy said with absolute certainty.

Peri had been listening in on the conversation. It beggared belief: the one he had always thought of as all powerful was in many ways the most vulnerable person he had ever met. 'Rain's right, your holiness. My family will find it easier to accept you if you disguise yourself to come among us ordinary people.'

The boy didn't look convinced.

'Remember the story of the Master and the blacksmith's bride?' Peri continued, recalling an old Magharnan folk tale of how the Master had attended the wedding of a worthy citizen incognito, turning the anvil gold with his royal touch.

'Of course. I know all the tales about me.'

'Then imagine this is like one of them. You'll need a name for us to use.'

The boy crinkled his nose. 'What's your name?'

Peri told him before going on to introduce the rest of the party. 'But you can't have our names. It's got to be one of your own.'

'Retsam,' suggested Rain. She shrugged at their bemused looks. 'It's master backwards. Just a thought.'

The boy tested it out. 'I like it. Retsam.'

'Blooming daft name if you ask me,' interjected Mikel, adjusting the course of the drifting vessel.

'I didn't ask you, bondsman.' The boy raised his brows when Rain started to giggle. 'What did I say?'

'I think you just made Mikel's day,' she explained. 'He always knew no one wanted his opinion and it's just been confirmed by the Master.'

'By Retsam,' the boy corrected her. 'But perhaps you could call me Ret?' He looked up at her through his lashes. 'That's what my friends call me.'

'Ret,' she repeated, her smile dazzling.

Peri shook his head at this byplay. If the Master wasn't careful, he was in danger of developing a serious crush on the little glassmaker. Peri couldn't blame him. Rain's compassion for everyone glowed like light passing through a lamp mantle. She made them all behave like better people just by sharing that brightness with them.

'So, Peri, now you've got us on board this chunk of wood, what do we do now?' asked Mikel, breaking into Peri's reverie.

'Land it as close to the barracks as we can. There's a dock not far from the gates; the fishermen use it to bring their catch ashore. At any rate, we want to end up on the same side of the river as the city if we can.'

Mikel nodded. 'I'll do my best, but the river's in charge of this little voyage.'

Rain got to her feet and picked up a coil of rope, paying it out to judge its length. 'Anyone swim?'

The scavengers shook their heads. Peri admitted to being able to manage a few strokes but no major skill.

'What about you, Ret?'

'Me?'

She smiled encouragingly at him. 'You'll have to get used to people expecting you to take part in things.'

'But I . . . no, I don't swim.'

'It'll have to be me then. I'm pretty good—my father made sure of that and the sea is a lot warmer where I come from so swimming's a pleasure. I used to go to the lagoon near my city most holidays in the summer. When we get near, I'll go ashore and get some help to pull us in.'

'You'll do no such thing,' said Peri, right on cue.

'I knew he'd say that. Someone sit on him, please. I can manage this, Peri. Let me do it.' She wriggled out of her tunic, leaving on her cotton shift, and then looped the rope over one shoulder and across her chest. 'If I get into difficulties, you just pull me back.'

Sly slapped Peri on the back. 'Let her do it, my friend. If she says she can manage, it's better than floating this crazy vessel all the way out to sea.'

Tight lipped, Peri nodded. 'All right. But give me the other end.'

With a huff, she placed the rope in his hand. 'You really need to work on that calm thing you mentioned. Will here do?'

Mikel shaded his eyes. 'Aye, I'll take us as close as I can. See that little platform there?'

'Yes.'

'I think that's the dock Peri was talking about. There are some people milling about on the shore—a market of sorts—doesn't look too threatening. Do your best, lovey.'

Kicking off her shoes, she gave him a salute and dived neatly over the side. The cold punched the air from her lungs but she surfaced quickly and began swimming strongly for the shore. The current was powerful but she made use of it, angling across rather than fighting it. It was harder work than it had looked from the barge but she eventually found herself entering the slack water around the docking area. Time was of the essence: if she didn't get the rope fastened quickly, she'd be towed after the barge as it sailed on by. Her icy fingers grasped the edge of the wooden staging and she struggled to pull herself up—only to find her wrists seized by the gnarled hands of a fisherman. He lifted her clear of the water and dumped her on the deck.

'As I live and breathe, a fey mermaid!' he laughed.

Relieved he seemed friendly, Rain shook her head, teeth chattering.

'Trying to land that there big fish?' he asked, seeing the rope around her.

She nodded and, before she could make a move, he'd taken it over her head and tied it off.

'Come on, mates, let's give the mermaid a hand.' Three fishermen joined the old fellow and began reeling in the barge.

A portly fishwife wearing stout wooden clogs, her bare legs roped with varicose veins, approached Rain and draped a tattered blanket over her shoulders.

'There now,' she said in her deep mannish voice. 'Can't have you catching your death, can we?'

Rain got to her feet and clutched the blanket around her, shivering with cold. 'Thank you.'

As the barge neared shore, close enough for Sniff to be seen, the fisherman's friendly expression changed to suspicion. 'What's this? Scavengers?'

'Some of them are,' admitted Rain.

The fisherman spat. 'Don't know why I'm lifting a finger to aid them when they're hoarding all the meat! They only think of their own kind, so why should we help?' He almost dropped the rope in disgust but Rain caught his hand in hers.

'Please. They're not like that. They came into the city to rescue me and my friend—he's a bondsman and I'm a servant.'

'You a servant? Nay, I was right first time: eyes like yours, you have to be a mermaid. Still,' he picked up the rope again, 'maybe they did help you.'

Conal threw a second rope once they were close to shore. The fishwife caught it and tied it to a mooring post to bring the barge alongside.

'Thanks!' shouted Peri, jumping on to the quay.

'You're welcome, scavenger,' said the fisherman coldly, watching Peri with ill-concealed hostility as the falconer lifted the gangplank and moved it to bridge the gap for the horses.

Rain refused to be daunted by the unfriendly atmosphere.

'Peri, this man pulled me out of the water. And this lady gave me a blanket.'

Peri looked up from his task, wondering why she was stating the obvious. 'That's very kind of them.'

'See, not everyone in Rolvint is like those looters. Some people are ready to come to the aid of others.' Rain gestured to the fish market on the quayside. 'Not everything has stopped working.'

'No, I can see that too.'

'Don't you think it would be a good idea if people like you and these fishermen got together to try and do something about the situation?'

'Rain!' he said in warning.

'It's obvious really: who else is going to step for-ward?'

He gave a growl of frustration. 'First you wanted to appeal to the Master and look where that got us; now you're saying it's up to us?'

'Well, yes.'

If she hadn't been dripping so charmingly all over the decking, Peri would have been tempted to shake some sense into her.

'Forget it, little mermaid, his sort aren't interested in other people,' announced the fisherman, turning to leave.

'Yes, he is. He just doesn't know it yet,' countered Rain.

Feeling a little ashamed of his impolite behaviour, Peri held out his hand to the man. 'She's wrong: I do know it, but I'm just not sure what to do about it. Shall we start with this?'

The fisherman looked at Peri's hand suspiciously. To touch it would be breaking a thousand taboos.

'Oh come on!' huffed Rain impatiently. 'He won't bite.'

The fisherman gave her a gap-toothed smile. 'He just might, but I'll risk it.' He took Peri's palm in his work-roughened fist. 'The name's Murdle. These here are my crew, Gator and Arlo.' He gestured to the two fishermen hovering at his back. 'And my wife, Marla.' The stout woman gave Peri a brief nod. 'Come find me when you've worked out what you want to do. Me and the other fisherfolk are here most days, or on our boats when things get dicey.'

'I'm Peri Falconer and these are my friends.' He quickly introduced the others as they led the horses off the barge. 'And I expect I'll be back soon.'

'Yes, I expect you will. No one turns down a mermaid.' The fisherman tipped his cap to Rain and returned to his friends by the market stalls.

His wife lingered a moment longer. She surprised Peri by poking him in the chest with her forefinger.

'Now you get this little one into the warmth,' she said threateningly. 'Or you'll answer to me.'

'Yes, ma'am,' said Peri quickly.

She strode off, her clogs clumping on the deck.

'Can we go home now, Rain, or do you have any more adventures planned for us?' Peri asked her, rubbing his rib where the fishwife had prodded him.

'No, that's it for today,' Rain said primly, squeezing out her skirt. 'At least, until I think of something else.'

Shard 11
Citrus Yellow

'I'm sorry, Peri, but I just don't like her.' Katia Falconer pounded the grain in the quern, beating out her bad mood. They had only been back a few hours but Peri's mother had already worked up a temper. Late afternoon light poured into the common room; most families were outside making the most of the warmth but the Falconers had guests for supper and too much to do. 'She's trouble.'

Peri said nothing, searching for an argument to change his mother's mind. She had taken in Mikel and Retsam without a protest but had treated Rain with cold suspicion the moment she saw her standing in the gateway wrapped in a blanket. Katia's motherly instincts had gone on high alert, recognizing a threat to her son, all the more dangerous for being prettily packaged.

'Look what she persuaded you to do today. I still can't believe you went all the way into the Master's palace. You all need your heads examining. What were you thinking! You could have been killed.'

'But we weren't.' Peri took the quern from her and brushed the flour into a mixing bowl. They had almost enough to make bread for the evening meal, but with three extra mouths to feed there wouldn't be much to go round.

Katia added a pinch of salt. 'She's manipulating you. You can't see it because you've fallen under her spell.'

'She's not a fey, Ma. She doesn't do magic.'

Katia waved her whitened fingers dismissively. 'Of course not. She's foreign. I meant she's charmed you into doing things which you know are foolish. That's not my Peri. You were always the calm and careful one—the only child I never had to worry about.'

A squawk of protest burst from the far side of the room as Ret took a ball in the stomach. Helgis stood in the doorway glaring at him.

'Don't you even know how to play catch?' Helgis asked in disgust.

'No, I don't, unclean one.' Ret rubbed his stomach, shocked that someone had dared inflict pain on him.

'Who are you calling unclean?' Helgis's fists were bunched but Ret was too inexperienced to recognize the signs.

'You, of course.' His tone was imperious.

Helgis took a swing, knocking Ret to the floor. He then jumped on top of him, pinning him to the ground. 'Apologize!' he snarled.

Peri crossed the room in ten strides and hoisted his brother off the boy.

'What's got into you?' Peri asked Helgis, giving him a shove away from his victim. 'Ret is new; I told you he's not used to playing with boys his own age.'

Ret got up from the floor, wiping at his nose which was trickling blood. 'I don't want to play with him, Peri.'

'I'm not surprised when he treats you like that. Helgis, what have you to say?'

Helgis scuffed the ball, kicking it out of the door into the sunshine. 'He called me unclean.'

Peri prayed for patience. 'Unfortunately, for Ret, that isn't an insult but a fact.'

'He's rude.'

'Not intentionally; he just doesn't understand, like a hatchling that needs training.'

'Sorry,' muttered Helgis, barely audible.

'No more name calling, agreed? Let's start again, shall we?' Peri brushed off Ret's dusty tunic. 'How's the nose?'

Ret was staring at the blood on the back of his hand in amazement. 'It's bleeding.'

'Welcome to life as an ordinary boy.' Peri held out a hand and shook Ret's solemnly. 'Congratulations.'

A slow smile spread over Ret's face. 'Ordinary: I think I like the sound of that.' Before Peri could intervene, he leapt forward, fist clenched, and swung at Helgis's nose. The punch missed but caught an ear. Helgis didn't waste time howling: he retaliated with a blow to the stomach. The two boys went down, rolling on the floor in an attempt to land a good hit on the other. Peri struggled to separate them, Ret's silken clothes making him as slippery as an eel, Helgis skilled at twisting free. Experienced at handling such scuffles, Katia rushed forward and threw a basin of water over the pair.

'Enough!' she scolded. 'Take it outside.' She grabbed them by the scruff of the neck and hustled them through the door.

Peri wondered if he should stop them, but if he didn't let Ret stand on his own two feet, he would never gain the respect of boys his own age. He trusted his brother not to let it get too far out of hand. Following them to the entry, he was relieved to see they were already running off together, united by a desire to escape a tongue lashing.

'Who is that boy exactly?' Katia asked, her mouth pursed in disapproval.

'I don't think you'd believe me if I told you,' Peri said cautiously. 'The main point is that he was abandoned by his family and we had to take him with us—the looters were all over his home.'

'How could parents abandon a child like that?'

'His father's dead and he never knew his mother. He was looked after by officials.'

'Strange.' Katia wiped her hands on her apron but was distracted from further questions by the arrival of Rain in the common room. After changing into dry clothes, she had been shown around the compound by Peri's oldest sister, Bel, and the two of them were chatting happily, giggling over something. Rosie trailed behind them, an awestruck smile on her face as she gazed in fascination at Rain's curly hair.

'Ma, you'll never believe it!' enthused Bel, rushing across the room to where they were cooking. 'Rain designs stained-glass windows back home—she's done some for the queen's temple, she says, but no one knows about it because the glassmakers are all narrow-minded bigots, don't like women doing such things. But not her father, he lets her do anything she wants.'

Rain blushed. 'Not anything, Bel.'

Katia brushed off the flour marks on the table. 'I see. Not a very useful occupation, is it?'

Startled at the hostility from Peri's mother, Rain glanced at Peri. She recalled that he held similar opinions. 'I suppose it might not seem as useful as hunting,' she conceded.

'Such useless luxuries are what got us in this fix in the first place,' Katia continued. 'The rich people spent money on fripperies while others starved; borrowed to buy whatever was in fashion even if it made no sense.'

'Ma, Rain isn't to blame for what went on here,' Peri said quietly.

Rain wished he'd offered a better defence. He was tacitly agreeing that her talents were worthless. 'I won't apologize for my craft, Mistress Falconer. I do good work and I'm worth my wage. My windows make buildings beautiful and I'm proud of that.'

'You must be upset at the depths to which you've fallen then.' Katia gestured to the unadorned windows which did not even have plain glass, only shutters to close at nightfall. 'You're eating the food provided by people who aren't afraid of getting their hands dirty, who've survived without fancy glass or ornaments.'

'You've never been in a glass foundry if you don't think we get our hands dirty too. I don't regard you or your family as beneath me.' Rain tried to think what she had done to offend the woman; Katia could not be clearer with her message that she resented Rain's presence in her household. It pricked her pride. 'And if you don't want me to share what you have, then I suppose I'll have to go elsewhere.'

'You'll do no such thing.' Peri stepped between his mother and Rain, alarmed that the argument had escalated so quickly.

'Ma, you're being mean!' protested Bel, taking her new friend's arm in hers, preventing Rain from leaving.

'It's all right, Bel; I won't stay where I'm not wanted. I expect the fisherfolk will take me in if I ask.' Rain disengaged her arm.

'You're not leaving,' Peri said firmly. 'Ma, tell her she's welcome here.'

Katia puffed a strand of her hair out of the way that had fallen across her eyes. 'She can stay. But I don't want her causing any more trouble.'

Rain folded her arms defensively, hugging her sides. Rosie tugged at her skirt, wanting to be lifted up but Rain shook her head.

'That's hardly going to make her feel like we want her here.' Peri scooped Rosie from the floor. He was disappointed in his mother; she was normally so fair but today she demonstrated a prejudiced side that he had not suspected her of having. She was doing untold damage to Rain's view of them. 'I invited her here. She's my guest, my responsibility.'

'My guest!' agreed Rosie, stretching her arms out to Rain.

But their visitor was already beating a retreat. 'Thanks for coming to find me, Peri. I'll just go and tell Mikel that I'm off. You're not to feel responsible for me.' Rain slipped past Bel and was out of the door before Peri could stop her.

'Ma!' exclaimed Peri and Bel together. Rosie began to cry.

'I can't believe you said those things to her,' continued Bel. 'She's nice. You've not even tried to get to know her.'

Katia began kneading the dough. 'She's a threat to your brother. I look after mine first.'

Peri gave a frustrated sound. He gave Rosie a hug before passing her over to Bel, then hurried after Rain.

'Wait!' he called, catching her outside the mews.

Rain slowed.

'You mustn't listen to my mother. She's got it into her head that you're a bad influence on me.'

Rain gave a shrug, pretending not to care. She was sick of being made so unwelcome in Magharna. 'Perhaps she's right.'

'No, Rain, she's wrong.' Peri caught her arm and pulled her into the mews where they could be alone. The birds on their perches were quiet, sleeping the afternoon away. The smell was unpleasantly strong to Rain's nose, unused to the odour of droppings and feathers that never quite left the place no matter how clean the falcon handlers kept it.

Peri ran his hand down her hair and drew her close, soothing her as he would one of his charges. Her stance was stiff, braced for rejection.

'Listen, sweetheart, I'm not letting you go anywhere. We had a deal: I took you to the palace and then you came here.'

'I didn't promise to stay.' Her voice sounded muffled against his chest.

'That was understood as part of the agreement.' Rubbing up and down her spine, he coaxed her to relax against him.

'But your mother's made it clear I'm not wanted here.'

'My mother is a muttonhead.'

Rain smiled. 'You shouldn't say things like that.'

'Only when she deserves it.'

Rain did not pull away when he circled her loosely with his arms. Instead, she looped hers around his waist. She didn't understand what it was about Peri: he was either driving her to distraction or making her want to get as close to him as she could. She felt his lips brush across the crown of her head.

'I think I want to kiss you again,' he whispered.

'Is that a good idea?' Rain shivered.

He pulled her snugly against him. 'It's the best idea I've had all day.' He leant over and gently kissed her, lingering to enjoy her taste.

'Aw, yuck!' Helgis emerged from the shadows further down the mews, dragging Ret after him. 'Let's get out of here.'

Ret didn't seem as disgusted as Helgis; he was rather intrigued by all that kissing, but he followed his companion's lead and pretended to gag as he ran by.

'So much for my romantic timing,' Peri said, watching the boys disappear out of sight. He held on to Rain, not ready to release her yet.

'The choice of place leaves something to be desired too.' Rain wrinkled her nose at the smell.

'I'll take you out into the fresh air if you promise there'll be no more talk of you leaving.'

Rain sighed. 'I promise I won't let your mother scare me off.'

It wasn't a perfect agreement, but Peri decided it had to be enough for now. 'Let's go find out how Mikel is settling in with Pa.'

In the days that followed, everyone but Rain found their niche in the scavenger compound. Despite the rocky start, Ret and Helgis forged a friendship united against adults and Rain often spotted them around the mews where Helgis initiated the guest into the mysteries of looking after a sparrowhawk. Mikel had been easily accepted by not just Peri's family but all of those in the compound. He made himself useful doing odd jobs, but spent most of his time sharing his vividly expressed opinions with anyone who would stop to listen. Rain wanted to work too, but every time she offered, Katia would say she wasn't needed and send her away. Bel told her she was lucky; that her mother never passed over a chance to send her on chores; but Rain knew it was not kindness that kept her idle. Katia didn't want her to wheedle her way any further into the family than she had already.

To Rain's disappointment, she did not spend as much time with Peri as she would have liked as he was kept busy with the hunting parties. They went out in large groups for mutual protection so even when he wasn't flying one of his birds he was needed to make up the guard. Conal and Sniff were almost always with him and Sly was busy with his butchery, so that left Rain with large stretches of empty time on her hands. Not feeling welcome at the falconers' end of the common room, she took to staying in the little chamber she shared with Rosie and Bel, laying out the shards of glass she had collected in the summer palace. First she formed them into geometric patterns, then the shapes of trees like those on the Master's palace fence. Her choices were limited by the colours she had available. She'd gathered many shades of brown, dark blue, and a few precious pieces of yellow, but she had no golds, pinks, or light greens. Still, it was exciting to form the pictures she had in her mind, even if she had to break them up every night.

Bel caught her at it one day. 'That's amazing—it's a willow, right?'

Rain nodded. 'There are lots of them down by the river. I saw them when we landed the barge; they're just coming into leaf.'

'Can you make this into something?' Bel looked longingly at her empty window.

'Sorry, but I'd need lead and a proper frame to set the glass. This is just playing.'

'That's a shame. I'd love something really pretty in my bedroom.'

Rain curled her knees up to her chest and leaned back against the wall. 'My papa made me a rainbow.'

Bel sat next to her, mimicking her position. 'How?'

'He blew lots and lots of glass droplets and hung them from the ceiling. When the sun shines in, the light splits in many colours.'

'I'd love to see it.'

Rain closed her eyes, recalling every detail of her room back in Tigral. Homesickness washed over her like a breaker knocking a swimmer off her feet. Though she sometimes wondered what her future might be like if she stayed here with Peri, mostly she dreamt of going home, but that chance seemed as fragile as a glass teardrop. She pictured the droplets dangling, spinning, recalling that they weren't held in a frame but suspended on thread.

'Bel, you've given me an idea!' Rain jumped up.

'Can you get me some fine cotton?' She began gathering the shards carefully together, packing them back in the cloth she used to protect them.

'Yes, of course, but what idea?'

Rain laughed happily. 'It's a surprise—something for you and your family.' She really meant it as a gift for Peri and hoped he would realize it. How else could she hint that her feelings for him had deepened? She wasn't the sort to blurt out a confession, particularly when she was unsure if he wanted anything from her beyond a playful flirtation. 'I need to go to the mews.' She grabbed a stick of charcoal and one of her pieces of paper. 'I won't be long.'

For the next week, Rain worked hard on her project. She had chosen Rogue as her subject because he had helped save her from the bandit leader, Krital. She carefully studied his sleek flint-blue coat and creamy stomach, his ebony eyes set in citrus yellow rims. Borrowing a chopping board from Sly, she laid out the pieces of glass, choosing the shapes that looked most like feathers. Her design suited the small fragments, allowing them to overlap as she netted them to a smooth twig Helgis and Ret had found her. Bel had sworn she wouldn't sneak a look at the mobile until it was finished, though Rain had caught her glancing at the space under the bed where she hid it each night.

'When will it be ready?' asked Bel.

'Not long now. I'm having problems finding enough cream-coloured bits.'

'I could go and drop one of the milk pitchers if you like.'

Rain swatted Bel playfully. 'Don't you dare! Your mother already thinks I'm single-handedly responsible for every foolish thing your older brother does; I don't want her to start blaming me for what you get up to.'

The final touch were the eyes. Using a whetstone, she ground two pieces of yellow glass into circles and stuck tiny black pebbles in their centre with glue begged from the compound's carpenter. She called Bel in when she had finished, keeping the present concealed under a blanket.

'I'm done. Do you want to see it or are you going to wait until I give it to your family tonight?'

Bel knew Rain had been looking forward to unveiling it for everyone, hoping to change their views about the value of her craft. 'I'll be good: I'll wait.'

Rain squeezed her hand. 'Thank you.'

The two girls were giggling like conspirators as they carried the board into the common room. The rest of the family were already there: Katia and Hern were cooking while Peri told Rosie a story. Helgis and Ret sat nearby, pretending not to listen.

'And then,' said Peri in a dramatic whisper, 'the fey lady disappeared in a puff of smoke, leaving the poor falconer all alone with no merlin, no meat, and no horse to carry him home.'

Rosie's eyes were wide. She took her thumb out of her mouth. 'What did he do then?'

Peri's gaze slid to Rain and smiled. 'What could he

do but set off for home a wiser man, walking all the way?'

'What a nasty fey lady,' Rosie decided.

'No, she wasn't nasty: she was fey, obeying her own rules. I expect the horse and the merlin had a splendid life in her kingdom.'

Bel and Rain put the board down on the table, pushing the bowls aside to create a space.

'Get that thing out of the way!' snapped Katia. 'Fey ladies may have their own rules, but here we have one which says that we clear the table for supper.'

'Ma!' protested Bel. 'Rain's got a present for us. She's worked really hard on it all week.'

'And your father and I have worked hard on this meal.'

Rain swallowed her disappointment, touching for comfort the necklace of tears she had rethreaded. This was hardly an auspicious beginning for her presentation.

Mikel came up behind her and put an arm round her shoulders. 'Rain, where have you been for the past few days? I've missed seeing you around the place.'

Peri lifted a corner of the blanket. 'Bel says she's been making something for us.'

'No peeking!' warned Bel, slapping his wrist. 'And, Ma, I'm sure it won't take long. Let her show us before supper.'

Hern stirred the pot. 'We've a few minutes before it'll be ready. What have you got for us, Rain? You know you needn't give us presents. We're pleased to have you with us.'

You may be but your wife isn't, thought Rain. 'It's just something I made with some odds and ends I gathered.' She threw back the blanket, revealing the jumble of glass shards on the board.

Peri tried not to show his disappointment: it looked a mess. 'Um, what is it?'

'Watch.' Rain kept her eyes on him as she picked up the twig, lifting the mobile clear so that the pieces hung free. It was like seeing a spell conjure a peregrine falcon out of thin air; what had been a bundle of rubbish transformed into the beautiful shape of Peri's favourite bird.

'It's Rogue!' he exclaimed in delight.

'Yes.' Rain held it up to the fire so that the light could glitter through the glass, enjoying his reaction. Could he not tell she'd made it from her heart? 'It'll look better in daylight; the colours aren't quite true in here.'

'Fabulous!' said Bel.

Rosie clapped her hands and reached up to touch it.

'Best not: it's delicate,' Rain told her.

Peri lifted his sister up so she could see the glass miracle from a safe distance.

'What do you think, Ret?' Rain asked the Master, knowing that he was used to the best craftsmanship.

'I like it; I've never seen anything like it before. Will you make me one?' He glanced at his new friend. 'And one for Helgis too?'

She laughed. 'If I can find enough pieces of glass. I've run out of most useable bits.'

'Plenty of broken glass in the city, lovey,' said Mikel, glowing with pride at her achievement.

Finally, Rain turned to Katia and Hern, almost afraid to see their reactions.

Hern rubbed his chin. 'Rogue's breast feathers are a bit whiter than that.'

'Pa!' Peri exclaimed.

Rain tried to hide her chagrin. 'Well, I only had a few colours to choose from.'

Hern's face broke into a smile. 'But all the same, it's the cleverest thing I've ever seen. You're sure you're not related to the fey people?'

Rain realized he had been teasing her. 'No, I'm not sure. I'm keeping an open mind on the subject.'

'Thought as much.'

Katia turned back to the pot, releasing a cloud of steam as she took off the lid. 'It's very pretty. Not that we've room for something like that.'

'I'll have it in our bedroom,' Bel said quickly.

'No, ours!' countered Helgis.

'Of course we've space,' Hern interjected, cutting them off before they started arguing. 'Look round the room: everyone's fascinated by it. I can't imagine anyone objecting if we hang it from the beam by the window here.'

Katia shook her head, stirring the stew vigorously.

Hern took the mobile from Rain's fingers and

climbed on the table. 'See, everyone, our guest has made us a present. What do you think?'

There was a swell of appreciative words, with a few suggestions that she should make one for the other trades represented in the common room.

'All right if I hang it down here then?'

'Aye, if you try and take it away, that's when there'll be trouble,' shouted Conal from among the hunters.

A laugh of agreement rippled among the people.

'That's settled then. Peri, get a hook in the beam and we'll put this up now.'

Much to Katia's annoyance, supper was delayed as Hern saw to it that Rain's gift was treated with due honour. But even Katia couldn't help smiling when the next morning she came in to find their end of the room danced with tiny rainbows as the light sparkled through the mobile.

Shard 12
Pale Blue

After this first experiment, Rain was inundated with work. Proud of their foreign glassmaker, the scavengers even ventured into the city to make sure she was kept supplied with the glass shards she needed. Peri set up a table for her in the good light by the common room window so that she did not have to hide away in her bedroom to craft her designs. She became a popular fixture in her corner, attracting callers of all ages to see how her latest project was progressing. People were hungry for beauty in an increasingly ugly world beyond the compound. To find someone still able to make things reminded them that there was much to value in the world and lightened everyone's spirits.

Perfecting her technique with each essay, Rain indulged her imagination and created a shaggy-haired dog for the hunters, a black bull for the butchers, and even a comical horse and cart for the refuse handlers. Each one hung from the ceiling over the heads of the families belonging to that profession, tinkling gently like tiny bells when a draught blew through the chamber. On each one she etched a swallow, so small none noticed what she had done, but to her it was a promise that she would never forget who she was and what she was capable of if given more than fragments to play with.

Peri liked to spend his free hours sitting beside Rain, mending his equipment or cleaning his weapons. They got so used to each other's company that words were not necessary and they would often share a comfortable silence for long periods of time while each was absorbed in their tasks. He liked it best when she accepted his invitation to walk with him whenever there was a fine evening. Then he could touch her, taking her arm as they circled the compound at a slow pace. When he thought no one was watching, he would steal a playful kiss or two, but it was rare they were really alone. As the days became weeks, he had the strangest sensation that the bonds joining them multiplied each day, like the intricate web she wove in cotton to hold the fragile shards in place.

One afternoon in early April, he sought her out, finding her as he expected absorbed in her newest piece. He sat down and began working on his hunting quiver, glancing up from time to time to watch the flicker of her sooty lashes as she examined each shard with care, the chestnut gleam of her hair tied back to keep it out of her way. It had begun to worry him that she still spoke of returning home. He as good as told her every time he kissed her that he cared for her but was still waiting for her to confess her feelings for him. When she had produced the mobile for his family, he had taken heart that she had spent so many hours making a gift surely calculated to please him, but he wasn't sure if it was a gesture of friendship or something more. Fear of rejection prevented him from asking straight out; he wanted a clearer sign. Did she not wonder if she might want to stay with him in Magharna? Part of him was secretly glad that she had no choice for the moment but to remain where she was. That way he had time to bind her to him as tightly as he felt bound to her.

'Peri?' Rain knotted the thread she had been working on.

'Hmm?' Peri looked up from the arrow he was fletching with some of Rogue's feathers.

'Did you go talk to the fishermen like you said?'

'You know I did. I took them the fish hanging you made for them: they were delighted. I thought I told you all that yesterday.'

She dabbed at a tiny cut on her fingertip which was beading with blood. Gently taking her hand in his, Peri drew a cloth from his bag and cleaned it for her. 'You should be more careful: you're cutting yourself to pieces.'

'Hazard of the job,' she said with a shrug. 'But about the fisherfolk, did you talk about anything else? About what to do? The lawlessness has gone on for over a month now.'

Peri put the cloth aside. 'I talked to Murdle. He said

the city is nearly empty; people have gone out into the countryside to find food, taking trouble with them.'

'Isn't it time someone stepped forward to restore some order? The strong might survive this, but what about the ordinary people, the vulnerable ones?'

'We discussed that, but we really don't think we have enough men for the job. The fishermen have about fifty; we've got almost a hundred; but you know how big the city is: we'd need an army to put down the looters.'

Rain toyed with a pale blue piece of glass, holding it up to the light to check its colour. 'I've been hearing rumours from the hunters. There is someone with enough men for the task.'

'Oh? Who would that be? Not the Master, because he's currently running around barefoot with my pest of a brother.'

'No, not Ret. I was thinking of Krital and the bandits.'

Peri had thought he had got used to the way Rain's mind worked, but she had managed to floor him with that suggestion. 'That was a joke, right?'

She put down the glass and stretched her arm behind her head, relaxing her tense muscles. 'No. In my craft, I've learned to work with what I can get. Krital's a criminal but, think about it: he's all that's left.'

'It's true that he's managed to keep the bandits together all this time, but only because they are knee-deep in riches.'

Rain had expected Peri not to follow her train of thought immediately; he was too much of a Magharnan to think the unthinkable as she did. 'Peri, Krital's done more than that. He's set up his headquarters near the old mine on the road to the port. He's got deputies that report to him, patrols keeping an eye on the land he considers his; he even holds hearings when there are disputes. Sounds like a little government to me.'

Peri rubbed his thumb across her knuckles. 'Bandits, Rain. Remember them? The people that killed everyone you were with and took you prisoner?'

'Of course I haven't forgotten—and I'm not excusing his behaviour or defending his glaringly absent morals.' Memories of that day cropped up frequently as her nightmares. 'But I'm thinking what we can do with the fragments that are left, not of what I would choose if we started from scratch. I doubt Krital chose his life as a bandit—he was forced out by the old system. If given the choice, isn't there hope he'll take the opportunity to change?'

'Krital wants me dead for taking you from him, remember?'

She shook her head. 'Surely he'll have forgotten all that by now.'

'I wouldn't bet on it.'

'He's a thug, I know that, but at least he is easy to understand. He will do what he sees as in his own interests. Have you not thought that if nothing is done the farmers will not be able to tend their crops this year. We'll all starve come winter. What's the bigger crime: letting people die of hunger or making an approach to people we'd rather not have to deal with? If we can persuade him that he will be better off on the inside of the new Magharna, rather than as an outcast on the road, I think he might help us.'

'He's not some misunderstood hero waiting for a chance to reform—don't deceive yourself that he has a good side.' Recognizing the slow-burn of panic inside his chest, Peri silently cast around for ways to stop her heading off on this disastrous course. 'He won't take any notice of you, so how exactly are you thinking of persuading him?'

Rain gave an awkward half shrug. 'With this?' She gestured to the latest design, a horse rearing on its hind legs.

'Sweetheart, your creations are wonderful, but even you aren't that good. Krital won't do your bidding for a bunch of broken pieces strung into a pretty pattern.'

'No, but it might make him pause long enough to listen to what we've got to say. I don't like him or his ways—frankly, he terrifies me—but we need him.'

'We?' Peri stood up. 'If you think for one moment that I'd risk asking Krital for anything then you've got another think coming to you. He'll run me through and not think twice about it.'

'I see.' Rain was disappointed. As with her designs, she felt she always saw the whole of what was needed long before others understood what she was aiming for. Magharna needed a force to impose order; the only order at present was in small pockets like the compound or out among the bandits. The conclusion was simple: the country needed the ones they'd thrown away if it was going to get back on its feet.

'Do you really see, Rain? Last time, I went along with your suggestion to go to the palace even though I didn't like it. I did that because, though I knew it was risky, I didn't think it a death sentence. You know we were lucky to get away with that. But this is different. You don't understand the bandits like I do. There's nothing you can say that will make them other than what they are: violent men out for themselves.'

Rain recalled the man in the employment office all those months ago who had been forced out of the city for no greater sin than being without a job. 'I don't think they are all like that.'

Peri threw up his hands in exasperation. 'There's no talking to you sometimes, Rain. You hear but don't listen.'

'You're wrong. I listen but I am capable of forming my own opinions. We keep coming back to this, don't we, Peri? You'd like me to go along with everything you say like some brainless sheep.'

'At least it would keep you out of trouble,' he muttered.

'Well, bad luck, I'm no more going to be like that than I'm going to fly to the moon.' She rolled up the cloth containing the finished mobile. 'You have no right to order me around—you often act as if you do, you know. I find it really annoying.'

'That's not true.' Peri felt a twinge of alarm: he didn't want to mix this disagreement up with their relationship, not after all the progress he'd made over the last few weeks to earn his place at her side. 'Don't change the subject, Rain: I'm talking about your less than inspired idea of asking a bunch of murderers to keep the peace for us.'

Rain sighed. 'So you won't come with me to see them?'

'Neither of us is going anywhere.'

'You're content to sit here until the chaos outside beats down even these walls?'

'That's a false choice—it won't happen like that.'

'Why not? I can't see anyone else doing anything to stop the slide. When people are desperate enough, they'll come back here and won't find a few hunting dogs enough to scare them away.'

'We have plans. We'll evacuate.'

'And go where?'

'There's a village in the marshes, easily defended because it can only be reached by a causeway. The people are used to us as we use it as a base for hunting.'

'Fine, so you've plans to save yourselves: but what about the rest of us?'

'You'll come too of course.'

'That's not what I meant.' Tired now, Rain wanted to drop the discussion. Her own mind was made up but so was his. She couldn't count on him for help so she'd have to do this alone. 'Let's go for a walk.'

Peri was quick to accept, mistaking her shift in subject for acquiescence. He took her arm through his and led her to the path running along the top of the wall around the compound. Too dangerous to go out, this was the closest they could come to a change of scene. The view beyond the compound towards the city was depressing: Rolvint lay in ruins, the facade of white buildings marred by burnt-out gaps like rotting teeth in a skull's grin. To the north stretched the untended plots of the city cemetery. He steered her towards the west with the vista towards the mountains. At least they hadn't altered, still dominating the horizon with their smooth profile, clouds skimming their summit like lather on a face about to be shaved. Neither Peri nor Rain mentioned that that was where the bandits lived.

Two more days passed. Rain was not so arrogant as to think her plan without flaw, but she was convinced no progress could be made in Magharna until law and order was restored. The scavengers were living a half-life hidden behind their walls, only to emerge in armed groups to make swift forays on the hunting grounds. They had been the lucky ones; Rain couldn't bear to think how other people must be suffering. As for herself, she would never be able to get home, nor her father find her, if the roads remained impassable.

Something had to be done, she thought, as she worked with her glass fragments, and it looked as if she was the one who had to do it.

She chose a day for her departure when Peri, Helgis, and their mother were out hunting with their birds. She took very little with her: just the horse mobile and a spare set of clothes, knowing it likely that anything she had would be taken from her. She toyed with the idea of adding a knife for protection but decided it was more likely to be used against her if she had one. There was no way she would win a fight so she would concentrate on not getting into one.

While Bel was helping her father with the washing, Rain scrawled a note to Peri in her bedroom. It was one of the hardest things she had ever done.

Dear Peri,

I think you can guess where I've gone and I know you'll be furious. Don't worry about me. Like the fey folk, I was always going to do what I thought right and you are not to blame if I am making a mistake. I'll return as soon as I can but please do not wait if you have to evacuate the compound. Whatever you do, don't come after me.

Thank you for everything you've done. Look after Mikel.

Rain

She hesitated over whether to declare her feelings

for him but decided that would be cruel. Better if he thought she took everything with her, including an intact heart, if he was to get over her departure. If he thought she did not care, then there was a chance he might feel so angry and let down by her that he would be dissuaded by his mother from coming after her— that would keep him safe. Rain folded the note, her hands shaking a little, knowing she was doing terrible damage to their relationship. When—if—she returned, she would try to explain. If he let her, maybe then they could explore what future they might have. She hadn't mentioned it to him, but she had even begun to imagine staying with him—that's if she could be sure that her father was not worrying about her. Or maybe she could persuade him to come to Holt with her? There were bound to be opportunities for a skilled falconer in her city. It was a lot to ask when Peri was clearly so close to his family, but her father needed her and . . .

Rain pulled back from her runaway thoughts. How could she be thinking of the future when the next step was one that would take her away from Peri? She could not afford to indulge in such daydreams. Before normal life could resume for anyone in Magharna, including herself, someone had to take a risk and begin the process of rebuilding the shattered state.

Leaving the note folded on her work table, Rain headed out towards the gate. She heard Bel and Hern laughing as they battled with a sheet in the stiff breeze. She'd miss the Falconers—with the exception of Katia. At least one of them would be happy this evening when they realized she had slipped away.

'Rain! Where are you going?' Ret popped out from behind the stable, a piece of straw clenched between his teeth.

'Nowhere special,' she replied wondering how she could shake him off her tail.

'I'm bored. Want to play catch? I'm getting good at it.'

'Not just now.'

Ret might have been slow to learn some of the skills of ordinary life, but he was by no means a fool. He spotted her bundle.

'You're going somewhere—somewhere you don't want Peri to discover,' he guessed.

Rain decided there was no point lying. He would find out soon enough and could not stop her. 'All right, I'll tell you: I'm going to ask the bandits if they would restore order in the city and the lands around. If nothing is done, the farmers won't be able to plant, the harvest will be lost and your people will be facing starvation this winter. Even bandits need to eat though they don't grow the stuff themselves.'

Ret nodded, her reasoning making perfect sense to him. He had learned to accept that scavengers were not unclean; why not turn to outcasts to police his city?

'That's a good idea. I'll come with you.'

She hadn't expected this development. 'What? No!'

Ret frowned. 'Why not?'

'It's too . . . I'm not sure what they will make of my request.'

'You were going to say it's too dangerous.' Ret pulled her bundle off her shoulder and looped it over his own. 'Then you should stay here and I'll go. I'm the Master; it's my country; you're the last person who should be risking your neck for us.'

Rain tried to tug the bag back. 'But I've a plan.'

'Tell me it and I'll do it.'

'You're not Master any more.'

'I am—I'm just in disguise, remember?'

Rain examined Ret's defiant expression. Years of training for a leadership role could not be undone in a few weeks. Add to that a sense of godlike vocation and she didn't have a chance. He'd made his mind up— just like she had. And if she didn't let him come, he might well spoil her only chance to leave. She would just have to make sure he was kept safe as far as it was in her power to do so.

'Then we'll go together. It's probably a stupid thing to do,' she warned him. 'Peri forbade me to do this.'

Ret grinned. 'But that won't stop us, will it?'

'No, it won't. But he probably won't forgive me either.'

Peri returned from the hunt with only meagre pickings. Spring was the hungry time of year and they had to be careful what they caught in case the quarry had young. To make matters worse, Rogue had gone into moult and wouldn't be flying for a few weeks.

Dispirited, Peri went in search of Rain, needing a few comforting words from her to cheer him up. He'd even welcome a good argument as it would at least make his blood run hot and drive away his dullness. She wasn't at her desk, which was odd. He looked round the common room but there was no sign of her. Going closer, he saw the piece of paper with his name on it. A sense of foreboding hit as he picked it up. Reading the contents quickly, he scrunched it up and threw it on the floor.

'Mikel!' he called, storming out of the building.

The old man hurried out of the stable where he'd been currying Nutmeg. 'What's the matter, Peri?'

'That idiotic girl has run off!'

'What? Why?'

Peri rapidly explained Rain's most recent hare-brained scheme.

'That's the stupidest idea I've heard in a long while. But why she go and do something like that without me?' Mikel was clearly hurt that Rain had not trusted him with her plans.

'She knew you'd stop her—just as I tried to do.'

'If we saddle up a couple of the horses, we can try and catch up with her.' Mikel headed back into the stable.

Peri checked the position of the sun. It was dipping towards the horizon, the shadows already lengthening. 'Wait! We need to know how much of a head start she has. If she's had enough time to reach the mountain pass, she may have already met up with the bandits.'

'So? I didn't take you for a bleeding coward, falcon man.'

Peri shook his head. He felt so angry with Rain, but he refused to let that blind him to the facts. 'I'm not a coward. We have to have a plan if we are going to rescue that infuriating girl from her own stupidity. There's no point riding in and becoming prisoners ourselves.'

Mikel threw the curry comb into a bucket. 'All right, all right, find out, then let's decide what we can do.'

Peri ran to the muster bell that hung in the centre of the compound and rang it. Scavenger families rushed out of their homes to see what the emergency was, gathering around him in an anxious flock.

Peri jumped up on a wagon. 'My friends,' he called. 'Rain has disappeared. Can anyone tell me when they last saw her?'

Bel hurried out of the mews. 'Rain? She's gone? Why?'

He waved away the question, too eager to have his own answered. 'Anyone see her this afternoon? Who's been here all day?' He looked round the crowd. 'Pa? Ret?'

Helgis jumped up beside him. 'Peri, I can't find Ret either.'

Peri closed his eyes briefly. It wasn't hard to imagine

what those two were up to; neither of them had the least idea what real life was like. He could imagine that Rain had easily persuaded Ret that the tiger of a bandit leader was really a pussy cat, but she should never have led a boy on such a suicidal mission.

'So we've two people missing. Have you seen either of them since the morning?'

Silence met his question. He would have to assume that Rain and Ret had a whole day's start.

'Thanks—that's all I needed to know.' He made a move to jump down from the wagon.

'But, Peri,' called Conal, 'are you going after her? Do you know where she's heading?'

'Yes, she's gone to tell the bandits to play nicely and police the city for us.' He gave a hollow laugh at their aghast expressions. 'What can I say? She's foreign.' And she'd left him without even bothering to say goodbye face-to-face. He tried to quell his sense of hurt but it was hard to take this as anything but a rejection of him and everything he had to offer. Had he been so wrong about her having feelings for him?

'But you'll go after her?'

Of course he would: she might reject him, but he would never abandon her. He had done that once on her first day in Magharan and sworn never again.

'When I've decided how best to get her out of this.'

'Many of us are willing to go with you. We like Rain. We know she means well.'

A murmur of agreement spread through the crowd.

Katia Falconer chose that moment to step up beside her son. 'No one is going anywhere tonight. The girl has chosen her own path and asked us not to follow her.' She held up the scrunched note Peri had discarded. 'It's time we stopped worrying about her and thought about ourselves. Stores are running low. We've got to get ready to move. We need to be somewhere to grow our own crops this summer and we've only a few weeks left before it'll be too late to plant.'

'But I don't know anything about being a farmer!' protested one butcher.

The discussion headed off on this new track, leaving the matter of Rain unresolved. Peri jumped down, leaving the stage to Katia. His mother could say what she liked; but he was not going to give up on Rain. First he was going to find her, then shake some sense into her, and if that failed, kiss her until she forgot anything but him.

Mikel was waiting for him. 'So, what's the plan, Peri?' He also had taken no notice of Katia's announcement.

'Thanks to the start she has on us, our choices are pretty bad,' admitted Peri, as Conal, Sly, and Bel gathered at his shoulder. 'The best I can suggest is that we ride out under cover of darkness, camp out in the hills near the bandits' headquarters and try to sneak in just before dawn when the guard will be least vigilant.'

'Then what?' asked Conal.

'Pull them both out whether they want to come or not.'

'I'll saddle the horses,' said Sly.

'I'll get Fletch,' offered Bel.

Peri caught her arm. 'No birds, not this time.'

Bel studied his face. 'You think you might not come back. Peri, no! You can't go.'

He gave a sigh and hugged her against him. Battered by Rain's decision to walk out on him, he was feeling particularly vulnerable. 'I'm sorry, Bel, but I can't stay.'

'Ma's right: she's bad for you.' Bel's loyalty to her new friend buckled now she saw she might lose her brother.

'Don't say that—Rain isn't to blame for my choices.'

'And you aren't responsible for rescuing her from hers.'

'Maybe not, but I can't help myself. And there's Ret to think about.'

Mikel led Nutmeg from the stable. 'Come on, lad, let's get going.'

'Uh-oh,' said Bel, pushing away from Peri as their father approached. 'Too late.'

Peri braced himself for another confrontation, but Hern surprised him. He handed his son a sword then checked the fit of the girth on Nutmeg.

'Don't take unnecessary risks,' Hern said gruffly, patting Peri on the back. 'Only go in if you think there's a real chance of rescuing them, promise me that.'

'I promise.' Peri swallowed against the lump in his throat.

'Off you go, before your mother tries to stop you. She means well.'

'I know. Tell her I'm sorry to worry her.'

Hern nodded. 'I'll close the gate behind you.'

Shard 13
Chestnut Brown

'How do we find the bandits, Rain?' Ret asked, taking an anxious glance at the sun which had just dropped below the hills. Long shadows stretched across the road winding along the valley bottom. His feet were aching in a pair of Helgis's ill-fitting shoes but he didn't want to admit this to Rain who had walked without complaint for hours. She'd taken back the bundle when she had noticed him struggle.

'Don't worry, Ret, if I'm right, they'll find us. You mustn't be scared. If we don't fight them, I doubt they'll hurt us.' At least that was what she was hoping. 'If you like, you could wait here and I'll go on. You can be my lookout.' She wished he'd take this option so that at least she wouldn't have to be concerned about him in what was to come.

'No, Rain, we're in this together,' he said determinedly.

Rain couldn't help smiling. 'You know, Ret, I think you would make a splendid Master given the chance.'

'Thank you, Rain. I'm certainly learning a lot. I just didn't realize.'

'Realize what?'

'That all this was out here—that my people were like Helgis and his family. I feel like I've been living in a box.'

'And we took off the lid and tipped you out,' finished Rain.

'Yes. I should've done it myself.'

'Don't be hard on yourself. You're twelve. At that age, I was only just thinking about what I wanted to do with my life. It's when I made my first designs. I was lucky I had a father who paid attention.'

Ret kicked a stone. It bounced into a pothole and disappeared. 'I only ever saw my father on state occasions. Everyone says he was a good Master.'

'Maybe he was, but I think you'll be even better.'

'If I ever get the chance. It seems impossible that I'll ever live in the palace again.'

Rain adjusted the loop of her bundle across her chest. 'Is that why you're here: to make that chance happen?'

'Yes—and no. My people come first. I'm not sure it matters what happens to me.' He sounded much older than his years, which didn't seem right to Rain. Even a ruler deserved the chance to be a child. He shouldn't be carrying the burdens of the world all the time.

'Of course, it matters!' Rain took his hand, swinging it to and fro playfully. 'You may not have had anyone

228

to pay attention to you, but I'm here now. Think of me as your big sister.'

'Like Bel?'

'Yes, like her.'

He responded to her teasing tone. 'Does that mean you'll pull my ears like she does to Helgis?'

She gave the nearest one a tweak. 'Absolutely.'

They both laughed, and so didn't notice the bandit patrol until the two men stepped out on the road before them.

'Glad someone's happy in Magharna,' grunted the first man, holding out a staff to block their passage. Rain stepped in front of Ret, gesturing him to keep back.

'Either that or they're mad—I vote for that,' commented the second, beckoning Rain to drop her bundle. 'Must be, if they've come here. What've you got in there, girl?'

Rain took a calming breath, knowing that how this conversation went would decide whether or not they got their interview with Krital.

'A gift for your leader.'

'That's a new one.' The one with the staff looked her over contemptuously. 'Everyone gives all they've got to Krital whether they like it or not. What's with the hair, girl? Have an accident with the curling irons?' He flicked the staff towards her.

'I'm not from your country. I've met your leader before. I've made something special for him.'

The man stared at her, searching for an elusive

memory. He tapped her lightly on the chest, pushing her backwards. 'You're the foreigner—the one caught in the raid six months ago?'

Rain stilled. She had told herself if she was to do this she had to prepare herself for meeting men who had shed her cousin's blood, but face to face with one of them it was hard to disguise her revulsion.

'Krital said you got away from him—something about a bolting horse and a falcon man. He was in a foul mood for weeks after.'

Rain gave him a brittle smile. 'There you are—I've come back and I have something to cheer him up.' Her bravado sounded hollow to her but the man was impressed.

'Is that so? Well then, little foreigner, let's see what he makes of your gift. Follow me.'

The bandit led them further up the valley, leaving his companion to guard the way. The efficiency of the watch on the road confirmed Rain's view that these bandits did indeed have the discipline needed in Rolvint. She took Ret's hand and squeezed it, partly to comfort him, but also to bolster her own spirits.

The climb up from the road was steep, following an old stone track used to transport the slate down the mountainside. When they emerged on the plateau, Rain saw that the area around the abandoned mine had been transformed since she had last laid eyes on it. The level ground where wagons had once waited in line to transport the slate to market now bristled with new buildings, many of them little more than shacks hastily thrown together, but two or three of the dwellings looked more permanent. The bandit led her to the largest of these, a long low hall with smoke curling from the centre of the roof, though even this was dwarfed by the mountain peak looming above the mine encampment, a black shadow against the starlit sky. Their escort pushed open the double doors, revealing a crowded chamber. Food was laid out on trestle tables; men and women lounged at their ease while serving maids passed among them with trays of tankards. The mood was boisterous but good humoured. The most objectionable thing to Rain was the smell: the rushes on the floor hadn't been changed for weeks and it appeared that washing wasn't high on the agenda for any of the brigands. Krital hadn't set his sights very high if he was content to reign over this bunch.

They proceeded through the crowd, heading for the table nearest the fire. Rain was grateful that they did not attract much attention, giving her time to prepare what she had to say. Her eyes were locked on Krital who was seated in the centre, feet up on the board. His gaze was fixed on the ceiling, watching the smoke winding its way out of the hole in the roof. An attractive woman wearing a bright yellow jettan robe, spoils of a raid on a convoy, perched on the arm of the chair beside him, trying to amuse him with her conversation, but it was not going as she had hoped; Krital's face was stony, his expression one of boredom. Two muscular men stood behind him, arms folded, on hand to prevent anyone taking their leader unawares. Krital understood that a man who had earned his place by violence could expect more of the same to be dealt out to him.

'Boss!' called the guard as they came within earshot. 'I found something of yours on the road.'

Krital turned his eagle-eyed gaze on the newcomers; his fist, which had been propping up his square jaw, dropped to the arm of his chair, dislodging his companion. 'The girl.'

The room fell silent as those nearby realized that something interesting was happening at the top table.

'Aye. She says she's got something for you.' The guard beckoned Rain forward. She stepped nervously into the space between the table and the fire, feeling the flames hot on her back, the hostile looks of the yellow-robed woman. She sensed rather than saw Ret keeping close, alert for any threat to her.

'What are you doing here, chestnut?' Krital asked, his eyes narrowed in calculation. 'Are things so bad in the city that you thought you'd do better with me, even though you know I'll enslave you?'

Rain decided it was best to ignore this threat. It was unlikely that markets still existed for the sale of bonded labour; he was probably just testing her.

'I . . . er . . . I actually came to give you something.' She wished she was more eloquent but nerves were getting in the way and her fluency in Magharnan faltering.

Krital raised a black eyebrow. His hair was as short

as ever, but instead of his black skull cap, he wore one of red velvet like a splash of blood on his scalp. He would have won no beauty contests with his mashed nose, hard-beaten features, and mud-brown eyes narrowed in suspicion, but there was no doubt that he was in command here.

'Everyone gives me things—with or without their agreement,' he said coldly.

'But I imagine no one has ever made something specially for you.' Rain shook out the contents of her bag and held up the roll of canvas. 'Don't you want to see?'

He waved a hand towards her. 'Why not.'

Rain was now grateful that she had the fire behind her. Gripping the top of the mobile, she let the rest shake into place, revealing the rich colours of the leaping horse, the image of the one he had ridden away from the raid on her convoy.

Krital sat up in his chair, his boredom forgotten. 'You made this?'

'Yes.' She bit her lip nervously. Did he not like it?

'For me?'

'Yes.'

'Why?' His brows drew together in a frown.

'It's a kind of . . . ' she searched for a word to explain, 'a kind of peace offering.'

'That makes no sense. Why risk your freedom in bringing it here?'

Before Rain could stop him, Ret stepped forward. 'We brought it to you, sir, because we believe that you can see the value of creating something beautiful out of fragments.'

'Who's this?' barked Krital.

'My friend,' said Rain.

'I am the Master,' declared Ret at the same moment.

Krital threw back his head and laughed. 'The Master? Master of what?'

Ret flushed. 'I am the Master of Magharna. And though that no longer means much, I still believe I have a duty to my people. And that duty has brought us here.'

Krital beckoned him forward. Ret approached the table cautiously, coming within reach. Rain held her breath, wondering if she should pull him back. She could sense the menace under Krital's gesture.

'You know, boy, what I think of masters?' said Krital in a hoarse whisper, his fist bunched.

'Nothing good, I'm sure,' replied Ret, determined not to flinch in the face of a threat.

His wit surprised the bandit. Krital relaxed his hand and laughed. 'I would've shown you with a punch, but you beat me to it, lad. Enough of masters, explain what you mean.'

Rain wanted the attention back on her to get Ret out of the line of fire. She held out the mobile. 'There's not much left in the city, just bits and pieces no one wants.'

Krital sat back. 'I know that.'

Time for her plea—if he would only have the

patience to listen. 'But do you know what it means? The city is dying, and so is the land around. People are being forced to fight for survival, retreating to protect themselves. Farmers are too afraid to work their land and what little they have is often raided. What will happen when the seed corn is eaten? Where will the next crop come from?' Rain picked up a piece of flat bread from a platter on the table and crumbled it on to the floor. 'What will you eat when there's no more food to steal?'

Krital shrugged. 'We'll be the last to suffer, little foreigner.'

'I don't doubt that, but you admit that you too will feel the effects eventually?'

'Maybe. But what do you suggest I do about it?'

She passed him the mobile. 'Gather what's left and make something of it.'

He shook the horse, smiling at the tinkling sound that came from it. 'Very pretty. But you don't mean this, do you?'

'No.' She looked round the room, realizing that everyone was listening to her so she had to get this right. 'You have, what? Several hundred men?'

He nodded.

'If you took over the city, you could restore order to the streets. Once people feel secure, they'll go about their normal lives, growing, making, selling.'

Krital started to laugh but then sobered. 'You are serious?'

'Yes. Who else is there?'

'But we are outlaws.'

'When there is no law, how can you be outside it? Isn't it time you made your own?' She scanned the faces of those listening. Many bore the signs of a tough life, scars on arms and faces, bitterness in their expressions. Did she really expect them to rise to this challenge? 'I know you were thrown away before by the authorities, but the people who did that have gone. Why can't you step into the gap and remake the city as a place where you can live in a lot more comfort than out here? Wouldn't it be better to earn people's gratitude than be despised and feared?'

Krital didn't appear convinced of that. He passed the mobile to the woman in the jettana's robe. 'Hang this in my chamber,' he ordered. 'Where I can see it.' He turned to the guard who had escorted Rain inside. 'Take our guests to the holding cell.'

Rain's hopes took a dive. 'You're not going to do it?'

He arched a brow at her. 'Did I say that?'

'No.'

'You've given me something to think about—leave me in peace while I consider what you've said.' He banged his empty cup on the table. 'More beer!'

The hubbub resumed as Rain and Ret were led away.

'I think that went well,' whispered Ret, his eyes darting with curiosity around the boisterous gathering. 'He was really paying attention.'

'But that doesn't mean he's going to do what we want the way we want it.'

'Of course not. But him doing something is better than the nothing we've had so far, don't you agree?'

'I hope so. Either that, or we've made a terrible mistake coming here.'

'Can you see them?'

Hidden in the hills above the bandit settlement, Peri peered over a ledge, watching the comings and goings in the camp.

'I think so,' he said in answer to Mikel's question. 'Two short prisoners were led from that big building to that hut over there.'

'Did they look all right?'

'If it's them, then yes, I'd say they were unharmed. They walked in unassisted.' He had been relieved by this glimpse of Rain, but it also brought back his anger at her rashness. What had she been thinking to venture into this place of her own accord? He'd already spotted two drunken brawls and seen how tightly the camp was guarded. Getting out of there without losing anyone was going to be very difficult.

'What now?' asked Conal, slithering on his belly to come up alongside Peri. Sly was a few feet further back, admitting that he didn't have a head for heights.

'I think two of us should climb down from here and try to get to them. It's the only route that's not well guarded.'

'That's because the slope is nigh impossible to scale,' Conal observed drily.

'And how will we get them up here?' asked Mikel. 'I don't have a good feeling about this.'

'Nor do I, old friend, but do you have any better suggestions?'

Mikel shook his head and unfastened his cloak. 'I'll go first. At least if I fall, I won't knock you off.'

Peri eased back from the edge. 'I know you want to do this, Mikel, but we stand the best chance if Conal and I are the ones climbing.' He slipped off his shoes, flexing his toes. 'I'm sure you know that.'

Mikel scowled. 'But I've looked after her like a daughter these past months. She's my girl, my responsibility.'

'I take it we're going to have to flip a coin as to who gets to tell her off for this madcap adventure of hers? I know: I do the rescuing, you can do the scolding. Do we have a deal?'

With a little more grumbling, Mikel agreed.

'If things go badly, which is more than likely, I'll whistle. We'll try and meet up by the broken bridge. If we don't make it, go back to the compound and tell them what happened.'

Conal peered over the edge and gulped. 'You think there's a way down?'

'It's not as steep as it appears.' Peri let himself drop over the edge, feeling with his bare feet for a ledge. 'Climbed worse when looking for falcon nests.'

'Bet you had a rope then.' Conal waited for Peri to make the first few moves successfully before following him, not taking exactly the same route but trying his luck to one side. His feet lost purchase and he found himself hanging by his fingertips briefly before he regained control. 'I hate this.'

He continued chanting this as he edged down, cursing the slippery slate for every time it gave way under him. Peri grinned at his vehemence—but only when they were both safely on the ground.

Keeping low, they crept across the open ground to the little building set on its own. The small windows and heavily barred door made it plain that its purpose was to keep people in rather than let them see out. Peri cursed under his breath: Rain had been lucky she'd been made a prisoner and not had her throat cut on sight—a point he was going to make to her if Mikel didn't.

'Down!' whispered Conal, pulling him behind a pile of shale. Three men were approaching the hut. One went inside while the others waited for a moment before retreating back the way they had come.

'Was that Krital?' wondered Conal.

'I don't know—couldn't see him clearly—but Rain and Ret are on their own in there with one of them. Let's not debate.'

They scrambled over the open ground separating them from the hut, relying on the darkness to hide them from the patrol guarding the encampment. Breathing heavily, backs flat against the back wall, they paused to draw their weapons. Peri selected an arrow from his quiver and strung his short hunting bow. Having already confronted Krital once, he did not relish the prospect of hand-to-hand combat with someone so much more skilled than him. Conal's eyes glittered in the moonlight, watching Peri for the signal.

With a nod, Peri stepped forward to stand in the open doorway.

Rain and Ret sat side by side on the narrow bunk as Krital paced before them.

'Your idea has legs—I can run with it,' said Krital. He tugged the velvet skull cap from his short hair and scratched his scalp. 'It's true I've had enough of being an outlaw: time I got back inside the walls. Better in the city than out here this winter. I take it the boy here knows the layout of the palace buildings?'

Ret sat up straight, resisting the urge to finger the pendant tucked under his clothes. 'I do, sir.'

'How bad was it when you left them? Roof still on?'

'Yes.'

'We could probably move everyone in right away then,' said Krital, thinking aloud. 'Start by securing the palace then take it from there.'

Rain was conscious she had set in motion a process over which she had no control but she had to try. 'When you've done that, will you create safe places for the vulnerable ones?'

Krital looked surprised by the suggestion. 'Why would I want to do that? I'm not a charity, true? I'm not playing nursemaid to a bunch of women and children.'

Her wish that he would have a change of heart suffered a blow. 'No one's asking you to, just to give them somewhere safe to go. I can make the rest of the arrangements.'

Krital leaned over her, one arm against the wall behind. 'You are a continual surprise, little foreigner. You've got guts coming here and telling me what to do. You're getting me thinking things I never thought before.'

'Move away from them!'

Rain looked up in shock. Peri stood in the doorway, arrow trained on Krital. The bandit leader swore.

'The scavenger! So this is all a trick?' He seized hold of Rain and pulled her up on to tiptoe. 'Why?'

'It's not a trick!' she protested. 'I didn't know he'd followed me. Please, listen!'

'Guard!' roared Krital.

'Move away from the girl!' ordered Peri, cold sweat trickling down his back. He'd never shot someone before but if Krital did not let go of Rain, he would.

Krital dropped Rain and swung round to face Peri, feeling for the dagger he carried in his belt. 'You've made your last mistake, falcon boy,' he snarled.

Seeing Krital's hand move to his blade, Peri loosed his arrow.

'No!' screamed Rain, surging forward.

Ret yelled a warning, but too late: Peri's arrow hit Rain high on the shoulder, knocking her back against Krital. The bandit's dagger went flying as he caught the girl as she fell. The bandit gave a great roar of fury, but could not retaliate as Rain was slumped in his arms.

Peri stared in horror at the blood seeping from the wound he had inflicted.

'Peri, they're coming,' said Conal. Men were pouring out of the hall, grabbing their weapons from the doorwarden.

'I've got to stay,' Peri said numbly.

'No, you're leaving—now!' Conal pulled him firmly from the hut. 'Ret?'

'I'm staying,' the boy said without hesitation.

'Good lad. Look after her!'

Conal dragged Peri back towards the cliff. His shock had mutated into anger: if Peri didn't do something they were going to get caught by a horde of vengeful bandits. 'Get a grip, my friend, or we're both dead!'

'I shot her.'

'Yes, but you don't know how bad. Dog's breath, Peri, you've got to move! Rain won't want you dead.'

This argument made some impact and Peri stopped dragging against Conal's grip on his jacket.

'I'll get you out of this,' Peri vowed.

'You'd better, because they're not far behind.'

Peri glanced behind to see the men fanning out through the camp, looking for the intruders. 'No time to climb,' he panted. 'We'll have to take the quick route out.' He gave a whistle, the prearranged signal to Mikel and Sly that plans had changed. At the same time, he shifted direction and ran for the entrance to the abandoned mine.

'Quick route?'

'Slate wagon. They had a track on stone runners down the mountainside. It's probably still working.'

'Probably!'

The ground underfoot became more treacherous as they approached the old mine. The slag heaps slumped over their path so that they had to wade across them to reach the entrance. A chill breeze emanated from the shaft.

'Couldn't we just hide in there?' asked Conal.

'And then what?' said Peri, pulling off a ragged tarpaulin covering an empty wagon. The wheels looked rusted into place. 'We'll be cornered like a fox in a hole—they'll tear us to pieces when we come out.'

Conal shuddered. 'Thanks—I could do without the imagery.'

'Get in. I'll lever it from the back. Then we press thumbs,' said Peri, referring to the traditional plea for 'good luck'.

Conal didn't waste time arguing. He knew as well as Peri that they would be incredibly fortunate if the track was still intact. He vaulted inside, landing in three inches of muck and grit. Peri dug through the debris until he found a thick wooden post. Wedging it under the rear wheel, he heaved, cursing as it refused to shift. Inside the wagon, he could feel Conal rocking the car forwards to dislodge it.

'I think it's moving!' Conal bumped on to the front wall, making the whole thing shudder.

Seething with self-hatred for what he had done to

Rain, Peri found strength he had not known he possessed. With a final heave, he forced the wheel to turn; the wagon began to creep forward.

'Get in!' ordered Conal.

Pushing from the rear, Peri ran a few paces, then jumped on board. With a grinding creak and rattle, the wagon was away, heading down a sharp slope for the valley bottom.

'Next problem is how do we stop this thing?' asked Peri as they kept low, bracing themselves across the car. Outside, he could hear shouts as men spotted the wagon careering out of the camp.

'No idea.' Conal gave a mirthless laugh. 'But I think we're going to find out one way or another.'

Peri found he couldn't rouse himself to care; he felt he had already crashed when he let loose that arrow.

Shard 14
Midnight Black

Ret was profoundly grateful that Rain was unconscious. He ran beside Krital bearing Rain's bundle as the bandit leader carried her into the hall near the fire and kicked a table over to clear it of the evening meal. His bodyguards set it upright so he could lay her on it.

'Where's the scholar?' he shouted.

'Coming, sir,' answered a reedy voice. A scrawny man with two thin black plaits emerged from the private quarters at a run. He had a quill tucked behind his ear.

'Tutor Nighman!' exclaimed Ret, recognizing one of his former teachers who had made himself noticeably absent from the palace since the beginning of the troubles.

'Master!' Nighman tripped over his feet in shock, before bending into a low bow.

'Scholar, stop that rubbish and do something.' Krital pushed him towards Rain.

'But I'm not a doctor!'

'You're the closest we've got. If you don't, I'll practise my surgery on you.'

With this threat, Nighman's protests subsided. He
huddled over Rain, pulling the collar of her dress away
from the wound. 'I'll need boiled water—and a knife.
What kind of arrow?'

'He had a hunting bow,' said Krital, waving to one
of his guards to fetch the water.

'Peri carries small tipped arrows, for hunting game,'
added Ret.

'Barbed?'

'No, I don't think so.'

'Thank the Master,' Nighman mumbled automatically, before blushing.

'Forget him,' growled Krital. 'Save the girl.'

'The arrow went in high—no major organs hit,'
muttered Nighman, speaking his thoughts out loud. 'If
we can ease the head out, then I think the main risk is
the wound going bad.' He peered closer at the entry
point, blinking as if trying to see it clearly.

'Where are your glasses?' whispered Ret.

'Damn things broke. It's all right: I can see enough.'
Dipping the knife in the boiled water, he gently used
the tip to ease the arrow out of the wound. It slipped
free, allowing him to staunch the bleeding. 'Good,
good,' he muttered.

Rain moaned.

'Oh no, my dear, don't wake up just yet. I need to
see to this. Does anyone have a clean needle and
thread?'

The bandits looked blank but Ret dived into Rain's bundle, knowing she kept cotton in there. 'Will this do?'

Nighman nodded, looking distinctly green. 'Keep her still. This needs a few stitches, I think, but I've only ever read about how to do it.'

'Time to get practical then, scholar,' bit out Krital.

The bandit leader braced Rain's legs while Ret held her head. Nighman took a deep breath. After a few fumblings, he got the idea and managed to sew up the wound and bind it in clean cloths. Rain remained unconscious through the procedure, much to everyone's relief.

'Unless she's very unlucky, I think she'll recover,' Nighman said when he had finished. 'Now, Master, if it be your will, please tell me what you are doing here?'

Ret opened his mouth to answer, but Krital pushed him aside. 'I'm master here, scholar. Get your patient into bed, then come back to me. We've plans to make. We're taking over the city.'

Peri flipped on to his back and considered the stars spinning above his head. The wagon had hurtled down the hillside until it collided with a rock left on the track. The consequent jolt had tipped the car sideways and thrown the two passengers out on to the boggy ground at the valley bottom. The mud had cushioned his fall but the water was now soaking through his clothes. He knew he had to move before one of the bandit patrols found him or the men from the camp caught up.

'Conal?'

A groan from his right told him that his friend had survived the rapid exit from the wagon.

'Are you hurt?' Peri felt as if his nose had taken the worst of the impact as he had gone face first into the marsh. He wiped mud from his eyes.

'Nothing broken,' reported Conal.

'Let's go.'

Holding on to each other for support, they staggered out of the patch of muddy ground and back to the path. Peri did a quick inventory of his weapons. His bowstring had snapped—good riddance to the thing—but his sword was still at his thigh. He drew it.

'Krital must have a guard on the road,' he said hoarsely, spitting out the rank taste of marsh water. 'I'd prefer to slip by rather than fight through.'

Conal nodded. 'We've one advantage.'

'What's that?' Peri waited for a cloud to pass over the moon before crossing the next stretch of open ground.

'We're well camouflaged.'

It was true. No patch of skin had avoided the mud bath. Conal was very difficult to see in the dark even though he was but feet away.

By mutual agreement, there was no more talking. The two scavengers took a leaf out of the bandits' own book and merged into the scenery, becoming one with the muddy black shadows of night.

As arranged, Sly and Mikel were holding the horses for them at the meeting point of the broken bridge and no one wasted any time when Peri and Conal arrived, leaping into the saddle and urging the mounts into a fast retreat. Sly and Mikel did not need to be told that the attempt had failed: the fact that Peri and Conal came alone said it all.

Once out of the hills, Mikel drew his mount level with Peri, his silence asking the question for him.

'It was a disaster,' Peri said tersely. 'We're being pursued. I shot Rain.'

'What!' Mikel pulled on his reins to slow his horse but Peri slapped the creature's rump to make it go on.

'She stepped in front of Krital. But it's no good. They'll kill us if we turn back. Ret stayed. He'll do his best.'

Mikel swore and tugged on the rein again. 'They'll kill you perhaps—you bleeding well deserve it—but I've got a girl who needs me.' Without another word, he steered the horse back the way they had just come.

Conal made to stop him but Peri shook his head. 'No, he's right. Rain needs more than Ret at her side. If I didn't know I would be executed on sight, I'd be following him. Come on, let's get home.'

The older members of the Falconer family had spent a sleepless night waiting for Peri and his companions to return. Hern had kept the fire going in the common room in anticipation that the rescue party would need hot food and drink when they returned from their arduous journey. He sighed with relief when he heard Peri, Conal, and Sly at the door, but when they came in his expression shifted to unease. They were alone.

'You didn't find her then?' asked Hern, seeing the look of devastation on his son's face.

'I shot her.'

'By mistake,' Conal added swiftly, casting an anxious look at Peri. He'd never seen his friend like this, all life drained from him.

'She's dead?' squeaked Bel, throwing off the blanket wrapped around her legs.

'We don't think so. I hope not.' Conal replaced the cover and patted her shoulder comfortingly. 'He was aiming at Krital—the arrow went in high.'

'And Ret?' asked Helgis, crawling out from under the table where he had been sleeping.

'He stayed with her.'

'I should've stayed,' whispered Peri, the mud on the back of his hands cracking as he curled them into fists. 'I should've stayed.'

'He shouldn't have done,' contradicted Conal, meeting the eyes of the others in the common room. 'It would've meant his death. Rain will understand. And Ret will be fine. For some reason the bandit listened to both of them. From what I heard, Krital plans to enter the city.'

'He does?' Katia shook her head in disbelief, her

gaze not leaving her oldest son as he paced before the fire. 'But why?'

Conal shrugged. 'Prefers a comfortable life under a roof than out in the mountains, I would guess. Rain must've been very persuasive.'

'But she doesn't realize she has a tiger by the tail,' added Peri, his voice hoarse. 'He'll turn on her and us.'

Hern looked round the chastened group. 'And Mikel?'

'You know that old badger, stubborn as anything.' Peri gave a grim smile. 'Insisted on riding into the camp to nurse her—said nothing would stop him. She'd looked after him when he was sick; he wants to do the same for her. We had to let him go.'

Katia gave a groan. 'Another one she's led into disaster!'

'Stop it, love,' warned Hern, catching the flash of anger in Peri's eyes. 'I'm glad Mikel's gone. She'll need him and the bandits are unlikely to harm an old man. He did well.'

'But next we're going to have these outlaws on our doorstep! Did she think of that when she invited them to take over Rolvint? And who is she in any case to decide what's best for us?'

Peri began to laugh, a sound drained of any real humour. 'Actually, Ma, she's doing it all with the support of the Master.'

'What nonsense is this?'

'No nonsense. Ret is the Master. We found him abandoned in the palace, remember? It's really him.'

'The Master's a boy?'

Helgis looked suitably impressed. 'It's like one of them stories.'

Peri leant against the wall by the window over which Rain's mobile hung and thumped his head on the stone. 'Yes, but they have happy endings. The Master's currently the captive of a bunch of thugs. I don't think for one moment they're interested in restoring him to power.'

Hern drew Peri away from the wall and put his arm around his shoulders. 'You know, your little lady is quite right, we don't have to sit back and wait for others to resolve this mess.'

'What do you mean, Pa?' Peri let himself sag against his father.

'You say the bandits are about to move into the city?'

'Yes.'

'They will be less likely to run wild if someone else got there before them and started the job she asked them to do.'

'Hern Falconer, we are moving to the village, not running Rolvint!' said Katia, glowering.

'Why not, Kati? Rain was right: soon there will be no more bolt holes. Better to take the initiative now than when it is too late.'

'But won't we just end up fighting the bandits?' asked Conal taking a seat on the bench next to Bel.

'Not if we prepare the ground so that there's a place

for them.' Hern's eyes gleamed with an idea. 'Everyone has a place in Rolvint, remember? That's the number one rule.'

Peri could see what his father was saying. Give the bandits a blank canvas and they would scrawl whatever they liked on it; present them with some attractive but limited choices, they could be channelled in less violent directions.

'A ruling council with representatives of all the professions that are left in the city,' suggested Peri. 'Krital to be the general of the new army—not that we could stop him. It would just be acknowledging the inevitable.'

'So we need a civilian force to keep his men in check,' said Sly, coming out of the shadows to join the group at the table. 'Do the day-to-day business of maintaining order rather than the fighting.'

'That'd be us then—and the fisherfolk will help,' Peri added. 'I've already talked to them. All they are waiting for is a direction.' Peri saw that Rain had been right all along, though her methods were reckless. While everyone had been looking at the fragments of their old life breaking apart in their hands, she had already seen the potential for reconstruction.

'That's good. You talk to them; I'll go to the other scavengers. The butchers will want to help.'

Conal stood up. 'I'll go with you. The huntsmen will be on your side, I can vouch for them.'

'You're all mad!' exclaimed Katia.

'No, Ma,' said Peri. 'I think we're finally seeing sense.'

Mikel made it through to the encampment after surrendering his horse to the party of men pursuing Peri and Conal and undergoing a brief but brutal interrogation. He found Rain asleep in a bed in Krital's private quarters, Ret at her side looking wide-eyed and spooked like an owl startled by daylight. He was accompanied by a thin young man in midnight black robes who hovered at his shoulder. He was talking in a low voice and treated the boy with odd deference. Mikel's escort turned him loose.

'If you make trouble, we'll kill you, true?' the thug warned.

'Yes, true. Bleeding bandits,' muttered Mikel, closing the door on them.

Ret rushed to him and for a moment both were uncertain how to greet the other, until Mikel folded the boy in a fatherly hug. 'I reckon you've been a bit scared, young 'un,' he said gruffly. 'But you did good staying with her. How is she?'

Ret stepped out of the embrace, surreptitiously wiping his eyes. 'She's all right. Tutor Nighman treated her.'

Mikel eyed the thin man suspiciously. 'Know him, do you?'

'He used to teach me Magharnan history.'

Mikel gave a snort of disgust. 'One of the rats that bailed out when you needed them, eh?'

254

Nighman tugged at his dirty black robe awkwardly. 'You have to understand, it was very confusing—I never dreamed no one was looking after the Master—I would've stayed if I'd known.'

'Yeah, right. Blooming coward.' Mikel went to Rain's bedside and picked up her hand. She felt cool to the touch which was encouraging. 'Has she woken?'

'Once—only to take a sleeping draught I'd prepared,' reported Nighman stiffly.

'Get over it, man,' growled Mikel. 'I only called you a coward; I didn't say you were completely useless. You've done a good job here as far as I can tell.'

'Who are you?' The tutor resumed his seat. 'Her father?'

Mikel smiled at the thought. 'No, that position's already taken. I'm her friend. I kept the gate at the summer palace when she worked there.'

The tutor looked rapidly between Ret and Mikel, his weak eyes blinking. 'You're a bondsman? Master, I'm so sorry—you've been forced to mingle with those beneath you—had to talk to them in person!'

'I've been living with a scavenger family,' Ret added, smiling at Mikel.

Nighman gave a wail of distress.

'I think he's a bit behind the times, your history tutor.' Mikel stroked Rain's hand. Her fingers curled into his, reassuring him that her sleep was not a deep one.

'Yes, that's all done with. I'm Ret now.'

'But, sire!' Nighman protested.

255

Ret folded his arms. 'Let's put it another way. I'm the Master, so if I decide that what we thought was unclean is now clean, then I can.'

Nighman gave a jerky nod.

'Good, because I've decided.'

They were diverted from their discussion by Rain stirring on the bed. Her eyes flickered open, startling Mikel once more with their blueness.

'Mikel?'

'I'm here, lovey.'

'What happened?'

'That idiot falcon boy shot you.'

'He did?' She tried to move and then winced at the pain in her shoulder.

'He was aiming for Krital,' Ret said quickly before she got the wrong impression.

'Oh.' Her face clouded with worry. 'I remember now. Is he all right? Did he escape?'

'Yes. Both he and Conal should be back in the barracks by now,' said Mikel.

'Then why are you here?'

'To look after you, of course.' He brushed her hair off her forehead. 'You shouldn't've come here. I'm very angry with you.'

She closed her eyes and smiled. 'Is that all the scolding you're going to give me?'

'Until you're well.'

'It worked though. Krital's going to take his men into the city. I need to get better so I can make sure he behaves.'

'And how exactly are you going to do that?'

'I don't know. I was going to think of something.'

Mikel shook his head but let the matter drop. Rain wouldn't be fit to tame Krital for some time, not that her chances of success had ever been very great.

'Rest now, lovey. Ret and I will look after you.'

Shard 15
Emerald Green

It took a few days for Krital to finalize his plans for the take-over of Rolvint. He milked Ret and Nighman for every detail they could remember about the palace complex, though Rain suspected that Ret kept some secrets back. She applauded the decision; they would need as many advantages as they could manage now that the bandit leader was on a mission. Krital had changed from the gruff brigand into a man convinced that his new destiny was as a ruler. He inspired his men with the same belief—at least as long as they stood a chance of a more comfortable life with him.

When they moved out from their camp, it was in formation, the rough bandits bullied into ranks like the army Krital aspired to control. He also insisted that Rain be taken with them. She needed the attention of the scholar, he claimed, to ensure she recovered fully from the injury gained in his defence. He did not want to admit that he had come to think of her as something of a personal mascot, and though he joked about her giving her fey blessing to the enterprise, Rain suspected he half believed the superstition.

Still too weak to ride, Rain travelled in the middle of the column on a stretcher carried by Krital's own bodyguards, Ret, Mikel, and Nighman at her side. The bandit leader rode in the vanguard, flanked by his most trusted men. This honour guard spent much of the ride keeping watch on the brigands behind, knowing they posed the greatest threat. But for now, lured by the promise of a city to command, the outlaws held together, submitting to the discipline they were not used to obeying.

The city gates were open when they approached. Rain strained to sit up on her pillows to glimpse the scavengers' barracks but they passed through so quickly she saw very little.

Mikel noticed her restlessness. 'Do you want to stop, lovey? I can ask them to take you to the compound.'

Rain shook her head. 'No, I can't do that. I'm responsible for what happens here. I have to see it through.'

'It won't be your fault,' Mikel said cautiously. Rain could tell he was gloomy about the prospect ahead.

Rain watched the ruined streets of Rolvint pass. She tried to remember how they had looked when she lived at the House of the Indigent, but the images of burned out buildings and shattered windows had supplanted her memories of the beautiful houses and fragrant gardens. She wondered if things had gone too far to pull them back. Then, as they turned into the district near the palace, she detected the first signs of change. Some of the doors on the mansions had been replaced. There was an air of order about the squares, the fountains trickling water again and the worst of the rubbish cleared. She had the impression that until the brigand army had been spotted, there had been people on the streets. A basket loaded with flat bread had been abandoned at the entrance to one alley. A bucket hung empty by a well, swinging on its chain like a pendulum.

'I don't blooming believe it,' muttered Mikel.

'What's happened, do you think?' asked Rain. 'Have the jettan families come back? Are we making it worse by bringing the bandits here?'

Ret grimaced. 'I doubt it's them. They don't do this kind of work. Must be the people—the ordinary people. My people.' He looked inordinately proud of his former subjects, getting life back together without him.

The column stopped moving on the approach to the palace. Rain strained to see what was taking place at the front, but they were too far back. Then, with no explanation, the army was marching again, entering the palace grounds without opposition.

'Ret, can you find out what's happening?' Rain pleaded.

He winked. 'Of course. I never thought you'd ask.'

He ducked out of the column and sprinted to catch up with Krital.

'Have I been really stupid?' Rain asked Mikel despondently. 'Are the bandits going to make it worse just when it was getting better?'

Mikel wasn't sure what to reply. His face suggested that he believed it probable, but he thought it cruel to tell her. 'Not your fault, love. We created these bandits; it'll be our fault if they take revenge on the city that kicked them out. Blame us Magharnans for what happens next, not yourself.'

Peri stood in the white cavernous entrance hall to the palace with the other members of the ruling council, watching nervously as Krital approached at the head of his men. Conal was at the bandit's side. The greeting at the gate must have gone well; the two were talking amicably; Krital appeared eager to learn more before taking any rash decisions. He obviously hadn't recognized Conal from the rescue attempt; or if he did, held no grudge.

There was a flicker in the rhododendron bushes, a shifting of the heavy pink blooms and a glimpse of a boy's head. Ret was shadowing the bandit leader, weaving in and out of the bushes with a skill for evasion that Helgis must have taught him. It was a relief to find him alive and well; but what about Rain and Mikel? Where were they?

Hern, who had been nominated the city's

spokesman, smoothed his tunic and cleared his throat nervously. Peri tore his attention from Ret and met his father's eyes with a confident smile.

'You'll be fine, Pa. Just stick to what we agreed,' he said in a low voice.

'I'm not made for this kind of thing,' Hern confessed. 'Give me a good bird and a clear run at my quarry, then I'm your man; but this!'

'You'll be fine,' repeated Peri, willing it to be so.

After a brief discussion with Conal in the courtyard, Krital entered the palace with his core guard of nine men. As he took in the twenty strong reception committee, made up of representatives of all the professions that had remained in the city, he drew off his riding gloves and bunched them in his hand.

'This is a surprise,' he said coolly. 'Where did you lot spring from?'

Hern stepped forward, his bold demeanour giving no hint of his earlier doubts.

'We are pleased you could join us. We're the temporary government of the city.' He briefly named each member. 'We've been looking forward to your arrival. We badly need some good strong fighting men to help us keep order.'

'We're not mercenaries for hire,' snapped Krital.

'We know. You're Magharnans, like us. The job of ruling this country is too big for any one of us; that's why we need you—and you need us.'

'I need no one,' sneered Krital. 'You're irrelevant.'

Hern ignored this piece of rudeness. 'Allow me to introduce your fellow council members. Marga here is responsible for the welfare of widows and orphans—unless of course you want to do this?'

Krital shook his head curtly.

'We are reopening the houses of the indigent under less rigid rules. Ustavan is looking into restoring city markets.' Hern waved to a sharp-looking former purveyor. He paused. 'Unless of course you want to do that too?'

'You know I don't,' growled Krital.

'Murdle here is ensuring the supply of fish to the city. Tasmin is investigating the possibility of restoring the currency in some form. Medic Hort is contacting any doctors who have gone into hiding, assisted by Nurse Bedwin who is doing the same for midwives. Your escort, Conal Hunter, is in charge of a local watch system, dealing with incidents of theft and violence. Need I go on?'

'You've made your point.' Krital crossed his arms and tapped his foot irritably. 'What does that make you—and where does it leave me?'

'I'm temporary spokesman for the council until such time as we can identify an appropriate leader. As for you, we were hoping you'd like to take charge of defence. We need an army and yours is the only fighting force left to defend Rolvint.'

'Why should I do that? Why don't I just push aside your little council and get on with things my own way?'

Peri knew that that indeed was the crucial question. He wondered what his father would say.

'Because, sir,' said Hern, 'you listened to a little foreigner when she came to you. I think you see that there is no point destroying the fragile efforts we've made to reconstruct our city. We're not working against you; we'd like to work with you if you'd allow. Surely we've all had enough of chaos and bloodshed. It's time to declare an amnesty and make a new start.'

Krital scanned the faces of those gathered in the entrance hall until his eyes lighted on Peri. He gave a thin-lipped smile.

'All right, falconer, we'll work together for now. On one condition.'

'And that is?' asked Hern nervously.

'That we banish that boy from Rolvint. He shot that foreigner you mentioned. I won't work with you if he's here.'

Hern began to protest but Peri stepped forward.

'No, it's fine, Pa. I'll go if that's the price he wants.'

'Pa?' Krital looked at Hern with new hostility. 'You can forget the offer of co-operation if he's anywhere near me. Unless, that is, you'd like to give me your son so that we can settle our differences *personally*.' He bared his teeth at Peri.

Peri had been carrying a great burden of guilt ever since he'd shot Rain. In a strange way, he felt relieved that he had a means of paying his debt.

'I'll go. But please, just tell me if Rain is all right.'

'She is, no thanks to you, falcon boy.'

'I'm not sending my own son into exile,' protested Hern.

Krital slapped his gloves in his hand. 'I'm in charge of the defence of the country, true?'

'Yes,' agreed Hern.

'Then give me the boy. I've a vacancy for a guard on the road to the port. I'm sure he'll enjoy serving under Morg, my commander in that district.'

So this was his revenge: to send Peri where Krital had just come from and make sure he suffered under his control as an outsider in the bandit army.

'Peri has important work to do here,' countered Hern.

'Really?' drawled Krital. 'More important than mine?'

Peri handed his father the scrolls detailing the foot patrols he had been working on for Conal. 'It really is fine, Pa. He knows we need him. There's no point dragging this out.'

Hern reluctantly agreed, but he couldn't let it rest there. He drew Krital aside and spoke right in his face. 'You treat my boy well, Krital,' he hissed, 'or you'll rack up a personal debt with me that I will insist you pay in full.'

Krital pulled away and laughed. 'I'll treat him exactly as he deserves, falconer. Morg, congratulations, you've just been appointed commander of the western district.' The bald-headed bandit, who had first found Rain hiding from the attack on the convoy, stepped out from among the bodyguards, a malicious grin on his face. 'Take our lad here and induct him into my army. You can have my old quarters as your own.'

'Thanks, boss.' Morg took Peri by the back of his neck. 'You're coming with me, scavenger.'

Krital folded his arms with great satisfaction as he watched Peri being frogmarched out of the palace. 'Now that's settled, I suggest you show me to my living quarters. We need to discuss the position of head of the ruling council, true?'

Morg thought it amusing to lodge Peri in the same hut in which he had shot Rain.

'Here you go, bird boy, your new palace,' he quipped, kicking over the pallet bed and stomping on the straw-filled mattress until it burst.

Peri supposed he should be grateful that the door was unlocked and he was free to move around the camp, but his first few days as a new recruit to Krital's army left him wishing he could bar the entrance and stay inside. The dozen bandits given the job of guarding the pass on which they had once preyed, enjoyed having a target to bully. For them, it passed the boring hours off duty.

It started when one man threw his muddy footwear at Peri when he came into the hall for the evening meal. 'Bird boy, clean my boots.'

Peri debated replying that the bandit should clean them himself, but knew this was a test. If he failed, it would give them the excuse to beat him up. On the surface, they may be reformed characters acting to uphold order, but their old nature lay not very deep beneath. Peri had always had a deep supply of patience in his dealings with wild birds; this was really no different. He had to train them to ignore him. He scooped the boots off the floor and said to the room at large. 'Anyone else?'

The jobs continued to come to him—cooking, fetching and carrying, taking messages up and down the hillside in the middle of the night—but the bandits got less amusement from the falconer than expected. Peri conducted himself with dignity, undertaking the humiliating tasks they demanded of him with no complaint, not letting it touch him, picturing one of the hillside stones shedding rainwater from its surface.

As no one had forbidden him to do so, on his first free afternoon, he returned to the compound and fetched Rogue. Perhaps it had been a little selfish to take the falcon from the mews but it did not feel right to Peri to be without at least one of his birds. When he exercised Rogue, he noted that no one bothered him with pointless errands or insulted him. If the bird hadn't required the peace of his perch for large parts of the day to avoid overstimulation, Peri could've gladly carried him on his wrist at all times.

The novelty of taunting the falconer wore off. Krital had miscalculated. Without his presence to remind his men why the boy was so out of favour, they got distracted by their own concerns. Morg went from being pleased at his appointment to being fiercely worried that he was missing out on the real action in the city. He made frequent trips ostensibly to report, but really just to keep up with news. The bullying reduced to a bearable level, a knee-jerk reaction to any reminder of Peri's difference from the rest of the men guarding the pass, but in truth it was withering away.

One morning, two weeks into his new life, Peri had been given the watch on the road. His companion was stretched out in the sunshine behind a rock, having told Peri to do the ruddy work while he caught up on his sleep. That suited Peri. He could keep an eye on passing traffic while flying Rogue to the lure.

The falconer stood on the summit of a hillock over-looking the track; his bird soared overhead. The emerald green of the late spring grass whipped to and fro in the breeze, white clouds moved swiftly across the sky. Peri had the sensation that the world was in flight, shifting on to the next thing. Rogue sensed it too, skimming the crags with exuberant sweeps, shrieking his joy at mastering the air with his skill.

Towards midday, Peri spotted two men coming up the pass from the direction of Port Bremis. He summoned Rogue by swinging the lure, then hooded him. Unless he wanted to wake his companion—which he didn't—it would be better to confront a pair of strangers with his best defender on his gauntlet. He jogged down the slope and took up position on the road.

'Halt! State your business,' Peri challenged them.

The two men stopped some feet from him, their uncertainty apparent in the confused looks they exchanged.

'We traders from far country,' the younger man said in poor Magharnan.

Peri studied the strange clothing of the pair, the odd moustache covering the speaker's upper lip like some bushy creature Rogue might have hunted. His hair was brown, proving his claim to be a foreigner. The older man had a pepper-and-salt thatch of curls and a deeply lined face. He looked both tired and worried.

'What country?' asked Peri, though he was beginning to guess the answer.

'Holt. We seek the glassmakers. Not know that your country have problem.'

'Problem? That's one way of putting it.' Peri gave a wry smile. 'Why are you here?'

The older man spoke up for the first time. 'I seek my daughter. She is small by your measure,' he indicated in the air, 'long curly hair, blue eyes—very blue.' He clenched his fists against his chest. 'I would give my life to know she is all right.'

'And my brother. Brown hair like mine. A glass trader,' added the other.

Peri held out his free hand. 'Master Torrent, welcome to Magharna.'

'How do you know my name?' gasped the older man.

'Your daughter told me.'

His palm was seized in a vice-like grip. 'Is she well—where is she?'

'She is in the city. And yes, I think she is in good health, now at least.' He thought it best not to mention to her father that he had put an arrow in her shoulder. 'I know she is most anxious to be reunited with you. It's not been an easy time for her.'

'My brother?' the other man asked. 'Is he with her?'

Peri thought back to his first meeting with Rain and realized that he knew the answer to that too. 'I'm sorry, but I fear your brother was killed soon after arrival, on this very pass. Rain was the only one to survive the attack.'

'Attack? My brother?' The younger man struggled to follow Peri's terrible words.

'I'm so sorry, but he is dead. It happened months back. Please, come with me and I will make sure you get an escort to the city. Rain can tell you what happened.'

'Can you not take us?' asked Torrent. He released his grip on Peri's hand and put an arm around his nephew to comfort him.

'Unfortunately not, sir. I'm not allowed. But I'll make sure you have a reliable guard. Your daughter is a favourite of the chief of our army; you'll be well treated, I promise.'

Rain had been given Ret's old bedroom for her

recovery. He didn't seem to mind, making do with a mattress in the cupboard he had hidden in, preferring to remain with her now his old home had been turned over to the new government. Mikel had found her a bed and mattress through means known only to him, and Ret had mysteriously turned up with a bright gold satin bedspread one evening and laid it over her with no explanation.

Rain didn't remain in bed long. After two days' rest, she set up a worktable in the window and began again with her designs. She had many visitors, including Helgis who, she suspected, came mainly to tempt Ret outside into the gardens, and Bel, who brought her schoolwork with her to keep her company, but none of them was Peri.

'Where's your brother?' she asked Bel a week into her stay in the palace.

Under orders not to upset Rain with news about Peri's punishment, Bel muttered something evasive about him having something to do on the hunting grounds.

'When will he be back?'

'I'm really not sure. When he can.' Bel smudged her slate with her sleeve, wiping out the last answer. 'He was really upset that he hurt you.'

But not worried enough to come and see how she was doing now, thought Rain. That didn't seem like the Peri she knew, more like the falconer who had left her at the bath-house months ago. Had her letter so destroyed anything he had felt for her that he preferred not to visit? The idea that this was true formed a hard knot in her chest, causing more pain than the residual effect of her wound.

Stamping on the stairs heralded the arrival of one of her most frequent visitors. Krital marched into the room, wearing a long scarlet robe but with none of the slashing favoured by the jettans. Their style was now out of fashion.

'General.' Rain stood up and curtseyed. She knew him to be a tough and brutal man, but his new responsibilities had changed him for the better. He was working with the government and making sure his army kept within limits. But she had no illusions he had suddenly become a saint; he just saw his best interests now lay in preserving order rather than wreaking havoc.

He took her hand and kissed it. 'My fey lady, what have you made today?'

She showed him the latest design, a tree in blossom, which she intended for Bel.

'Excellent, true?'

Bel murmured her agreement.

Krital rubbed his hands together. 'I've come with good news. My council has found enough glassmakers to start up one of the furnaces. We need new windows to replace the broken ones.'

'Yes, indeed. Do you have materials as well?' asked Rain.

Krital waved a hand dismissively. 'Someone's dealing with that. But I came to say that we decided you should take charge. I proposed it and Hern seconded it. You're not to do any heavy work, mind, but you are, as of this moment, the representative for the glassmakers and have a seat on the council.'

'Me?' Rain's voice squeaked with astonishment. 'But I'm an outsider. Why?'

'Because you can't fiddle around with fragments for ever, fey lady. Do you accept the task?'

'Well, yes.'

'Thought you would. Put some of your magic in our glass for me, won't you?' He strode out, bellowing orders as he went.

Bel put her slate aside. 'I believe that man has a soft spot for you.'

'I'm his lucky charm,' admitted Rain, awkwardly aware that she was now the favourite of the man who had murdered her cousin. But the amnesty meant no justice would be given to his victims; the page had turned on many ugly sins on both sides of the bandit's balance sheet. She rolled up the last mobile on her workbench and handed it to Bel. 'Looks like I need to find my forge and see where things stand.'

Rain was pleased with her new workforce. The glass-makers who had been left behind in Rolvint tended to be the apprentices who had not had the means to flee the capital during the troubles. They'd hidden along with everyone else and only felt safe enough to crawl from their bolt-holes now that the palace glass foundry had reopened. Due to the fire risk it posed, the foundry itself was on the eastern outskirts of Rolvint in an area Rain did not know well, a district of orchards and tanning fields.

The most urgent need was for clear panes. Many of the foundry tools had been looted but Rain and her apprentices salvaged enough to begin the production of crown glass. This was one of Rain's favourite processes. After the molten gather had been blown into a cylinder shape, it was then spun on a potter's wheel to make it flatten and spread outwards. The wavy sheets of glass were then cut into small panes and fitted in lead frames in the houses able to afford the replacement, paying with bartered goods and services until the new currency was made ready. The first building to be done was Krital's office in the palace complex. After that, Rain insisted that the houses of the indigent be next in line before she would consider any private commissions. Those who dealt with the little glassmaker soon learnt to respect her determination to get her way. It took only a few days working for her for the apprentices to become staunchly loyal; they would not hear a word against her, especially from those still suspicious of the outsider.

When Torrent finally caught up with his daughter, he found her checking the latest batch of glass for flaws. He stood for a moment, drinking in the sight of her bending over the workbench, her hair flopping forward as she rubbed at a bubble trapped under the surface.

'Raindrop,' he called softly.

She sprang up. 'Papa!' She couldn't believe it! He was here!

Torrent crossed the workroom in three big steps to sweep her into his arms. 'My God, girl, don't do that to me again! I thought you had to be dead.'

'I'm not; I'm fine.' She clung on tight, thinking that she'd probably never let go now she had him back.

'More than fine from what I hear. I called in first on the palace and they told me all about you. I met a splendid chap called Mikel who seems to think you float above the ground, you are so perfect. Even the thug they've got in charge of the army adores you and I noticed one of your creations hanging in pride of place in his office.' Torrent eased her back to the ground. 'He said you were injured by an arrow.'

'Peri shot me—but it was an accident,' she added rapidly seeing the thundercloud gather on her father's brow.

'I think I met your Peri.' Torrent's frown deepened. 'Out on the pass across the mountains. He was the one who told me where you were. But he didn't mention wounding you.'

'Peri? In the mountains? That's not right.'

Torrent shrugged. 'Maybe he's not your one—but he did seem to know you well.'

'What's he doing out there?'

'On guard. Said he wasn't allowed back into the city for some reason.'

Some of the delight on Rain's face leached away.

She had been wrong: Peri had not turned from her; he had been forced to go. 'Krital. He hates Peri—not because he shot me but because he took me from him in the first place.'

Torrent couldn't follow her reasoning, not that it mattered just then. Soon he'd have her back home, away from these Magharnans with their chaotic state and their fragile government. 'I see we have much to catch up on, love. But first, is it true that your cousin is dead? I'm here with Timber; he's waiting outside.'

Rain bit her bottom lip. 'Yes, I'm afraid it is. He didn't even make it as far as Rolvint.'

'I'm very sorry about that. Come, let's go and tell Timber together. He already knows the truth but he should hear it from you in person.'

Learning that Rain's family had arrived to reclaim her, Hern insisted on holding a celebratory meal for them all that night. Katia for once was happy to welcome Rain to her table, hoping that this would mean the foreigner would soon be gone and her family return to normal.

'It's not that I wish her ill—indeed I hope she is happy when she gets home,' Katia confessed to her husband as they prepared the rabbit stew together. 'But she's no good for Peri. I can't get past the fact that she's the reason he's not here tonight.'

Rain stopped in the doorway, embarrassed to be caught eavesdropping. Katia's attitude to her was no surprise, but this confirmed what she had feared. She only hoped her father hadn't overheard.

'Um, Papa, can I introduce you to Hern and Katia Falconer?' She tugged him into the room, Timber just behind them. Her father was smiling, so she guessed his basic Magharnan learned in Port Bremis and on the road hadn't been good enough to catch what was said.

Timber accepted the Falconers' commiserations on the loss of his brother with suitable gravity. His eyes glistened with tears as he thumped his chest.

'I feel I've lost half of myself,' he said, before tucking heartily into a bowl of stew.

Rain spent the evening acting as translator between her family and her new friends. Hern and Torrent hit it off from the start, as Rain thought they might. Timber was frustrated by his lack of fluency so spent the evening grilling Bel for new words and phrases. Rain made a mental note to thank her later for putting up with him.

'So, Rain, what will you do now?' Timber asked her towards the end of the meal.

'She's coming home with us, of course,' answered Torrent, holding his daughter's hand in his lap.

But what about Peri? thought Rain. Her father had made it clear that he expected her to go back with him immediately. Now he was here, she realized she no longer wanted to leave. There was so much she and Peri still had to settle between them. Would he still want her after she had left him to go to the bandits? At the very least, she had to see him one last time to explain. She had never actually told him that she loved him and now it might be too late.

'We'd be very sad to lose her,' said Hern. 'And, seriously, I'm not sure our general will let her go. He seems to think she guarantees the success of our attempt to rebuild our shattered nation. We're only barely keeping him under control as it is. We need you, Rain.'

Katia gave a snort.

'Uncle,' Timber said after Rain translated Hern's speech for the two visitors, 'you should bear in mind that my lovely cousin has been put in charge of the glassmaking industry—an amazing opportunity.' Timber smiled at her, smoothing his moustache, drawing what Rain considered quite unnecessary attention to it.

Bel giggled.

'The girl needs to be in her own home with her own people, Hern,' said Katia, pronouncing her sentence on the troublemaker.

'Eventually,' countered Timber when Rain had translated for him, 'but such talent as hers should not be squandered. She may be just what your industry needs to get back off the ground.'

'The decision, my dear, is yours,' said Torrent.

'I think,' said Rain, 'I think we should stay—just for a bit, Papa.' She repeated her decision in Magharnan.

Hern filled her cup. 'I'm glad—and I know someone else will be too.' He gave her a wink.

279

Shard 16
Bright Orange

Determined that the least she could do for Peri before she had to leave was win an end to his exile, Rain waited by the door to Krital's office. Inside, he was briefing his men and giving them orders with a characteristic mixture of bribes and threats.

'We've only got twenty square miles or so under our control, true? That's like a clean spot on a cow's bum; the rest of the beast is a ruddy mess. I want the whole of Magharna sorted by the end of next month.'

'That's impossible,' whined one commander. 'We've not got enough men.'

'Then recruit some more. Find out who used to do the local law enforcement and drag their sorry butts back on the case.'

'We're being turned away by some of the jettan estates,' added another.

'Then beat down their gates. We're the government now; no one holds out against us. The man who tells me he's secured the road to the border with Kir gets the next bonus.'

'How much this time, boss . . . er . . . general?'

'A mansion on Peacock Street. Roof on, most windows repaired. I'll bump it to the top of the waiting list with the glassmakers if you get this done. So get out there and do what I'm paying you miserable rascals to do!'

The bandit officers filed quickly out of the office. They were a motley bunch, the only sign of uniform being the red sash Krital insisted all his men wore.

'Next!' roared Krital, scaring his secretary, Nighman, into dropping his record of the meeting. 'Nighman, you're such a frightened rabbit.'

'Yes, boss,' agreed the secretary.

Rain poked her head round the door. 'Just me.'

Krital beckoned her in and put his feet up on the table, his hands linked across his chest.

'Do you think I'm getting soft, fey lady?'

She gulped back her laughter. 'No.'

'I'm sitting around all day, barking orders. I think I'm becoming one of those bureaucrats I hated.' Krital looked a little lost, surrounded by paper in the elegant surroundings of his office. With his unshaven jaw and meaty arms, he was as out of place as an oak block in an ice sculpture.

Rain perched on the chair opposite his. 'Then why not go out with your men sometimes? Go on patrol. Join in the training. I don't think you're made for this.' She gestured to the files waiting for his attention and the lines of people queuing up to see him outside.

'You're right.' He yawned. 'I thought I'd like running a country, being the power, but to be honest, it's boring. Only Nighman's in his element. True, scholar?'

'True, boss,' replied Nighman, amusing Rain with his lapse into bandit slang.

'Met your father,' Krital continued. 'Wants to take you home, doesn't he?' He reached up to touch her mobile of the horse, making the glass tinkle.

'Wouldn't you in his place?' Rain asked cautiously.

'Probably. So what are you going to do?'

'I was thinking of asking you a favour,' admitted Rain.

He laughed. 'Got someone you want me to get rid of? That idiot of a cousin of yours perhaps?'

Rain found the suggestion tasteless seeing that he had already caused the death of Shadow. It reminded her that Krital, however much he had changed since leaving banditry behind, still had ugly sides to his character. He needed careful handling at all times.

'No, nothing like that. I want Peri back. I know you sent him away, but I really want him to return to the city.'

Krital's face set in harsh lines. 'Sorry, fey lady, can't do that. Bird boy and I don't mix well.'

Rain stood up. 'All right.'

'That's it? You're not going to argue this any further?'

'No. I'm just going to make arrangements to go home.'

Krital slashed at the mobile, ripping some of the delicate threads so that glass showered on to his desk. 'You can't do that!'

Nighman ducked behind his writing table.

'Why not?' Rain held very still, knowing that, when unleashed, Krital's temper could be dangerous; but she stood her ground.

'Because you bring us good luck,' Krital blurted out before he could stop himself. He looked embarrassed to admit his superstition.

'I don't feel very lucky when one of my best friends is exiled from the city.'

'He hurt you—he deserved it.' He turned his back to her and stared out of the window.

'But it wasn't about that, was it?' Rain approached the desk and began collecting up the pieces. 'You were annoyed about what happened that first day.'

'He made a mockery of me.'

'No, he didn't. He gave you a choice and you picked the horse over me.' She tried to lighten the situation with humour. 'If you think about it, I'm the one who should be upset, not you.'

Krital turned around to face her. 'You'll stay if I let that bird boy back?'

'Yes, at least for a while, until I'm not needed.' She rubbed her hands nervously—her father had not given up the idea of leaving as soon as possible.

He frowned at his mangled mobile. 'Can you mend it?'

'Yes.'

'Do so and the bird boy can return.'

'Thank you.' Rain swept the pieces into her apron pocket.

'But, fey lady?'

'Yes, general.'

'Tell him to keep out of my way.'

Torrent sat beside his daughter as she mended the mobile. She did not break her concentration even after a full day at the forge, painstakingly matching colours and weaving the cotton web. The candle was guttering low in its socket by the time she was near to completion.

Torrent yawned. 'Isn't it well past the hour you should be in bed?'

'No, Papa, I've got to finish this. It's Peri's ticket back.'

'Shame to see you working with these sharp fragments. I can't help thinking your talent is going to waste. We need to get you back to the stained-glass windows.'

'Oh, but it hasn't really been a waste.' She riffled through the shards, selecting a chocolate-brown piece. 'I've got lots of ideas—I've even done a few designs. You know the summer palace I should've been working on? Well, I spent a lot of time there and made some sketches. I thought the windows should be gateways to the fey kingdoms the Magharnans talk about in their tales, magical doors for the imagination. There's a lot of work to do here.'

Torrent let his daughter rattle on, enjoying the expressions passing across her face even as she peered carefully at her mobile. He then realized what she was really saying.

'You . . . you want to stay?' He shook his head. 'No, no, you can't. I want you safe. This place is going to be as volatile as a flawed batch in the furnace for a long time to come. I can't leave you here.'

Rain bit her bottom lip, turning the shard in her fingers. 'But it's complicated, Papa. There's Peri to think about.'

'You have an understanding?' Her father did not look pleased at the prospect.

'Not exactly,' she answered truthfully.

'Then you don't owe him anything and you are free to go home. He can come with us if he wants. See what develops between you somewhere safe.'

Rain sighed. It wasn't just Peri. She felt responsible for what happened in Rolvint.

After another thirty minutes, her father yawned again. 'That's it for me. I'm turning in. Promise you won't stay up much longer?'

'I'm almost finished.'

He kissed the top of her head. 'Good night, Raindrop.'

'Good night.'

Rain threaded her needle and lit a second candle, dripping the wax on to the window ledge to keep it steady. Mobiles were much easier to make from scratch. This reconstruction was a fiddly matter, but she was determined to get it done. Peri should not have to spend another day out of the city on her account.

She heard footsteps approaching softly behind her.

'Ret?' No, it couldn't be him. He had gone to bed in his little cupboard bedroom some hours ago. 'Who's there?'

'Just me, cousin.' Timber stepped out of the darkness. Rain wondered how long he'd been watching her; she hadn't heard him climb the stairs.

'What are you doing here?'

'Come to keep you company. You're so busy during the day at the forge, and in the evening you're with the Falconers; I hardly get any time with you on my own.'

Which was the way she preferred it.

'It's very late.'

'I know. You're working too hard.' He rested his hands on the back of her chair, examining her creation over her shoulder. When Peri had done that in the past, she had felt safely surrounded; with Timber, she thought of nothing but being trapped.

'That's not really your business.'

'I wish I could make it mine.' He lightly ran his finger along the chain of her necklace to her pulse. She knew he could feel it spike with alarm. 'You must stop.' He shook the last piece of glass out of her fingers and pulled her up from the chair.

'I don't want to. I think you should leave. And, please, let go of me.'

He smiled a shade hungrily. 'Don't you like me, Rain? I always thought you had a bit of a crush on me as a little girl.'

'Then you thought wrong.'

'Everything points to us getting married, you must see that—my role as sole successor to your father now my brother is lost to us, your new position here, deciding the direction of the Magharnan glass industry. Between us, we could make a fortune for our family.'

'I'm not interested in such things.' She wondered if she should call Ret. Timber would have to back off if another person was in the room.

Timber traced his finger down her cheek then tapped the end of her nose. 'You should be. Sleep on it. Let me know if I feature in your dreams, my love.' He hovered, making Rain fear that he meant to kiss her, but fortunately he thought better of it. 'Goodnight, cousin.'

Rain shuddered as he walked away. That had been a near thing. She would have to make sure she wasn't cornered by him again.

Rain used some of Mikel's favourite curses as she realized this batch of glass was flawed. Something must have gone wrong in the mixture—it was too brittle and cloudy.

'Tobart!' she called, summoning her head apprentice.

He ran into the office, tugging his cap off his head as a sign of respect. 'Mistress Rain?'

'Look!'

'By the Master, I've not seen that before. What's wrong with it?' The young man appeared genuinely peeved.

'I imagine someone got the measurements wrong when they weighed out the sand—or the sample was impure. Who was in charge this morning?'

He flushed. 'That would be me. But I swear that I didn't mess up. I was really careful, like you trained us to be.'

Rain sighed, wondering if her father had this trouble telling off his apprentices. Tobart must've made a mistake, but he was so sincere she couldn't find it in her heart to give him a proper scolding.

'Check the scales and make sure everyone is clear about the procedure. We'll have to discard today's gather and begin again tomorrow.'

'Yes, Mistress Rain. Sorry, Mistress Rain.'

She folded her arms. 'We all make mistakes. My father always says it is how we learn. He'll be about somewhere. Why don't you ask him to help you set this right?'

Tobart's glum face brightened. 'I'll do that. Thank you.' He rushed out to get to work.

A round of applause broke out behind her. Rain turned to the window and found Peri at the open casement, looking tanned by the sun and fitter than ever. Her face lit up with pleasure—he was back!

'Masterfully done,' he congratulated her.

'Peri! Come in!'

He didn't wait for a second invitation but took the most direct route, vaulting through the window.

'I understand you earned my reprieve for me.' He didn't touch her, not being sure of his welcome. 'I'm very grateful.'

She beamed at him. But why didn't he greet her properly? 'You should never have been sent away in the first place, but that's Krital for you.'

'I hear you've got him wrapped around your little finger.' Peri studied the glass samples on her desk, avoiding her eye. He couldn't help feeling jealous of everyone she had charmed. She looked beautiful, dressed in a bright orange tunic and loose trousers with her long hair fastened back in a matching ribbon, like a flame from one of her furnaces.

Rain shook her head. 'Hardly.'

'I deserved my banishment. If I hadn't been so quick to take things into my own hands, thinking you needed rescuing, I wouldn't have hurt you.'

She closed the distance between them and touched his cheek with her palm. 'Peri, it was an accident. I don't blame you—you thought I was in danger.'

'You could've died.'

'I didn't.' She let her hand drop to reach for his fingers. She laced them together with hers. 'I'm sorry I hurt you when I left.'

He rubbed the back of his neck. He couldn't deny she had crushed his feelings like a glass bead trodden underfoot.

'I let you think I didn't . . . well . . . *care* enough to do what you asked.'

'You care?' He risked a smile.

'It seems that I do. And it didn't work—you still came after me, revealing what I had always suspected.'

'What's that?'

'That under that calm exterior of yours, you are as reckless as me.'

He laughed and pulled her to his chest. 'I sent your father to you. Did he tell you?'

'He wasn't sure if you were my Peri or not, seeing that you failed to mention that you'd put an arrow in me.'

He groaned. 'Don't remind me.' Though he liked the sound of 'my Peri'.

'He wants to take me home soon.'

'But your home's here now.'

But she needed more than that to stay. If he didn't propose to her soon, she would be on a ship to Tigral. 'My father would like a word with you.'

Peri ran his fingers through her curls. 'I'm trembling in my shoes already.' He gave a shudder that was only half an act.

'You should be. Oh, and Mikel wants a word.'

'No, he doesn't. He just wants to thump me.'

She nuzzled his chest. 'I won't let him.'

'May I kiss you?' he whispered in her ear. He wanted to restore the closeness they had enjoyed before he risked asking her to marry him. The gap that had grown up between them needed a bridge for him to feel safe enough to cross.

'You don't need to ask.'

As he leaned down, Helgis burst into the room, closely followed by Ret.

'Not again!' complained Peri, shifting position to tuck her under his arm, his perfect moment spoiled, his bridge swept away in the flood of the boys' entry. 'Can't you knock?'

Helgis looked entirely unrepentant. 'You've got to come. Krital sent us to get you back into the palace, Rain. He doesn't want you stuck out here.'

'Why? What's happened?' asked Rain.

'A big party of jettans and their men are approaching the city,' explained Ret. 'We think they're coming to try and seize control.'

'By force?' Peri frowned.

'Why else come marching in with weapons drawn?' said Helgis.

Rain quickly ran through what had to be done to secure the foundry. 'We'll have to evacuate the forge and extinguish the fires. Give me a moment.' She ran to the door, shouting for her father and Tobart.

Peri closed the shutters and picked up Rain's work-bag and cloak. 'Come on, boys, let's go.'

'We should try talking first,' suggested Hern. 'Invite their representatives in and see if we can avoid a fight.'

The ruling council was meeting in the old throne room of the Master, among the marble columns fashioned into the shape of a grove of trees. The mess left by the rioters had been cleared and the chamber restored to its former glory. The throne, too big to steal, stood empty; the council sat instead around a long oval table brought in for their use. Rain had a seat at it, as did Hern, Conal, and Sly. But as their survival was the matter under debate, this session had been declared open to all interested parties, so Peri, Ret, her father, Timber, Mikel, and the other Falconers observed from the side of the room.

Krital lounged in his chair at the head of the table. 'Why bother with talking? They won't want to put themselves under the likes of us. Remember these pig-brains think we're dung. I've got my men waiting. We can take them.'

'But with the loss of how many?' interjected Conal. 'They've got over a thousand men with them. They must have been planning this for some time and pulled everyone together in hopes we'd give in to their superior numbers.'

'We've enough food supplies to withstand a siege,' said Sly, raising one possible course of action.

'The wells are in good order,' added Katia.

'But we've not enough men to guard the entire circuit of the walls,' said Peri. 'Rolvint's not a defendable city—it wasn't built for that purpose. I'm with my father: let's see what negotiation can get us.'

Krital flicked his council papers angrily. Rain could tell that he was impatient with making decisions this way. He'd prefer to stick with what he knew and that was force.

'We wouldn't lose anything, would we, general, if we tried talking?' asked Rain.

'I suppose not. Stinking jettan class—just like them to think they can walk back in as if they still owned the place.'

'Then we must show them that they don't. If we act like a responsible government, then they cannot claim that we aren't needed. We'll keep the people on our side.'

Krital rubbed his chin. 'That's a good point, fey lady. I hadn't thought of that. The jettans can't do anything if the city stands united against them.'

'I haven't heard anyone shouting for their return, have you?' asked Hern drily.

'The silence has been deafening,' agreed Conal.

Krital slapped his papers. 'That's it then. I move that we get the ringleaders of that miserable lot in here and give them a choice: work with us under our authority or get lost. What do you think?'

A rumble of agreement resounded in the room.

Krital gestured to Conal. 'Go get them, hunter. Take

bird boy with you.' Krital knew full well that Peri was in the room but so far had refused to look at him. 'I'm sure the jettans will appreciate being invited in by a couple of scavengers.'

'Will do,' said Conal, rising from his chair.

'Don't forget to take your creatures with you. I think that would be a nice touch, true?'

After many protests, the jettans finally agreed to send in a deputation. They demanded that the city provide hostages in their place, so Conal and Murdle the fisherman were left behind as a guarantee of safe passage. The jettans were led into the council chamber by Kirn, whom Rain had last seen lording it over the workers on the summer palace site. The former chief adviser to the Master still wore his fancy slashed robes, today's being an ostentatiously clean white silk edged with gold. He obviously hadn't yet caught up with the news that this fashion had fallen out of favour. Markets were selling simply-cut gowns and tunics, a pattern chosen for being the exact opposite to the old style. Rain's own dress in forest green, that she had slipped into after discarding her work-soiled tunic, exemplified the new taste, but something told her Kirn would not notice.

'This is outrageous!' the jettan declared, striding into the throne room as if he had a right to it. 'You greet us with the impure and claim to be in charge. I have never heard anything more preposterous in my life!'

Rain, standing next to Krital at the head of the council table, feared that the former bandit would lose his temper, but he surprised her. 'Who is this joker?' he asked with mild amusement. 'Anyone know?'

'I think you'll find he's called Kirn. He's the one who was in charge of the summer palace,' whispered Rain as the jettan delegation scowled at the people gathered to see them.

'Ah, a builder,' Krital said in a carrying voice. 'We need builders, don't we, Hern?'

'Aye. Lots of work for a man who knows his hammer from his chisel,' agreed the falconer, cracking his knuckles.

'Kirn the builder, and friends, welcome to the new Rolvint,' announced Krital jovially. 'As you can see, since you so hurriedly left us all to rot, we've made a few changes. We now have a ruling council and we are expanding our control over Magharna bit by bit, restoring order after the chaos you lot caused. My name's General Krital. My fellow members are drawn from all the professions. No one gets a seat at our table unless they've got something to offer the new Magharna.'

'It isn't your Magharna, bandit!' spluttered Kirn. 'I have a thousand soldiers camped not far from your gates. You should be suing for mercy, not insulting me.'

Krital's eyes turned hard. 'You've got that wrong, Jettan. When you walked out on your responsibilities, you lost any claim to rule this country.'

Rain could sense the heat rising in the room. Krital did not have it in him to be a peace maker, and from the looks of it, neither did Kirn. She didn't blame Ret for nudging Helgis and both of them slipping out of the room. The meeting was likely to turn ugly.

'And what were you doing, eh, bandit?' sneered Kirn. 'I know exactly who and what you are. It was your thugs raiding our goods that got us into this mess in the first place!'

'Yeah, and why were we out there? 'Cause you lot had booted us out of your precious city, telling us we were scum and of no use to anyone. We declared war on you and your sort when you gave us no choice. Then you fled and, well, that scum has done a better job of keeping things safe round here than you ever did. Ask the people who they want looking after them. My men aren't saints, but at least they don't run at the first sign of trouble.'

Kirn waved his arm at the throne, his sleeve wafting like a flurry of snow. 'People? What have the people got to do with it? Rolvint is the Master. He is the nation.'

Krital was about to respond when a high voice spoke out from behind the throne.

'I am glad you realize that, Jettan Kirn.' A boy stepped into sight, dressed in stunning robes of golden fabric and the white crystal crown of Magharna.

'Master!' gasped Kirn, his knees bending before he could think twice about it.

Rain managed not to smile. She knew that Ret had

been hiding something from them all. He had concealed his robes of state and regalia throughout the crisis, only displaying them when he knew that they would be most needed.

'I am gladdened to see my faithful subjects returning to the fold.' Ret didn't sound too convinced. 'But you cannot be surprised that, during your regrettable absence, I have made some changes to how I run things.'

'Of course not, Master. Just let me get rid of these bandits and scavengers for you and we can discuss what needs to be done.'

Ret swept his robes round in a practised gesture and took a seat on the empty throne.

'Ah, Kirn, I see that you do not yet understand. The changes are that these bandits and scavengers, as you call them, are now my most trusted ministers. The jettan families proved sadly lacking in constancy and faith so I was obliged to find replacements.'

'But Master!'

Ret's expression conveyed every bit of scorn he felt for his old protectors. 'Do you question my actions?'

'No, of course, but—'

'Did you not just say that I am the nation?'

'Yes, I did, but—'

'Then you should be asking for my mercy because just at the moment I'm feeling very angry with you all.'

'Sire!'

'You left me to starve in my empty shell of a palace.

The only one who cared enough to come looking for me was a foreigner.' Ret held out his hand to Rain. She took it and curtseyed. 'The only ones to protect me were scavengers and bondsmen.' Ret beckoned Peri and Mikel to his side. 'Even my outcast bandits came to my aid when I asked them to restore peace for my people.' He nodded regally to Krital, who appeared to be enjoying the show even if his memory of what had happened differed in some vital aspects.

'But Master, you can't—'

'I can, and I will. Here are my orders: disband your men. Those that wish to enrol in my new army should present themselves to the general or one of his commanders. The jettan families are welcome to return to Rolvint but they must understand they have to earn their place like everyone else.'

Kirn looked confused. Nothing that he knew was the same. 'Please think, sire. You are throwing away centuries of our traditions.'

Ret flashed a grin, a glimpse of the impish boy shining through. 'Yes, and making new ones. The class system is no more. No one is impure.' He rose. 'The Master has spoken.'

Knowing it was best to quit while he was ahead, Ret walked from the room through a door Helgis held open for him.

'Well, I . . . I—' spluttered Kirn.

'Yes, Jettan Kirn?' gloated Krital. 'It seems you've got your orders. In a few minutes, news will be spreading through the city that the Master is back. I imagine your men will hear the same. I can't think they'd want to refuse a direct command.'

Kirn wasted no more time arguing when he knew he had lost. The delegation departed swiftly; though they muttered angrily, they were powerless now their authority had been trumped.

Krital waited for the double doors to close behind them before guffawing. 'What a boy! Perhaps there's more to this Master stuff than I thought. He did a damn good job, true? Call him back, someone.'

Rain went off in search of Ret, locating him by the sound of laughter as he and Helgis relished their victory. She found the two boys in a cellar hidden behind a secret door in one of the antechambers. The room was filled with treasures and several ceremonial robes, though she thought they had chosen the most impressive one for the Master's appearance. Ret had done magnificently to preserve these priceless artefacts for the nation.

'You're wanted, your masterfulness,' she said.

'Coming!' Ret called. 'I'll just lock up.' He used the same pentagonal key to seal the room. 'This is a secret, right? I told Helgis about it a while ago but I don't want Krital to know where this is.'

'Understood,' said Rain. 'Your faithful bandits do have serious flaws.'

He grinned. 'Er . . . yes, they do. But I prefer them to two-faced cowards like Kirn.'

Rain took the boys back to the throne room, to find the room had been rearranged in their absence. The table had been moved so that the throne now stood at its head. Krital had shifted his seat to the right-hand place. The council stood up when Ret entered. Peri came over and looped his arm around Rain's waist. 'I'm impressed, Master. Welcome back,' said Peri.

Krital gave a shallow bow, the first he'd ever performed. 'Master, the ruling council would like to invite you to resume your throne.'

Ret was taken aback. 'Me?'

'I suppose we could ask someone else,' Krital said drily, 'but we decided we'd got used to the old one. What do you think?'

'Really?'

Krital laughed. 'Yeah, really.'

Hern spoke up. 'It would not be quite like before, Ret, I mean, Master, you have to understand that. You'd be working with us. You'd be our figurehead. But the country needs someone it can rally round.'

'And you're it, sprout,' said Peri in a low voice.

Ret turned to Rain. 'Do you think I should?'

'No question. I already told you that you'd make an excellent Master given the chance.'

Ret cast a speaking glance at Helgis who gave him a sober nod. 'I'm behind you.'

Squaring his shoulders, Ret faced the council. 'Then I accept.'

Shard 17
Apple Green

While the most stubborn jettans decided to return to their estates to moan about the loss of the old ways, the majority of their followers chose to join the new army. Krital finally found his vocation bullying his new recruits into shape, taking a bloodless revenge on them for all the years he had been harried by their kind into living on the margins of society. He resigned his leadership of the council to Ret, handing over Nighman and a vast pile of unopened files.

'Here you are, Master,' he said with evident satisfaction. 'Power behind the throne, that's me, not a ruddy scribe.'

Foreseeing himself rapidly drowning in responsibilities, Ret immediately appointed Hern as his deputy and delegated the task of sorting out the affairs of state to a hand-picked group of twelve men and women. Katia and Hern also relieved him of the paperwork, insisting that he be allowed time 'to be a boy' as they put it.

Helgis took more direct action by blacking his eye in a boisterous wrestling match in the throne room.

Hearing the commotion from his office where he was working with Conal on the police patrols, Peri took Ret with him to his quarters to treat the injury.

'Best thing for that is ice, but we don't have any,' Peri admitted, putting a cold cloth on the eye instead.

'We will do soon. The looters left the door open on the ice house but it wasn't damaged,' said Ret. 'Helgis and I checked this morning.'

'I thought Tutor Nighman was supposed to be giving you both lessons.'

'Yes, well . . . '

'Have you become familiar yet with my father's application of a wooden spoon to the top of a head?'

'No. He wouldn't. I'm Master.'

'He would. To him, you'll always be Ret first.'

Thinking about that, Ret smiled. 'Good.'

Holding the cloth in place, Ret wandered over to Rogue, sleeping in his niche in the corner of the room. He ran his finger lightly over the falcon's breast feathers. 'So, Peri, when are you going to marry Rain?'

'W-what?' Peri dropped the bandage he was putting back in his falconer's bag.

'Don't tell me you aren't thinking about it. The pair of you are so soppy when you're together, Helgis and I are a bit fed up. We talked about it and decided that if you get married, you can start acting normally. We won't have to worry about walking in on you stealing kisses from her and all that icky stuff.'

Peri wasn't so sure about that.

Ret folded his arms and leant back against the wall, his bruised eye a strange contrast to his silken robes. 'You'd better hurry up because her father is talking about taking her home and that cousin of hers is hanging around her all the time. He told your mother that they're unofficially engaged.'

'He did what!'

'I heard him, last night at supper. Slimy goat. Even your mother didn't sound too pleased.'

'Yes, I think she's finally forgiven Rain for letting me shoot her.' Katia had relented now that she no longer saw Rain as a threat to her son.

'Oh come on, Peri! I couldn't bear it if Rain married him just because you were too slow to ask her. He'd take her back to Holt and I want her here.'

'We all want her here.'

'I don't understand you. Why aren't you at the forge? That other man is. And she's started on the first of my windows for the summer palace. You should at least go and look.'

Peri practically ran across the city to reach Rain's workshop. He had no rational explanation for why he felt such a sense of urgency. Ret had purposely spurred him on, Peri knew that, but he felt impelled to settle this either way today. Rain liked him, that was plain, but he worried that she didn't love him enough to give up her old life.

If that was the case, he'd offer to go with her instead. She shouldn't be the one to make all the sacrifices.

Uncharacteristically ruffled, like one of his birds on a gusty day, Peri arrived outside the forge. He ran his hand over his hair and straightened his tunic, then walked in.

The work had finished for the afternoon. The apprentices were cleaning up the foundry, chatting happily. Torrent sat in their midst, peeling the rind off an apple as he smiled at their tall tales.

'Where's Rain?' Peri asked.

'Ah, the falconer,' said Torrent. 'I want a word with you.'

'Could you just give me a few minutes with Rain first, sir?' Peri edged towards her office, guessing that was where she would be.

'No, I cannot. I've been having a little talk with her about you. You and I have some things to sort out, young man.'

'What things?' Peri's old feelings of inadequacy rushed back. He was a scavenger. A man like Torrent would want someone much better for his daughter.

'Don't look so scared. Rain doesn't want to go home with me. My Magharnan is not very good yet, but I have enough to ask a simple question. Do you love Rain?'

Peri was very conscious of the audience of apprentices, none of whom were even pretending to work now. He would never live this down if he admitted his feelings then Rain rejected him.

'Yes, I do. I'd give my life for hers.'

Torrent nodded. 'I understand you've already proved that on more than one occasion.'

'I want her happiness above anything.'

'Good. You'll do.'

Peri gaped. 'Is that it?'

'Yes—I trust my daughter's judgement. Or do you want me to ask you some more?'

'Er . . . , no.'

'Have a bit of apple.' Torrent held out a slice.

Peri took it automatically.

'Like it?'

'Yes, sir.'

'Sweet with a sharp edge, so never boring. Seems like you and I have the same taste.'

Understanding they were discussing something other than Magharnan apples, Peri nodded. 'And it's a flavour I find I can't live without.'

'She'll drive you mad.'

'Probably.'

'You'll argue frequently.'

'I know.'

'Like I said, you'll do.'

Rain wandered out of the back door of her office into the orchard across the lane. She had her sketchbook with her, wanting to draw one of the trees from life for her window design. The late afternoon sun cast long shadows across the ground like dark slashes in the earth. The sky glowed, intense orange on the horizon, fading to pink, then to blue above her head. Swallows revolved in the air, transforming the catching of their meal into an elaborate dance.

'Rain?'

She looked up from her sketch to see Timber standing before her. She was tired of him springing out on her at unexpected moments. It was making her nervous.

'It is time, my dear.'

'Time for what?' she asked cautiously, rubbing at the charcoal line she had just drawn. She had vowed never to be alone with him again, but it was impossible to avoid him completely.

'I've given you an opportunity to consider my proposal. I'd like to announce our engagement to your father tonight. I've got pressing business back in Holt and I've been discussing arrangements with some of the tradesmen here for bringing in the goods they need. Further delay will lose us money.'

Rain decided she had to stop this once and for all. Placing her sketch on the ground she stood up and brushed off her hands.

'Cousin Timber, thank you for asking me to marry you, but really I have to refuse. Please do not delay your return to Holt with the idea that I will change my mind. I won't.'

'I don't think you understand, my dear.' Timber stood over her, trying to impose his superior height on her. 'I know you have little regard for me, but it is your duty to your father to accept. He signed over the forge to my brother and me. With very little difficulty, I could have him thrown out of the guild, particularly if I mentioned the role a certain daughter played in his business.'

The blow was low but she should have seen it coming. 'You're blackmailing me into marrying you?'

'I prefer to see it as persuading you to take the best course for all concerned.'

Rain didn't know what to say. She'd almost forgotten what it was like to live under guild rules. She knew her father intended to return to Holt soon. Would Timber really go so far as to ruin him to revenge himself on her? Or was it a threat he never intended to carry out?

'You may not believe me, my sweet, but while you've been away, your father has paid proper attention to training his boys. The forge is better placed to survive without him than ever before. In short, Torrent Glass no longer needs him.'

She pressed her fist to her forehead. 'You don't even like me, do you?'

Timber shrugged. 'What's that got to do with marriage? Together you and I can become rich, raise a family in style, build a strong business between this country and ours. I do not turn away from such opportunities.'

'And if I marry you and refuse to go along with your little schemes, what then?'

He curled his hand around the back of her neck. 'Then, my dear, we fall out—seriously fall out.'

His hand was abruptly removed and ended up twisted behind his back. Peri stood over Timber, breathing hard from having run the length of the orchard as soon as he saw what was going on.

'Touch her again and I'll kill you!' Peri growled.

Timber tried to shake him off. 'Let go of me. I can touch my future wife if I wish.'

'Peri, don't hurt him. He's threatened to ruin Papa,' pleaded Rain, scared that Timber would get so angry he'd do what he said to spite them.

'And that's a reason for going easy on him? Sounds like an excuse to do this.' Peri kicked Timber on the rear, sending him flying forwards on to the ground. 'He's pathetic. If he has to bully you into marrying him, he's not worth worrying about.'

'But Peri, you don't know what it's like in Holt. He'll—'

'Hush now.' He put his fingers to her lips. 'Holt man, you're not wanted here. Get going.'

Timber picked himself up and brushed off his tunic. 'I warned you, Rain. You should've listened to me. When you come to your senses, I might accept an apology.' He stalked off, kicking a fallen branch out of his path.

'Peri—'

'Ssh, love!' He gathered her to him how he liked her best, her head on his heart. 'Whatever he said, I'll fix it. Trust me?'

With a sigh, she nodded.

'You can't marry him, in any case, because you're marrying me.'

'I'm what?' She pushed away to look up at him.

'Marrying me. It's quite simple. I love you. I want to spend the rest of my life with you either here or in Holt. And I promise not to call you "my dear" in that pompous way he does, or grow a silly moustache. So, what do you think?'

Rain was tempted to smile at Peri's brusque proposal. For all his declarations that she was wedding him, he was clearly worried she'd turn him down.

'Let me think.' She tapped her chin. 'You've abandoned me, threatened to tie me up, and shot me.' His face fell. 'How could I not marry you?'

'Is that a "yes"?'

'Yes.'

He picked her up and spun her round, the apple trees whirling dizzily.

'Good decision,' shouted Peri. 'Now let's go and take a chunk out of old Timber. I know just how to handle him.'

Epilogue:
Rainbow
Tigral, ten months later

'Your Majesties, may I introduce the Master of Magharna,' announced Prime Minister Melletin. King Ramil and Queen Taoshira rose to greet the head of state of an allied nation. Now in his prime after twenty years on the throne, Ramil looked very fine in a green velvet robe over a silver tunic, complementing his dark complexion. Yet he would be the first to admit that he was outshone by his wife, her long fair hair streaming to her waist, her slender figure clad in a pale blue gown embroidered with silver dragonflies.

Down the centre of the long audience chamber walked a youth dressed in a deep orange robe threaded with glittering jewels. He wore a most unusual crown made of many-coloured glass arranged in a glorious rainbow, set in gold. Behind him followed his ambassador, bearing a magnificent peregrine falcon on his wrist, and the diminutive head of the Magharnan glassmakers' guild.

'He's very young,' whispered the Queen. 'About the same age as our little Lagan.'

'According to Torrent Glassmaker, the Master is about as mischievous as our son. That's why I've asked Lagan to show him and his companion around Tigral after the ceremonies.'

'Is that wise?'

'Probably not, but it should be fun for the three of them.'

The King and Queen descended the steps from their thrones to stand on the same level as the Master.

'Your Majesty.' Ramil bowed.

The Master returned the gesture.

'Welcome to our court,' the King continued.

'Thank you,' said Ret in Common tongue. 'I have heard much about you from my friend here.' He beckoned the head of the glassmakers' guild forward. 'I've borrowed her from your country but I fear I have no intention of returning her to you.'

'Rain Glassmaker, isn't it?' Ramil smiled at her. 'News of your exploits has travelled ahead of you. Your father is very proud.' He turned back to the Master. 'I'm rather afraid I might have to go to war with you over this. I understand you've stolen our best designer of stained-glass windows.'

'I have,' said Ret, his delight evident. 'You should see what she has done to my summer palace. I'm turning it into a school, but it has the most wonderful windows. Not a stroke of work is going to get done; everyone will be dreaming of escaping into her landscapes.'

'Perhaps we will travel to see her designs,' said Queen Taoshira. 'I've always loved stained glass.'

'Oh, but you don't have to go far. I did yours too, Your Majesty,' said Rain, blushing as she realized she had spoken out of turn. She tugged nervously on her necklace of teardrops.

The Queen laughed. 'How wonderful! And is it true that you have said you will only trade with our glassmakers' guild if they allow women into their craft?'

Rain's blush deepened and the Magharnan ambassador reached over to take her hand reassuringly. 'Yes, Your Majesty. Their attitude was standing in the way of progress.'

'Good for you, Mistress Glassmaker,' commented King Ramil. 'You've succeeded where I could not.'

'It was my husband's idea.' Rain smiled up at the ambassador. 'Peri told me that the way to their heart was through their purse.'

'Excellent. Your husband is a very wise man.' The King signalled to his servants. 'But enough of ceremony, Your Majesty. We've a feast prepared tonight and a hunt with our falcons tomorrow. Darling, would you lead the Master in?'

The Queen offered her hand to Ret. 'Please, come with me.'

The King, Queen, and Master filed out, leaving Rain alone with Peri in the throne room.

Peri bent down and kissed her nose. 'Well done, Mistress Glassmaker.'

'Well done, Ambassador.'

'Ready for the feast?'

'Definitely. But you must promise that you won't leave me alone with Timber. He's still going on at me about giving his trading company preferential treatment.'

'He's lucky you let him trade in Magharnan glass at all, love.'

'He can't help being awful.'

'And you can't help being too kind to him.'

Rain tugged his hand, leading him towards the banqueting chamber. 'I can afford to be generous. I got you, didn't I?'

Light poured into the passageway through a stained-glass window depicting a flock of birds. Peri stopped in the pool of multicoloured sunshine.

'One of yours?' He cocked an eyebrow.

'Of course.' Playfully she trapped the shadow of the swallow in her palm and pretended to press it to his heart.

He kissed her. 'A miracle.'

They stepped out of the light together and headed into the celebration beyond.

Julia Golding is the author of over fifteen books for children. Her stories are set all over the world (and in some new worlds too) and span the centuries.

In her first year as a published author, she won a Nestlé Gold Prize, was shortlisted for the Costa Children's Book Award, longlisted for the prestigious Carnegie Medal, and won the Waterstone's Children's Book Prize.

Julia Golding lives in Oxford with her husband and three children.

dragonfly

Julia Golding
Winner of the Nestlé Gold Prize

Princess Taoshira and Prince Ramil must marry in order to unite their kingdoms against the mighty Fergox Spearthrower. Unfortunately, it's more like hate on first sight rather than love. That is until they are thrown together, on a breath-taking adventure to save their people and their lands. They must learn to trust one another, and themselves, in this epic tale of loyalty, love and courage.

Because before Rain and Peri there was Taoshira and Ramil.

The Fourth Crown Princess of the Blue Crescent Islands had sixteen rituals to observe from the moment of waking to when she broke her fast. These included getting out of bed on the right-hand side; turning to the east to bow to the sun; submitting to having her hair groomed with forty strokes from a silver-backed brush by the Under Mistress of the Royal Chamber; and—

Princess Taoshira paused. *What have I forgotten? Goddess rot the Etiquette Mistress's rule book, I know there's something else.*

'Your fingerbowl, Your Highness,' intoned the Senior Mistress of the Chamber, holding out a bronze basin.

Fingerbowl! Why do I always forget the fingerbowl? Taoshira rinsed her fingertips delicately and dried them on a white linen towel.

Probably, chimed in another voice in her head, *because when you were at home—before you were chosen as princess—you had to wash your hands under the pump in the yard, jostling the serving girls for your place in the line.*

Taoshira, or Tashi as she used to be known to her family, almost smiled at the recollection—then remembered that the Crown Princess was not allowed to show emotion until she had said the Four Blessings, the true beginning of the day in the Royal Palace, and accompanied the words with the appropriate gesture.

'Eternal Goddess of Mystery, give our people wisdom (*touching her head*);

Gracious Mother of Mercy, look upon our people with compassion (*right hand on heart*);

Kind Sister of Healing, bless all who are ill (*hands outspread*);

Joyful Child of Hope, prosper our work this day (*fingers arched, thumbs touching in a triangle*).

The four attendants gathered in her bedchamber gave the required response in unison: 'As the Goddess wills.'

Tashi was relieved that was over. She liked the morning prayer to the four faces of the Mother Goddess but had not yet got used to the fact that she was now an official priestess for the entire nation. If she forgot to say it—or even fluffed the words—her people believed that dire consequences would be felt throughout the land. It had been very different mumbling the same prayers to herself up on the hills of her family's estate on Kai, the northernmost of the islands that made up the Blue Crescent, named for the curving shape of the isles in the Sapphire Ocean. In those

days, as a faithful Kaian, she had said the words with only her goats to hear her as the sun broke over the jagged crests of the Marine Mountains. She had never dreamed that she would be snatched from that life as abruptly as a kid is plucked from the ground by a bird of prey. From insignificant daughter of an impoverished matriarch, she had become one of the four most powerful women in her world.

Tashi stood with arms outstretched as the Assistant Under Mistress of the Chamber removed her nightgown. That was another thing that had taken a lot of getting used to: standing stark naked in front of her attendants with only her long fair hair to veil her while they went through the ceremonial dressing. Over the last four years, from blushing furiously she had progressed to thinking of other things while they fussed over her. The ceremony had its set order: first placing on the white silk under-robe, then the sleeveless orange tunic of the Fourth Crown Princess, next the flamboyant embroidered gown (today was one of her favourites—the dragonfly design), and finally the orange sash.

Four items of clothing. Her life was ruled by that number. It had decided her fate when the last Fourth Crown Princess had met an untimely death at the age of twenty. The Blue Crescent Islands always had four crown princesses, one from each isle of Rama, Lir-Salu, Phonilara, and Kai. It had been the princess from the smallest and most northern island that had died, so the priests and priestesses of Kai had gathered to

identify the next candidate. Their choice was restricted to all eligible twelve-year-old girls of matriarchal families.

Normally, the choice fell on the greatest and most wealthy households, but it seemed that in Tashi's year something had gone awry and she—the youngest daughter of a family whose claim to matriarchal nobility was largely on paper—had been chosen. Her family had long since ceased to be noticed at court, their wealth dwindling until they had become hill farmers in an obscure province.

There had been no question that she would accept the role. Tashi had known that her family would benefit hugely from having their daughter at the seat of government—and she also shared the belief that the Goddess's hand was behind such decisions, no matter how imperfect her human agents. Though Tashi had wondered many times over the years that had transformed her from free-living goat herder to a key part of the most formal court in the known world, whether the Mother had not chosen her for a bit of light relief from her three co-rulers. She sometimes felt she was more court jester than ruler as she struggled to submit to her new life.

Only to herself would she admit that the ceremonies and duties were driving her mad; and yet she was committed to repeating the same pattern day in, day out for the rest of her life, for the good of the nation.

The Etiquette Mistress, one of the highest ranking officials in the court, arrived even before the breakfast.

'Now, Crown Princess, shall we revise our lesson on the right degree of bow to give the Gerfalian ambassadors?' she asked, opening her scroll at the correct place.

'As the Goddess wills,' replied Tashi, keeping her face inscrutable.

Ramil ac Burinholt, Prince of Gerfal, had risen before the sun for the hunt. The dawn had found him and his friends riding pell-mell through the Royal Forest, leaping fallen trees, whooping with excitement as they picked up a trail. Ramil loved the reckless speed of the chase and rode like the wind when the mood took him. His mother had originally come from the hot deserts of the far south, princess of a dark-skinned people known as the Horse Followers. His friends always said it was her blood in him that caught fire when he and his stallion, Leap, set off on one of their mad careers through the forest, leaving all the others behind. The professional huntsmen just shook their heads in despair and let the young Prince go, knowing from experience that he would return when it suited him, having caught nothing.

At one with his galloping horse, Ramil entered a state of mind of pure happiness. The greens, oranges, golds, reds, and browns flashed by as Leap streaked through the trees. Twigs snatched at Ramil's clothes but were unable to catch him. The rush of air was cool on skin. Harness jingled and leather creaked in a tuneful

counterpoint to the rapid thud-thud of the hooves. Leap's footing was sure, he was fresh, ready to run for as long as his rider wished. It was their great game; their moment of release from stable and council chamber.

Having covered a mile in this fashion, Leap barely slowed for the stream that crossed their path, jumping it in one bound. Once on the other side, he pulled up by a thicket of hawthorn and snickered to his rider.

'What's the matter, boy?' Ramil asked, patting his mount's sweat-stained neck.

Leap shook his black mane and snorted, shifting his hooves nervously.

In the joy of the ride, Ramil had almost forgotten the purpose of their outing this morning, but he trusted the stallion's instincts, not to mention his sense of smell. He reached for one of the short spears strapped to his back.

'We're close, are we?'

Ramil strained his hearing, listening for the tell-tale sound of snuffing or movement in the undergrowth. The ancient trees of the Royal Hunting Forest were particularly gnarled and squat in this part as if, like old men, they had stopped growing taller and started putting on weight round their middles. Dark-green holly and brambles swallowed up the space beneath the oak canopy. Plenty of places to hide; very hard to see. He nudged the horse forward. There! Definitely something moving through the bushes. Ramil shifted his grip on the spear and held it ready over his shoulder.

Twigs snapped aside as a boar erupted from the

undergrowth. Stubby tusks lowered, it charged towards the horse and rider. Leap side-stepped deftly, moving to give Ramil a clear shot with his spear. The boar passed them and reached the bank, trapped between huntsman and water. With gritty spirit, it wheeled round to face the spear, small black eyes glaring. Ramil rose in the stirrups, paused, and then let the weapon drop.

'Lucky for you that my friends were not here, brother,' he addressed the boar. Replacing the spear in its holster, he spurred Leap forward, jumping back over the stream, leaving a confused boar in sole possession of the bank.

'Fine prince I am,' chuckled Ramil, apologizing to Leap with a pat. 'But we have meat and he was magnificent—a fine sire for lots more boars just like him, don't you think?'

A horn sounded in the trees to the east, summoning the stray Prince to return to the hunt. Ramil and Leap trotted back at peace with each other. As they neared the old road, three young lords on fine horses joined them.

'There you are, Ramil!' called Hortlan, the Prince's cousin. 'So what have you caught?' He gave Ramil a huge grin, already knowing from the empty space on the pommel that the chase had been fruitless.

'I had him. I was this close!' replied Ramil, holding up a gloved hand, finger and thumb indicating the distance. 'A massive boar, enough to feed the whole household for a week!'

'And?' Hortlan mocked, giving no credence to his cousin's description.

'He charged and I—' Ramil began to laugh, both at himself and at his friend's expression of scepticism. 'And I ran for it.'

'Now that I don't believe!' Hortlan slapped Ramil on the back. With his long light-brown hair and blue eyes, Hortlan was as unlike his curly-black-haired, dark-eyed cousin as one could get. 'A Burinholt run from a little hairy pig? Never!'

Ramil shrugged. 'All right, all right, I made that part up.'

'And the boar too, if you ask me,' muttered Lord Yendral to the trees, but loud enough for all to hear.

'Ramil the Unblooded, that's what we should call you. Bane of every hunt,' quipped Lord Usk, son of the Gerfalian Prime Minister. A big-framed youth, he had the reddish-brown hair of his Brigardian mother. 'My father should propose a law to keep you in the castle come winter. We'll all starve else.'

Ramil bowed in his saddle. 'Thank you for that vote of confidence in me, my friends. Come, let us take back the tale of my heroic deeds to the castle and dine on fresh air and spring water in my honour.'

CPSIA information can be obtained at www.ICGtesting.com
Printed in the USA
LVOW04s1955261015

459795LV00036B/1924/P